The

JAKE
RYAN
C♥MPLEX

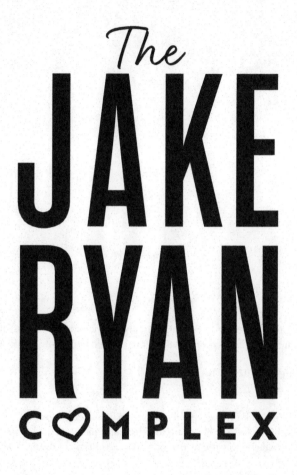

The
JAKE
RYAN
C♡MPLEX

BETHANY CRANDELL

Montlake

Published by Montlake, Seattle

www.apub.com

Amazon, the Amazon logo, and Montlake are trademarks of Amazon.com, Inc., or its affiliates.

ISBN-13: 9781542026000
ISBN-10: 1542026008

Cover design by Caroline Teagle Johnson

Printed in the United States of America

For Boog, G & Doozie,
my favorite trio

Chapter 1

"*Aaaaaaagh!* It feels like a watermelon's coming out of my butt!"

Despite my patient's distress, I can't help but chuckle. Of the nearly one thousand mothers I've cared for in my ten-year career, I've heard active labor described a lot of ways: *"A volcano exploding inside my vag," "Like an alien is trying to eat its way through my ass,"* even *"Satan playing jump rope with my guts!"* but I've never heard the watermelon-out-the-butt comparison before.

"Get it out!" she cries. "Get that little bastard out of me!"

Little bastard. I've heard that one . . .

"We're almost there, Rena," I reassure her with an encouraging nod. "Just a few more pushes and she'll be here."

"Oh, baby, you're doing so great. So, so great." Once again, the helpless father-to-be drags his palm across his wife's sweaty forehead, then smooths her black hair back from her face. "I'm so proud of you, baby. You're doing such a great job—"

"I swear, Jason, if you touch my face or call me *baby* one more time, I'll rip your head off and shove it straight up your ass!"

The usually mild-mannered preschool teacher swats her husband's hand away, teeth bared like a wild dog.

"This is all your fault!" she screams. "You did this to me. You did this to me, you dick! *What kind of man does this to his wife?"*

Jason Harrison stumbles backward, looking terrified. "Sweetie, it's okay. This will all be over soon—"

"Don't fucking patronize me! *This will never be over!* I'm going to spend the rest of my life shitting watermelons, and it's all your fault!"

And welcome to ten centimeters dilated.

"All right, Dad, time for you to take a seat." Moving with familiarity, Debbie, the veteran nurse I'm fortunate enough to be working with tonight, ushers Mr. Harrison to a chair in the corner and instructs him to sit down and keep his hands to himself. Wisely he doesn't object.

"Okay, Rena," I continue, focused on the task at hand. "One more big push should do it. Give me one more big one . . ."

"Come on, sweetie. You can do this," Debbie adds, encouraging her from the bedside. "Let's get this done. On three. One, two, three . . ."

"*Grrrrrrrrhhh!*" Rena lets out a deep, demonic-sounding growl that should probably make her head spin but instead provides her with enough strength to bear down against the stirrups and push one last time.

That's right. There you go. Your six hours of labor are about to pay off . . .

"*No!* Wait!" she wails. "I changed my mind. I don't want a baby. Put her back! *Put her back in!*"

"Sorry, too late." I grin beneath my surgical mask as the baby's head finally emerges, a coat of slick black waves covering every inch of it. "She's here, and with a headful of dark hair just like you, Mom."

I place my hands under the baby's slippery body and, with a gentle tug, proceed to guide her out into the world. *Hello, little girl.* As if rudely awakened from an afternoon nap, the baby opens her steely-blue eyes, and lets out an ear-shattering scream.

"Oh my god," Rena cries over an exhausted breath. "That's her. That's our baby. Jason . . ."

Forgetting their earlier grievances, the new dad explodes from the chair and races to his wife's side, pulling her into his arms and bathing her head with kisses, all the while keeping a nervous eye on me. "She's actually here?" he asks. "Our girl is—she's here?"

"Oh yes," I say. "She's definitely here."

Debbie and I move quickly, expectorating mucus from the little one's mouth and nose and tying off the umbilical cord. (Mr. Harrison made it clear that he wasn't interested in cutting the cord, so I don't even bother to ask.) Debbie wraps her in a warm blanket and then quickly hands her off to her parents. With tears streaming down her flushed cheeks, the new mom pulls the baby in close against her chest, burying her lips against the sleek, downy-soft locks covering her head.

"Hello, sweet Charlotte." Rena's voice is thick, wavering with emotion, and absent of all traces of demon possession. "I'm your mama. I'm so happy to meet you."

Hearing her mother's voice, baby Charlotte stops crying and blinks hard, as if trying to orient herself in this big new world.

"There's my little angel," Mr. Harrison says, a joyful strain in his voice. He tips his head thoughtfully, basking in the beauty and wonder of the tiny little person in front of him, and then, like all the good ones do, turns back to his wife and says, "I couldn't possibly love you any more than I do right this minute."

Sniffling beneath her tears, Rena smiles and nuzzles her way into that tender, safe space beneath the crook of her husband's chin and against his chest. I turn back to the work in front of me, trying my damnedest not to be jealous of her—not so much the baby but the man. Not that I'm in any way attracted to Mr. Harrison (besides his being at least ten years my junior, hipster beards and corduroy pants aren't really my thing), but because his unwavering love for her is so obvious—so *real*—I can't help but wish I had it for myself. Sadly, though, the universe has made it pretty clear that's never going to happen . . .

As I always do after a long delivery, I hit the Starbucks drive-through for a soothing cup of cocoa before I start the forty-mile drive home. I could have gone with a condo in the city, but I like the commute from downtown Chicago to Naperville; it's relaxing, when there's no traffic, and once I get there it's just like being home in my Michigan childhood, where churches anchor every corner and paperboys still deliver from their bicycles. It's the perfect place to live—or it will be once I can find a reliable handyman. There's always something going wrong with my old craftsman.

It's nearly ten o'clock when I finally turn onto my street. Lined with statuesque elms and old-timey lampposts, it's about the best greeting I could ask for after the day I've had—

My stomach sinks when I see a black pickup parked in front of my house, a Walsh and Son's General Contracting magnet displayed across the tailgate.

Dammit, now what?

I shield my eyes from the rotted-out woodpile (formerly my front porch) that's sprawled across my lawn and head up the long driveway. My house is dark, but the granny flat out back is lit up like the Vegas strip, which means that whatever catastrophe brought a contractor out in the middle of the night is happening at my twenty-two-year-old tenant / dog walker's place.

Crap.

Most nights Rerun, my elderly Labrador, is waiting at the gate to welcome me—his thick black tail swaying with anticipation—but tonight the only one standing watch is Gia. As always, she's the epitome of cool with her spiky platinum hair and retro cat-framed glasses, but based on the death glare she's firing at me, it's clear she's not very happy.

"Hey, what's going on?" I ask cautiously, motioning to the granny flat as I climb out of the Jeep.

Her glare tightens, and she settles deeper into her crossed-arms stance.

"Your house is a shit box. That's what's going on."

"What happened?"

"That fucking pipe burst in my bathroom again."

My shoulders sag. "It did?"

"Yes. But thankfully this time it happened while I was out walking Rerun, so it was probably only running for like a half hour before I found it. But still, there's water all over my fucking house, Mac. All my stuff is drenched."

"Is your artwork okay?"

Gia refers to herself as a "hijack artist," which basically means she replicates other artists' famous pieces and then embellishes them with some of her own flair. It used to be flowers or maybe a weird symbol, but lately it's all about Steve Guttenberg. She stumbled upon a random airing of *Police Academy* a few months back and has been inspired by him ever since. Steve's shown up—*naked, always naked!*—in more than a dozen pieces that have, surprisingly, sold for hundreds of dollars apiece, which is why she nearly strangled me when this exact situation happened last month and her latest Steve project (a naked Steve replacing Judas at the table in da Vinci's *The Last Supper*) was ruined from water damage. Not only did I have to pay to have all her things cleaned, but I also had to ante up $400 for the world's most sacrilegious painting.

"Yeah, my pieces are all fine, but only because there was a pile of clothes on the floor that sopped up the water. A few minutes longer and everything would've been destroyed."

Gia's messiness usually annoys me, but in this case her piggish style seems to be working to both our benefits.

"Well, thank god for dirty clothes," I say. Then I motion back toward the street, saying, "But the good news is it looks like you finally found us some help . . ."

Thankfully, she eases her stance a little. "Yeah. He comes into the flower shop all the time, left his card a few weeks ago. I remembered him saying something about being up for after-hours emergency work, so I figured I'd try him. He's inside assessing the damage now."

Along with her Steve art, Gia also works part-time at a local flower shop and picks up other odd jobs as the moods strike. I admit I was skeptical of her at first—septum piercings and come-and-go paychecks don't scream "reliable tenant"—but she's proven to be a great fit. Besides the fact that she's never late on rent, she adores Rerun and is more than happy to look after him when I'm not around. Considering the hours I keep, that's invaluable. And on a personal level, I like Gia. Sure, she's brash (and a little scary when she's mad), but she's also bold and lives her life with a kind of reckless confidence I've always wished I had. It feels good to be around someone like that.

"He seems like a pretty good guy," she goes on. "He came over as soon as I called."

"To come out this late on a Thursday night, he has to be."

Considering he even showed gives him a leg up on all those five-star Yelp reviews that did me no good.

"Rerun's completely in love with him," she continues. "He's been following him around all night."

"Rerun's in love with everybody."

"Not Mr. Feldspar." She grins snidely. "He took a dino-size dump on his lawn, right in front of him. The old fart was standing at his living room window watching the whole thing—"

"No! Not Mr. Feldspar! He's so fussy about his lawn."

"Yep," she goes on while I raise the cup to my lips for another swig of cocoa. "And we were out of poop bags, too, so I had to barehand it—"

Pffffitt—"*You what?*"

Cocoa erupts from my mouth, sending a spray of chocolate bubbles catapulting through the air and onto—

"*Whoa!* Hold your fire!"

My eyes spring wide, and I gasp as a tall, broad-shouldered man suddenly appears in front of me, his work gloves raised over his face in defense against my spray.

"Oh my god!" I sputter while swiping wildly at my mouth. My cheeks already feel hot beneath my hands. "I'm so sorry. I—I didn't see you there."

"It's okay," he chuckles. "Just confirm that you're done."

My blush deepens, and I raise my cup to underscore my apology, mortified. "Yes, I'm done. It's safe to come out."

He cautiously drops his leather-clad hands, revealing kind eyes and a strong, chiseled jaw that's blanketed with a sexy coat of day-old stubble.

"Well, that's a nice how-do-you-do," Gia says over a hearty laugh. "Mac, this is J.T., the contractor."

"H-hi. Nice to meet you." Blinking hard, I extend my hand to greet him, but before he accepts, he peels one cocoa-spattered glove from his right fingers, then scrubs his palm against his jeans.

Dear god, I just spit all over this beautiful man . . .

"Nice to meet you, too, Mac." He gives my proffered palm a solid shake, the calluses lining his warm skin prompting my insides to quiver with delight.

"I'm so sorry," I say again. "I don't usually spit cocoa on people when I first meet them."

"Yeah, she usually saves that for the second encounter," Gia mumbles.

"Really, it's fine." He looks straight at me and offers a charming, reassuring smile that extends all the way up to the cute little wrinkles kissing the edges of his brown eyes. "An unexpected shower is good every now and then."

On instinct, my gaze wanders to the cocoa splattered across his close-fitting T-shirt, partially hidden beneath his unbuttoned plaid flannel.

That's not the kind of shower you deserve—

Rerun suddenly bounds out of the flat, squashing my naughty train of thought. He thunders past J.T. and slams into my legs, groaning happily around the tennis ball in his mouth.

"Hey, old man." Easily adopting my doggy, baby-talk voice, I drop down to the dewy night grass and give him a hearty scratch. "You were a naughty dog tonight. Yes you were. You can't be pooping on Mr. Feldspar's lawn. No you can't, bud. You can't do that . . ."

"It was classic," Gia chuckles.

"No, it was gross," I scold her, sounding more like my mother than I'd ever want to. "You should never touch dog poop with your bare hands, or any kind of poop for that matter."

"Says the woman who plays with placentas for a living . . ."

Ignoring her remark, I stand and direct my attention back to J.T. "So, that old pipe is causing problems again, huh?"

"Yeah, but I don't think the pipe in the bathroom is the real issue. I think the problem stems from the supply line."

I scowl.

"It's actually not as bad as it sounds," he assures me. "Come on in and I'll show you."

With a courteous wave, he leads me into the flat while Gia hangs back in the yard to throw the ball for Rerun.

"Sorry about the mess," he says while navigating his long legs through the minefield of tools and soiled rags gathered in the hall outside the small bathroom. I can't help but chuckle. No different than any other day in Gia's flat . . . He drops down to one knee in front of the pedestal sink, his worn leather work boot grazing the baseboard behind him, and shrugs out of his plaid overshirt. He spreads it on the floor beside him and with a little pat indicates I should use it to kneel.

Who says chivalry is dead?

Holding back a nervous grin—mindful of the close quarters—I crouch beside him and feel my pulse spike unexpectedly when I find myself just inches from the taut biceps muscle that's peeking out from beneath the sleeve of his T-shirt.

Well, hello there—

J.T. points toward the metal pipes extending from the wall, reclaiming my attention. "You see how it's all warped back here . . . thankfully it's just this small section." He punctuates his point with a soft knuckle rap to the wall. "But it's definitely been leaking for a while."

I lean in for a better look.

"Oh wow. I never noticed that before."

I reach forward and press my fingers against the wall to where the paint is raised and rippling like lasagna noodles buried beneath a blanket of sandstone beige.

"And it's happening over here too," he says. I catch the faintest hint of peppermint on his words as he points away from me to his right, where the pipes come out of the wall and into the back of the toilet. I narrow my eyes. Sure enough, the same bubbly mess. "You've got a clog in the main that's forcing all the secondary lines to back up," he explains as he stands up, unaware of the tempting vantage point he's now offering me. "Have you had any leaks in the main house?" he asks, removing the glove still on his left hand.

Cheeks growing warm again, I shake my head as I slowly back-crawl out from beneath the sink. "Not that I've noticed," I say. "Though there are plenty of other things wrong with the main house."

He chuckles. "So I've heard. Here, let me help you."

My breath flutters as I reach up for his newly bared hand—

The light reflecting off his wedding band could land airplanes.

Ugh.

Of course . . .

Swallowing a silly, disappointed sigh, I lay my palm in his and allow him to help me up while simultaneously fighting the urge to punch myself in the face. How could I have possibly thought he was single? The universe doesn't offer me charming, chivalrous men with sexy calluses—I know that! I get the weirdos who only speak pig latin or live in their grandmother's basement. God, I'm an idiot . . .

"So, what's our plan of attack?" I ask, wiping my hands on my thighs as I quickly backpedal toward the door. He watches with a crinkled brow, then lifts his overshirt from the floor and puts it on again, this time buttoning the placket.

"Well, first I'll need to do a flush of the main line to get rid of the clog or roots or whatever's causing the trouble, and then I'll be able to get back in here and get this room squared away."

"Are we talking a total renovation?"

It's faint, but I'd swear I can hear the slurping sound of my bank account being sucked dry.

"Not at all." He shakes his head, the light dusting of gray along his temples shimmering with refinement beneath the LED lights. His wife must fall asleep with a smile looking at that. "We'll just change out the bad pipes, replace the damaged drywall, and do a quick touch-up with paint. It won't take more than three or four days."

"Really?"

The shock in my voice must be reflected in my expression, because he starts to laugh.

"You're used to the long, drawn-out approach, huh?"

"Oh yeah. And that's *if* they even come back to finish the work. I'm not sure if you saw the pile of wood on my lawn, but that used to be my front porch. And the guy who's supposed to be fixing it has been a no-show four times."

He frowns. "I'm sorry. Unfortunately, there are a lot of unreliable people in this business. But I'm here now, so I'll get you squared away. That is, of course, if you want me?"

If I want you . . .

A ridiculous grin erupts across my lips, so I quickly fake a cough, covering my mouth with my hand while I say, "Of course. Yes. I definitely want you to do the work."

"Great. I need to finish up another project first, but I should be able to get back over here sometime on Monday, and after this is done, we can talk about the rest of your to-do list."

I head back outside while J.T., the married contractor, Band-Aids up Gia's bathroom so she can continue to use it for the next few days.

"He seems like he knows what he's doing," Gia grunts while heaving the sloppy tennis ball across the yard for Rerun. "And he's kind of bangin', for an old guy."

I cast her a sideways glance. "He can't be much older than me." With those adorable little wrinkles, I'd say forty . . . forty-two, tops. "But he's married, so . . ."

"He is?"

I nod. "He's got a shiny gold ring on his finger."

"Huh. I've never noticed . . ."

No surprise there. Women don't develop wedding-band eye until well into their thirties.

"I guess she's why he's always buying the Sweetheart's Special when he comes in . . ."

The Sweetheart's Special.

I'm not even one for flowers, and that sounds perfectly charming right now.

"Now that you mention it, I did see him arguing with a woman outside the store a couple of weeks ago," she adds absently. "That must've been his wife. Now *she* was bangin'—looked like a swimsuit model."

I sigh. Of course his wife looks like a swimsuit model. Cupid wouldn't set him up with a troll . . . or a gangly, freckle-faced obstetrician.

Oh, no.

Cupid doesn't set *her* up with anybody worthwhile . . .

Chapter 2

Aside from Claire and Andy's minivan and Tracy's sleek Mercedes, the parking lot at the Windy City Women's Specialty Clinic is empty, which is to be expected. When Andy, Tracy, and I took over this practice five years ago, we agreed not to see patients on Fridays—unless they were in labor, of course. Instead we use that time volunteering at a free clinic on the South Side of town every other week. And on the alternating Fridays, like today, we gather for lunch to catch up on the boring businessy stuff that comes from running our own practice. Today we're discussing Claire's replacement. Claire is Andy's wife, my closest friend, and our part-time office manager. But with all four of their boys in school now, and each one playing at least one sport, she doesn't have time to run things anymore, so we have to find someone new.

The waiting area is also a very different place today: the comfy leather couches and armchairs sit empty, the *People* magazines rest unopened on the end tables, the kids' playhouse in the corner sits vacant. The only sign of life is Jaws, the teensy goldfish who swims around in a bowl filled with blue marbles behind the front counter. Jaws belongs to Ben, Claire and Andy's youngest. He won him last month at his school's Kindergarten Kickoff festival. He lived at their house for a whopping fourteen hours before Noah and Aidan, the oldest of their four hooligans—er, boys—threatened to force-feed him to Carson, the third born. He's been living here, in the safety of our offices, ever since.

I make my way toward the break room at the end of the hall. Along with the tempting smell of our favorite Chinese takeout, I can hear the three of them laughing before I even reach the door.

"Hey, guys," I say as I walk into the room.

They greet me in unison, and then Claire asks, "How'd it go with the Harrison baby last night?"

"Good." I drop down into the empty chair next to Andy, plucking a bean sprout from his plate. He winks at me as I pop it in my mouth. "She was stuck at five centimeters forever but then finally started making progress around six thirty or so. She refused the epi up until the bitter end, so of course she was still feeling plenty by the time the baby arrived."

"And baby was good?" Claire, always the mother, asks while she loads me up a plate of my own.

"Yep. Seven pounds even, with lungs for days."

"What did they name her?"

"Charlotte. After her great-grandmother."

"Aw, that's sweet." I see a glint of jealousy sweep across Claire's fair cheeks as she slides the plate in front of me. She'd sacrifice a lung to shop for dresses and hair bows.

"Who's got rounds this morning?" Andy asks.

"Steve Bradshaw. He left me a message this morning that everybody's doing well."

Because we're in private practice, the on-site hospital docs monitor our patients during our off hours. I'll look in on the Harrisons later tonight.

"Another healthy little nugget brought into the world," Claire says wistfully.

"Cut to the important details. Did she go *Exorcist*?" Tracy asks.

I grin as I snap open my chopsticks.

"What? *No!*" Andy smacks the table. "You're kidding. Please tell me you're kidding."

I shake my head, prompting Claire's pale-blue eyes to spring wide open in surprise. "Oh my god. She did?"

Tracy squeals, smacking her own hand against the table. "I knew it! I knew she'd cross over to the dark side. The sweet, quiet ones always cross over—"

"There's no way . . ." Andy shakes his head, stupefied. "She was my ringer—"

"Yeah, well, your ringer just landed you at the starting line in a tutu and go-go boots," Tracy chides over a delighted snort. "Claire, I hope you're planning on being at the race, because I'm going to need video documentation for future use."

"Damn straight I'll be there," Claire says while giving her husband a playful jab in the arm. "I wouldn't miss it for the world. I've been dying to see my little Opie in go-go boots."

Opie is Claire's pet name for Andy, which is appropriate given his boyish looks and mop of carrot-colored hair. Of course, that moniker could easily apply to fair-skinned, strawberry-blonde Claire or any one of their equally Richie Cunningham–looking boys.

"You're going to look so cute, honey."

"No, I'm going to look ridiculous," he whimpers. Then he turns to Tracy and says, "This is the last bet I ever make with you."

"Oh, I know," she says, and we all laugh. We've heard him declare that threat more than once.

Tracy and Andy have been gaming against each other ever since our resident days back at City General, where we all met. Because the residency program is so physically and mentally exhausting, they started drumming up ridiculous challenges and bets to add some levity to the otherwise stressful situation.

The fun started out benign enough, like seeing who could stuff the most M&M's up their nose, but soon their antics escalated into payoffs that included complete body shavings (Andy), running naked across our attending's front lawn (Tracy), and even regrettable Bugs Bunny lower-back tattoos (both of them). Now that they're older, and maybe a smidge wiser, they're limiting their bets to more family-friendly payoffs. In this case, Andy bet Tracy that my patient, the sweet, normally genteel Mrs. Harrison, would *not* fall victim to the horrors of the dilation demons, but Tracy was sure she would. And she was right. Now Andy will be running in the Humane Society's annual Donuts & Dogs 5K in go-gos and a tutu. And despite what he says, another bet is undoubtedly on the horizon; it always is.

We make small talk while we eat for a few minutes, before Claire takes the reins, saying, "Okay, so I've got a couple of candidates lined up for interviews—"

My phone suddenly rings, interrupting her train of thought.

"Sorry," I say, winding up another stickful of noodles. "I'll let it go to voice mail. It's probably just Hope again."

Hope is my little sister. She's already left me two messages this morning, and I've yet to listen to either of them. Not because I don't care about what she wants to tell me, but because whatever it is, it won't be the dramatic, life-changing event she'll make it out to be, which is what Hope does. She walks through life with an exclamation point trailing behind her. Everyday activities like eating lunch or changing a tire somehow become monumental events when Hope talks about them, and those exclamation points are strangely contagious—for most people. I could probably hate her for this annoying trait if she weren't so darn likable, or if she had any control over it, but she doesn't. It's a genetic defect she inherited from our mother, who I'm told *used* to be the same way, though I've only known her as a wretch of a woman whose mission in life is to destroy *my* life one criticism at a time.

"Again?" Claire inquires as the phone continues to ring.

I nod as I slurp up my noodles. "She's called a couple of times already, but I'm sure it's nothing . . ."

Andy and Tracy seem content with my response, because they just go on eating, but Claire most definitely is not. She sets her chopsticks

down firmly on her plate, and even though the phone has stopped ring-
ing and gone to voice mail, she says, "Mac, she's calling you for a reason.
There might be an emergency."

"Yeah, she might be lying dead in a ditch somewhere," Tracy teases
Claire over a mouthful of rice.

Claire glares at her and then turns her pointed look my way. "You
need to see what she wants. You're her big sister; you can't just ignore her."

I could easily remind her that if it were an emergency, my parents
would be calling too. Or that I've answered a lot more of Hope's calls
than I've ever ignored, but arguing with *mama* Claire rarely produces
good results.

I pull my phone from my bag and see that I was right. It was Hope,
and, as expected, she's left me another message.

I tuck some more food in my mouth and raise the phone up to
my ear while Claire looks on with a concerned expression. *Always the
mother . . .*

"Mac Daddy"—Hope's voice is as bubblegum and rainbows as
always—"where are you? Have you listened to my messages yet? I'm
getting married!"

I choke over the egg roll.

Married?

Di-did she say married?

"—can hardly even believe it!" her message continues. "Whitman
took me on a hot-air-balloon ride over the lake at sunset yesterday and
proposed! It was *so* amazing! The wedding is going to be over Memorial
weekend, so clear your calendar—and Michael's too! We're all so excited
we finally get to meet him. Okay, I gotta run. Call me back! I love
youuuuuu!"

Her message comes to an abrupt end, exclamation points wafting
through the air like a bad smell, while I'm left with my jaw hanging
open in horror, a chunk of half-eaten egg roll dropping onto the table
in front of me.

"*Ohmygod*, what's wrong?" The worry in Claire's voice mirrors her expression. She reaches across the table and grips my hand. "Mac, what is it? What'd she say?"

"She's . . . uh . . ."

"What happened?" Andy lays a concerned hand on my shoulder.

I blink hard. "She's . . . getting married."

"Oh my god," Claire gasps at the same time Tracy asks, "To who?"

"Whitman," I answer absently.

"Is he the attorney?" Claire asks.

I nod.

"Whitman?" Tracy grouses. "That sounds like an appliance, not a name."

"Wait, this is good news, isn't it?" Andy chimes in, oblivious to the root of my horror.

"Mac?" Claire prods, gently squeezing my hand. "What is it, hon?"

I inhale a deep breath that does nothing to calm my nerves. "The wedding is over Memorial weekend. And they're expecting me to bring . . . Michael."

"Oh my god!" Tracy barks.

Claire gasps, and Andy says, "Who's Michael?"

"The fake boyfriend!" Tracy crows.

"*Who?*" Andy's eyebrows arch high into his forehead.

"Michael." I hang my head and sigh. "The make-believe neurologist I've been dating since Valentine's Day."

"Michael the Neurologist" isn't the first lie I've manufactured to get my mother off my back, but he is the most recent—and definitely the most elaborate.

When I created him a few months ago, it was strictly for the purpose of silencing her harassing *"What are you doing for Valentine's Day? I'm sure I can find someone who'd be willing to go out with you!"* phone calls. But when February 15 rolled around, rather than tell her Michael was a creep I never wanted to see again (as is the sad truth when it comes

17

to my *real* dates), I've instead been perpetuating the stupid lie simply because she's *so* much easier to deal with when she thinks my life is *in order*. In the roughly nine weeks I've been "seeing" Michael, he has emerged as a once-engaged-but-never-married neurologist who lives in a high-rise downtown and enjoys cooking and hiking in his free time. He votes independent, attends a Methodist church on Christmas and Easter, and most recently started volunteering for Doctors International, which is why he was out of town last month when Mom and Dad drove down for a visit and hoped to meet him. Ordinarily I don't condone lying, but when it comes to my mother, it's a matter of survival. Like a life preserver to a drowning man, or a Valium drip for anyone who meets her . . .

"You made up a boyfriend?" Andy questions. "Why would you do that?"

"Because she's a habitual liar," Tracy answers snidely. "She lies about everything, don't you?" Her dark eyes narrow, and she leans across the table, chopsticks pointed directly at my chest like an accusatory finger. "Your name's not even Mac, is it? What's your real name? And who do you work for?"

"Oh shut up." I swat at her chopsticks. "I only lie to her because if I didn't, my ears would be bleeding from all her criticisms. It's just how I deal with her."

Warped as it is, I learned at an early age—thirteen, to be exact— that lying to my mother about the things *she* deems important was the key to surviving her. The realization struck me by pure luck: I was primping for April Osborn's birthday party (the first boy-girl party I'd been invited to) and was eager to make a good impression on the boys, so I decided to wear my new pink sundress. In my head I filled out the curves of the seersucker fabric like a svelte hourglass, but the reflection in the mirror was very much the opposite. Feeling desperate, I stupidly padded a handful of tissue into my bra. The resulting B cups looked like misshapen gopher mounds, but when Mom caught a glimpse of them, her face lit up like a Fourth of July firework, and she screamed, "Hallelujah! Your breasts have finally arrived!" (A stark contradiction to the "yardsticks have more curves than you" I'd been hearing.) Even then I was smart enough to recognize how misplaced her enthusiasm was, but I didn't care. It provided me with a delicious little reprieve from her constant pecking, so I rolled with it . . . and the Kleenex. I stuffed my bra until the *real* B cups finally appeared a year later. (And, sadly, I still haven't graduated to a C.)

Andy sighs. "Okay, so if you lie to her all the time, why are you so upset? How is this *Michael* lie any different?"

"Because all of my other lies have only involved my mom," I counter. "They're just between us. But now my whole family thinks that Michael is real—*Hope* thinks he's real, and if this blows up on her wedding day—*shit* . . ."

I turn to Claire, hoping to find one of her maternally sympathetic expressions looking back at me, but that's not what I get, not even close. Instead she's got her lips rolled so tight over her teeth to keep from laughing that her face is turning red.

I level her with a hard look.

She sputters over a stifled laugh and says, "I'm sorry, sweetie. It's not funny. It's just . . . *god*, what are you going to do? She thinks you've got a boyfriend. She's expecting you to bring *him*."

"I know!" I cry out over a laugh of my own. I'm not laughing because this is funny. I'm laughing because this is beyond pathetic. I'm a grown woman. I own my own home, have a robust 401(k)—*I deliver human beings into the world, for god's sake!*—but my instinct is still to lie to my mother rather than be honest with her.

"Can't you just tell her the truth?" Andy naively asks.

"No!" Claire and I snap back in unison, while Tracy says, "Hell no. She'd never let her live that down."

"I'm just going to have to break up with him," I say.

"You can't," Claire objects. "There's no way she's going to let you attend this wedding by yourself—not with the who's who of Grand Rapids in attendance. If you break up with him, she'll just arrange for Keith to be your date again, and that's the last thing you want."

I slouch back in the chair.

She's right. My mother, ever the show pony, will never allow me to attend this wedding without a plus-one, and she's been very clear on the fact Keith—the "successful attorney" with family money—is still available. Is it any wonder? She's the only woman alive who doesn't seem to be bothered by Keith always fondling his penis. (In his defense, he suffered nerve damage from a horrible skiing accident, so pinching his *friend* provides temporary relief to the incessant stinging, but it's still awkward, to say the least. Even George Michael had the decency to tug his boat in dark theaters, as opposed to the bright lights of upscale restaurants.) I'll just have to think of something else . . .

"Maybe I can hire someone," I offer up.

"Like an escort?" Claire asks.

"More like a prostitute," Tracy mutters over a mouthful of chow mein.

"*Not* a prostitute." I glare at Tracy. "Or an escort. More like an actor. I could hire someone to play the role of my boyfriend. I've got"— I do a quick mental count—"six weeks until Memorial Day. That's plenty of time to turn an actor into the perfect Michael—"

Andy chokes over the noodles in his mouth. "Wait, you're seriously considering this? You'd actually hire someone to be your date?"

Humiliation nips at my spine, but I still nod with conviction.

"But that's . . . ridiculous. It's just a wedding."

I slam him with a nasty glare that makes his green eyes open wide. "You're right, Andy. It is ridiculous. And to anyone else, it would be *just* a wedding. But this is my mother we're talking about. There's no *just* anything in her world. So as ridiculous as it may be, I don't have a choice. I have to hire someone."

"Oh for fuck's sake," Tracy groans.

"Sweetie . . ." Claire sighs. "You know the whole hiring-a-date thing was the premise of a movie, right?"

"It was?"

She nods slowly, the sympathetic expression I was looking for earlier finally appearing. "Yeah. It was that pretty redhead from *Will & Grace* and that other guy, Dylan McDermott or . . . Dermot Mulroney? I can never keep the two of them straight. Anyway, yeah, it was a movie. And a book before that . . ."

A book?

A movie?

I'm trying to solve my problems by living my life as the premise of a movie?

Good Lord.

I collapse face-first onto the table. "What am I going to do? My mother will lose her mind if I show up without a date."

"At least your mom cares enough to lose her mind," Tracy chimes in over a stomach-turning slurp of noodles. "Mine doesn't give a shit about my personal life. So long as I have a thriving medical career, she leaves me alone."

"Oh, T, that's not true, and you know it," Claire says. "Your parents were so happy when you were dating Martin."

"Only because he's a cardiologist. If he had been a gardener or something, they never would have gone for it."

"I don't think so—"

"Guys!" I raise my head, interrupting them. "Stay focused. It's all about me right now."

"It's all about me," Tracy singsongs over an eye roll, while Claire turns back to me, saying, "You're right. Sorry. We're focusing on you, babe."

I'm not usually a self-centered person, but come on! This is serious!

"I guess . . ." I exhale a painful sigh. "We're just going to have to *find* someone for me to start dating. I'll tell my mom that I ended things with Michael but that I'm now dating a new, even better guy. I've got six weeks. I can do this, right?"

"I'm not saying a word," Andy mumbles, shoveling another forkful of noodles into his mouth.

"Of course you can," Claire says encouragingly, while Tracy offers a weak nod.

Yes, of course I can.

I can find someone worthwhile to date in the next six weeks.

"Okay, so who can you set me up with?"

"Oh . . . uh . . . hmm . . ." Claire's bumbled response is strangled into silence as her lips start twisting the way they do when she's struggling not to say what she's really thinking. I know that maneuver well; she does it every time I wear my UGG boots.

I raise my palms. "What's with the face?"

She remains painfully silent, while Andy drops his gaze down to his plate, and Tracy stops midchew to stare at me. Her inky-black eyes are splayed wide, like she's in shock.

"*What?*" I ask again.

Tracy slides Claire a wary look, and then Claire clears her throat and in a weak voice says, "I think maybe it would be better for you to try and find someone on your own this time."

My eyes narrow. "What—why? You guys have set me up plenty of times."

"True. But . . ." Claire's voice trails off again, her lips pretzeling her into silence.

"*But what?*" I press.

Tracy sighs and sets her chopsticks down on the plate. "Don't take this the wrong way, but you're sort of impossible to please when it comes to men."

My jaw drops. "*What?*"

She shrugs. "It's true. Wiener pincher aside, you've got impossibly high standards that no man will ever be able to meet, which is why you drop them before you even really get to know them. It's a waste of everyone's time to keep setting you up."

High standards?

"What are you talking about?"

Beyond confused, I turn to Claire, looking for clarification, but she gives me only a sheepish smile in response. My eyes narrow.

What the hell is going on?

"How do *I* have impossibly high standards?" I ask, shifting my gaze between the two of them. "Do you know me at all? Just look at me." I hoist my left leg up onto the table and yank my yoga pants (which have never seen the inside of a yoga studio) up over my knee. I rub my hand across the forest of thick stubble. "I could injure someone with this mess—"

"When it comes to men," Claire interjects, undoubtedly nervous I might reveal some other areas in need of a good shave. "You have impossibly high standards when it comes to *men*, which is why you always end things—"

"For bullshit reasons," Tracy says over her.

"Because none of them will ever fit this perfect mold you have in your head—"

"For bullshit reasons?" I'm fixed on Tracy's ridiculous comment right now. I'll get back to Claire's in a second. "What bullshit reasons have I ever had for breaking up with someone?"

"Seriously?" She turns and looks at Claire and Andy, then back to me. "Okay. How about Seth? What was wrong with him?"

Seth.

Andy's golf buddy.

Ugh—

"Well?" Tracy prods.

"He has baby hands."

Andy shakes his head and groans, while Tracy levels me with a steely look that is clearly intended to solidify her point but doesn't. A man having infant-size hands is not a bullshit excuse; it's a very serious problem.

23

"It's creepy," I say. "His hands are way too small for his body. Ben's hands are bigger than his," I add, using Claire and Andy's kindergartner for illustration. "My hands are literally like three times the size of his. It made me really uncomfortable."

Claire's gaze drifts down to the table, while Tracy sighs and says, "Okay. Seth has teeny-tiny baby hands that make you uncomfortable. What was wrong with Joe?"

Joe. Tracy's twice-divorced neighbor who took me to that rib joint. Oh god, the rib joint.

I inhale a deep breath and on the exhale say, "He hums when he eats."

Andy chuckles under his breath, prompting Claire to grumble, "Shut up and eat your noodles."

Tracy sighs. "No, he doesn't."

"Yes, he does. He hummed through the entire meal."

"*No*, he doesn't. I've had lunch with him like a hundred times. He doesn't hum!"

"Well, then maybe he only does it at dinner!" The sharp tone of my voice makes my head pound. Or maybe it's just last night's wine. Either way, this conversation is getting frustrating. "I swear to you, he hummed 'More Than a Feeling' for almost an hour!"

"At least he's got good taste in music," Andy mumbles over a stifled laugh.

Claire elbows him, while Tracy rolls her eyes and says, "Do you even hear yourself? Tiny hands? Humming? So what! You're pushing forty, Mac. You don't get to nitpick like you did twenty years ago."

"I do if I ever want to listen to a Boston album without ramming scissors in my ears—"

"Whoa, whoa, whoa. Everybody just take a breath," Claire cuts in, aware that tempers are on the rise. "The point of us telling you was *not* to upset you, Mac. It was just to bring to your attention the fact that if you ever want to have a relationship that lasts more than a few weeks—"

"Or a few days," Tracy snips.

Claire glares at her. "You're going to have to readjust your standards."

"More like lower them."

"No," Claire snaps back at her. "That's not what I said—"

"Wait just a second!" I bolt upright, smacking my palms against the tabletop to silence their bickering. "I have had a long-term relationship, thank you very much. Just because you didn't like Brian doesn't mean he doesn't count."

Brian and I dated for over two years, back when we were all in the residency program.

Tracy sighs. "Yeah, and Brian was the *one* guy you actually had a valid reason to dump, and you didn't."

"He wasn't *that* bad," I say, which we all know is a total lie.

Claire casts me a tired glance while Tracy continues, "Um, hello? He was a deadbeat who couldn't keep a job and ended up draining your bank account and stealing the one nice thing in your closet!"

Despite the slam to my wardrobe, Tracy's right. Besides being a freeloader, Brian was also a thief. Not only did he skip town with the $3,000 I had tucked away in my savings account, but he also stole the Kate Spade handbag I'd treated myself to after graduating med school. I really *should* have ended things sooner—before I was broke and bagless—but I was pushing thirty and had never dated anyone longer than a few weeks before. I guess some insecure part of me (no doubt fueled by my mother's incessant nagging) felt like I had to prove to myself I was capable of something long-term, no matter how many red flags were being waved in my face.

"Look, babe," Claire continues, pulling me back to the frustrating present. "All we're saying is that you're never going to find a Mr. Right if you continue to measure them against this fictitious-perfect-guy mold you have stuck in your head."

"Fictitious-perfect-guy mold?" I raise my hands. "What does that even mean? Who is this fictitious perfect guy?"

Claire tips her head thoughtfully. "Jake Ryan."

I blink hard. "Jake Ryan?"

She nods, and Tracy adds, "Yeah, Jake Ryan. From *Sixteen Candles*."

I blast her with an exhausted look. "Yeah, I know the movie, Tracy."

Of course I know what movie Jake Ryan was in. I practically wore out the VCR after I was introduced to him. It was the summer of '97. I'd just turned fifteen, and our parents had ventured off to Europe, leaving Hope and me in the care of Amanda, our twenty-four-year-old cousin. Along with a carton of clove cigarettes and a case of Zima, she brought a library of her favorite eighties movies with her: *The Breakfast Club*, *Ferris Bueller*, *Weird Science* . . . All of them instantly claimed my affection with their angsty teenage drama and outrageous characters, but it was *Sixteen Candles* that stole my heart, just as it did for every other red-blooded female I've ever met.

"So, wait . . ." I blink hard. "Are you guys suggesting that I'm using Jake Ryan, a character from a movie I haven't seen in over *twenty years*, as a measuring stick for the men I date?"

The question sounds so absurd rolling off my tongue I can't help but snicker. These are two of the most intelligent, well-rounded women I've ever had the pleasure of knowing. There's no way they *actually* believe this. Clearly they're just messing with me. Trying to take the edge off all this wedding drama—

"Yes," Tracy says, and Claire nods in agreement.

"What?" Andy blurts out.

"*What?*" I echo him in a much-louder voice. "That's the stupidest thing I've ever heard. I don't look at every guy I date and wish he were wearing Top-Siders and a plaid shirt, or that he would steal the sex test someone passed me during study hall to see if I wrote down *his* name in answer to the *Who would you do it with?* question—"

"Over twenty years since you've seen the movie, huh?" Tracy mumbles.

I scowl at her; everybody knows that stuff. "I don't do that! I can't even remember the last time I said the name *Jake Ryan* until today!"

"You said it plenty of times when we were in Sonoma," Claire counters.

Sonoma?

I think back on the birthday trip Tracy and I surprised Claire with back in January, where the three of us spent a long weekend slurping our way through the swanky Northern California wine country.

"When did I talk about Jake Ryan?"

"That night when you were telling us about Caroline Fuller—"

Caroline Fuller: a patient of mine I know from high school. She tracked me down the day before we left for our trip. Her jerk of a boyfriend split up with her when she told him she was pregnant, so now she's going it alone.

"—and how you guys always used to play MASH during Spanish class, but instead of using boys you knew from school for the husband list, you used your movie boyfriends. You said that Jake Ryan was always at the top of your list."

Though the specifics of that night are buried beneath about a gallon of merlot, I do have a vague recollection of saying that, because it's true. Jake Ryan *was* always at the top of my MASH list. Quite often we ended up living in a shack in Tijuana with fourteen kids, but it still felt like a win because I was married to Jake . . . even if he was fictional.

"So *that's* how you established this ridiculous theory of yours? Because Jake Ryan was on my MASH list?" I stare at her, stupefied. "I also had Jack from *Titanic* and Ren McCormack on my list, so how come I'm not sabotaging my love life because of one of them?"

"Because you didn't blather on for half an hour about how you wished more men would take on the local preacher so you and your friends could dance in a barn," Tracy chimes in, her chin thrust high as if proud of her eighties-movie knowledge. "But you did about Jake."

"No I didn't."

"Yeah, you did," Claire confirms over an impish grin. "You went on and on about how more men should be like Jake; they shouldn't care about money or prestige, should be respectful to their elders, especially grandparents"—she pauses to tsk me with her finger, as if mimicking something *I'd* done—"and that they should be able to look past the Barbie dolls of the world and instead go for the girl with substance, even if she has smallish tits—"

Andy barks out a laugh, while I interject, saying, "I did not say that. You know I hate the T-word."

Tracy and Claire exchange an amused look. "Oh, I assure you, you said *tits*." Claire chuckles. "More than once."

"A lot more than once," Tracy adds.

My cheeks flush with embarrassment. *How drunk was I?*

"Sweetie, it's pretty obvious that you're hung up on Jake Ryan, or at least the *idea* of him," Claire goes on. "And nobody's saying it's abnormal. I mean, we all had a movie boyfriend that shaped the way we look at men—"

"Daniel LaRusso," Tracy cuts in. "He may not be Asian, but damn if he couldn't pull off that karate gi."

"Who was yours?" Andy asks Claire.

"Farmer Ted, obviously." She gives his red head a playful scratch after comparing him to the lovable dork from *Sixteen Candles*, then continues, "It's just that you're destroying any possibility of a relationship because, whether you recognize it or not, you're measuring every guy up to the Jake Ryan standard you set when you were fifteen years old, and unless you ditch that, you're *never* going to find someone."

Longing stabs me as the image of a married handyman spreading his plaid shirt on the floor taps the back of my mind unexpectedly. I shut it down, reminding myself I'm not on the hunt for a relationship. I just need a date for my sister's damn wedding.

Chapter 3

Forty days until the wedding . . .

Stephen Davison

Skip Overstreet

I glare down at the pathetically short list, rip off a chunk of bagel, and shove it into my mouth.

"All right, bud," I grumble to Rerun, who's sitting hopefully at my feet. "One of these two is going to be my Michael. Assuming neither of them have gotten married or come out of the closet lately." My gaze instinctively tightens in on Stephen's name. Stephen with a *ph* instead of a *v*. Stephen who was wearing a purple tie and loafers without socks the last time I saw him . . . *dammit.*

~~*Stephen Davison*~~

"Okay, maybe there's only one, but he is definitely going to be my Michael. Those girls think my expectations are too high. They think I only want to date Jake Ryan, but we'll show them, won't we, bud?"

Woof!

Rerun's commiserating bark earns him a scratch on the head—and the rest of my bagel.

Jake Ryan complex?

I shake my head.

Please.

◆ ◆ ◆

Despite his assurance that he wouldn't arrive to fix Gia's bathroom until later today, I still peek out the living room window to see if J.T.'s truck is out front. It's not, which is just fine. I need to focus on the task at hand, not lose myself in cocoa-filled fantasies . . . I pack up my gear for the day, then head out the back door, where I find Gia on her knees in the grass, spray-painting a canvas. Our atypically warm weather disappeared over the weekend, but that doesn't hinder her wardrobe selection. She's barefoot and wearing a tank top and shredded jeans. I cinch my jacket up tighter and make my way out to greet her.

"Morning."

"Hey, Mac."

"Is that another Steve project?"

She sits back on her haunches. "I'm not sure yet." She stares thoughtfully at the neon-yellow canvas. "I woke up this morning with a compelling need to immerse myself in yellow, so . . ."

Her explanation drifts away on one of her creative thoughts, leaving me, as always, clueless as to how her brain works.

"Okay, I'm heading into the clinic. I should be home around six or so. J.T. is coming by sometime today, so I guess just leave your door unlocked if you're not home." She nods in understanding but keeps her attention focused on the canvas. "And the old man is crashed out on his pillow, so . . ."

"Yeah, okay," she says, reaching for her spray can. "I'll check on him in a little while."

The Jake Ryan Complex

This is normally the point in the conversation where I'd take her disregard as my dismissal, but I can't go, not yet.

I swallow hard and, with a painful amount of hesitance, say, "Do you happen to know anyone you could set me up with?"

She shakes her spray can. "Are you just looking to bang it out, or are you talking about an actual date?"

The fact that she's even asking me that question is why I was reluctant to ask her in the first place. "Uh . . . an actual date. He doesn't have to be a forever kind of guy," I clarify. "Just someone . . . nice. And if he happens to look like Jake Ryan, then, you know, bonus."

I grin at my little joke, but the reference appears to be lost on Gia. "Who?" She finally raises her head to look at me.

"Jake Ryan. From *Sixteen Candles*."

She shrugs.

A tiny piece of my heart breaks, and I sigh.

She knows every Google-worthy detail of Steve Guttenberg's life, but she has never heard of Jake Ryan . . .

"Never mind. Just think about it, okay? I'll see you tonight."

Feeling monumentally old, I make my way out to the car and head into the city.

Daisy, Tracy's cousin, is manning the reception desk when I arrive at the clinic. She graduated with a master's in psychology last year but hasn't been able to find a job, so she works here answering phones and scheduling appointments. Well, she *sort of* works. Mostly she just plays therapist to anyone who speaks in her general direction, but we overlook her professional shortcomings because our patients have come to rely on her always-bendable ear (and occasionally helpful advice), and in the long run that saves us doctors time—and mental stability. Expectant and hoping-to-be mothers aren't always the most rational people.

"Morning, Daisy."

She's too busy talking to the always-crying Diana Chambers—twenty-three-weeks pregnant with triplets—to acknowledge me with anything more than a wave. I don't take it personally.

I duck into my office, where my patient docket waits on my desk. I take a quick look at the day's schedule while I swap out my jacket for my lab coat.

Interesting.

Caroline Fuller, my former high school sort-of friend, is coming in this afternoon.

She was pretty popular back in school. Maybe *she* knows a future Michael to set me up with—

"Paging Dr. *Ryan*." Claire pokes her head into my office, grinning.

I roll my eyes.

"You're hysterical, you know that?"

She smirks as she settles in against the doorjamb. "So, did you come up with some potential Michael candidates over the weekend?"

"As a matter of fact, I did." I grab my stethoscope from my desk drawer and start toward the door. "And it's a long list, too, so you geniuses better be prepared to eat your words when you see how fast I land myself a Michael."

"Ooh. Them sound like fightin' words," she teases, backing out of the way as I pass by her and head down the hall toward the exam room. "You're not trading Jake Ryan in for Rocky, are you?"

I shake my head, fighting the urge to laugh. My friends are idiots.

Ultrasounds and pelvic exams steal my morning and, thankfully, all my attention. I don't even think about the Michael situation until the afternoon, when I walk into the exam room and find Caroline waiting for me. She's got to know someone she can set me up with.

"What's up, hooker?" Offering the same greeting she has since high school, Caroline hops off the exam table and hurries over to hug me. Her mane of wild auburn curls presses against my mouth and nose, suffocating me beneath the heavy floral scent of her shampoo.

I swallow back a cough and say, "How are you? How are you feeling?"

"All right, I guess, except that I haven't taken a dump in like four days. Is that normal?"

Caroline's crass response doesn't surprise me. She's always been a little rough around the edges. Which is probably why my mother never approved of her . . . which subsequently only made me want to hang out with her more . . .

"Unfortunately, it is." I motion for her to hop back onto the table while I head to the sink to wash my hands. "Heightened progesterone levels tend to relax your muscles, including your digestive tract, so that can slow things down. Or it could be the extra iron in your prenatals. Are you getting much fiber in your diet?"

"I had a bran muffin for breakfast."

"That will probably do the trick, but if it doesn't, you can drink a little Milk of Magnesia. That should get things moving."

I unwind the scope from my neck, tuck the ear tips into place, and make my way over to the exam table.

"So, how's everything going? Work good?" I press the stethoscope against her chest.

Normal rhythm. Good.

"Yeah, it's fine. Just busy as hell. Tomorrow I'm flying out to New York for client meetings, and then Friday I'm heading to Seattle for a big pitch."

I gently guide her forward so I can listen to her lungs. I press the scope against her back, and she takes in a deep breath. Then another.

All clear. Good.

"What's in Seattle?"

I slowly ease her back down.

"Cannibeats."

"Canni . . . what?"

33

She laughs. "Cannibeats. Like *cannabis* and *eats*. It's a restaurant chain that uses weed in all of their recipes."

My eyes grow wide. "That's a thing?"

"Hell yeah, it's a *huge* thing. Anything weed related is selling like a motherfucker right now. This Cannibeats place started out as a food truck three years ago, and now they have fourteen locations in Washington and Oregon. They turned a profit of something like nine million dollars last year."

"Really?"

"Yeah, nine million dollars for pot brownies. It's insane! That's why I'm flying out there. They want to expand down into California now that they legalized. They're looking to run a huge campaign."

Caroline is a sales exec for a national advertising firm. She had been working at their Los Angeles office but was transferred back here to Chicago about a year ago. I guess it makes sense that they'd want her in on this deal, since she's the most familiar with the territory.

"I can still fly, right?" She interrupts my thoughts with a pointed look. "'Cause I have no problem telling those assholes I work for that I can't go. If it's too risky, I won't go."

Despite her ashtray vocabulary, I have no doubt that Caroline will be a good mom. She is always very conscious of doing what's best for her baby. Though I suspect *mama* won't be the first four-letter word that little one speaks.

"I think you're fine to fly now, but by next month we'll probably want to keep you grounded."

Even though there haven't been any complications, Caroline's still considered high risk based on age alone. Once she hits her third trimester, we're going to be extra cautious.

"Okay, let's see what this little one is up to."

I raise the hem of her shirt while she yanks down the elastic band of her maternity pants, exposing her rounded belly. Now at twenty-two weeks, her baby bump is really starting to show, like a cantaloupe she somehow swallowed whole.

"Have you felt the baby kicking yet?" I ask while reaching for the ultrasound gel from the counter beside me.

"I'm not sure it's kicking, but it's definitely doing something in there. Especially after I eat."

"Sounds about right."

I squirt some gel onto her belly, then press the Doppler against it and start seeking out a heartbeat. At first we just hear the whoosh-whooshing sound of the amniotic fluid, but with a little maneuvering, I land on my target. Caroline smiles.

"Oh my god. That's a heartbeat. There's a fucking person inside of me," she says, savoring the sweet sound like she does every time she hears it.

"Yeah, there is. A very healthy one from the sound of it."

We listen until the baby starts to move and we lose the feed.

I trade out the Doppler for a towel, and while wiping the gel off her stomach, I say, "So your ex is still being a jerk, huh?"

"And then some. That asshole won't even answer the phone when I call."

"He really wants nothing to do with his own child?"

"Nope. When I found out, he told me that he never signed up for a kid, so if I was going to keep it, I was on my own."

"God, that just makes me sick. How could someone be so cold and heartless?"

"You got me." She shrugs. "I mean, it's not like I was in the market for a baby, either, but here I am."

"Yep. And you're doing great," I assure her. "You don't need him."

"Damn straight. There are way too many penises in the pond to waste my time worrying about him."

Her penis metaphor makes me laugh but also reminds me what I need to talk to her about: the need for a penis in my own pond.

"Since we're on the topic of guys," I say as casually as possible while giving my hands another wash at the sink. "Do you happen to know anyone you could set me up with? I'm in desperate need of a date."

"Ooh. *Desperate* needs are the best kind . . ."

"No, not like that. I stupidly told my mother I was dating someone just to get her off my back, but now my sister's getting married, and if I don't show up at the wedding with my *boyfriend*, all hell will break loose. I just need to find someone to play the part—"

"No need to explain." She cuts me off with a raise of her hand. "I was there for Martina Day, remember?"

I sigh. As if I could ever forget Martina Day . . . It was my senior year of high school, and prom was quickly approaching. Because I hadn't been asked, I didn't even mention the dance to my mom. (Dances and pep rallies were her high school priorities, not mine.) But when she arrived on campus for a PTA meeting and saw the "Enchanted Evening" posters plastered across school, she pulled me out of English class and confronted me about whether I'd been asked right there in the hallway. With Caroline and my other classmates within earshot on the other side of the door, I couldn't very well lie—they all knew I hadn't been asked—so I was forced to tell her the truth. The result was a tirade of premenopausal wails, followed by accusations of *"It's because of your hair! I told you that short haircut made you look like that Martina Navratilova! That's why they're not asking you—they think you're a lesbian! It's that ridiculous hair!"*

Thankfully, some of her fellow PTA members started coming our way, so she quickly shut up—too concerned with looking foolish in front of them—but the damage had already been done. For the remainder of the school year, I was known around campus as *Martina*, my locker and car's windshield regularly adorned with heart-outlined images of the famous tennis player.

And I wonder why I continue lying to her . . .

"So, what are you into?" Caroline asks, bringing me back to the present.

My eyes narrow.

What am I into?

"Short, tall, black, white . . . What's your poison?"

"Oh right, um . . ." I grab a paper towel from the dispenser and lean up against the counter as I consider her question. I've never really thought of myself as having a type, but . . . "Well, I don't really care about ethnicity, but I guess I'd prefer that he be tall. A couple inches on me, if possible." Unlike Hope, who is five foot three on a good day and has always managed to make her plump curves enviable, I'm a five-nine beanpole with a shapeless silhouette and, as I apparently said on the infamous Sonoma trip, smallish tits. There's nothing worse than having your date be eye level with your boy chest.

"You want him to be local, right?"

"Definitely."

I'll need to squeeze in as many dates before the wedding as possible. Long distance is not an option.

"Is girth an issue?"

"Girth?"

"Yeah, do you like a thick dick or a candy stick? Oh my god, that should be a commercial." She snorts. "Do you see why I'm in advertising? This shit just comes to me."

Inwardly cringing, I fake a laugh of my own. "Yeah, you definitely have a knack for it. But, um, no. I'm not worried about that. In fact, I'd prefer you not have firsthand knowledge of their . . . size."

"Oh." A look of surprise settles on her face before she shrugs. "Okay, well, that will thin the herd a bit. Let me think on it, and I'll message you later."

I help her down from the table and, as I do with all my clients, walk her out to the lobby to schedule her next appointment, for one month from now. I'd ask Daisy to do it, but she's busy counseling Lydia Hernandez, thirty-nine weeks, baby number five.

God help you, Lydia . . .

At the end of the day, I'm packing up things and find Daisy standing in my doorway, a pinched look on her face.

"Hey. What's up?"

"There's something off about that woman."

My eyes narrow. "Which woman?"

"That Caroline woman you saw earlier."

"What do you mean *off*?"

"She's evasive."

"Evasive?" I fight the smirk threatening my lips. Daisy and her diagnoses . . .

"Yeah, she never gives solid answers to any of my questions, especially when I ask about the baby daddy."

"Probably because it's private." I give her a stern look. Daisy means well, but not everyone wants to lounge on her therapy couch when they come into the office. She really needs to learn some boundaries. "What do you have there?" I motion to the yellow Post-it note in her hand while I peel off my lab coat.

"Oh. Yeah. I took a message for you."

She took a message?

Like an actual phone message . . .

She steps into the office and presses the note onto my desktop, her raven-black hair swaying off her shoulder. "She said if you weren't going to answer your cell, she had no choice but to call you at work."

She?

Dammit.

There's only one *she* who ever calls me at work.

Scowling, I stare down at the note and shake my head.

Call your mother! Wedding emergency!

"She told you to use exclamation points, didn't she?"

Daisy crosses her arms over her chest and with authority says, "*That woman has control issues.*"

I wait until I'm driving home to return my mother's calls. There's something about the stress of bumper-to-bumper traffic that numbs the pain of talking to her. Probably because my hands are already strangling the steering wheel—

"Mackenzie Rose, it's about time you called me back. I've been trying to get ahold of you all day."

And my knuckles run white.

"Hey, Mom. Sorry. I was just really busy"—being an important doctor, not that you'd ever notice. "What's the emergency?"

"Well, we're working on the invitation list, and we need Michael's address."

My breath hitches. "Wh-why do you need his address?"

"So we can mail him an invitation."

"But . . . he'll be coming with me."

"Well, yes, I know that, but it would be impolite not to send him his own invitation."

I shake my head, hard. "No. No, it wouldn't."

"Nonsense. We're not a bunch of ticky-tackies, Mackenzie. Wedding invitations are keepsakes. We're sending them to all of our family members, and for this event Michael is considered part of the family."

Michael is considered part of the family. SHIT!

"Now tell me, what is his address?"

"Do . . . you mean his email address?"

She makes a horrific sound that lands somewhere between a gasp and a pig being slaughtered.

"*Heavens no!* We're not sending out emails, Mackenzie, honestly. What kind of wedding do you think this is?"

I fake a laugh, like I'm not slowly dying on the inside, but my horrified reflection in the rearview would say otherwise.

"So . . . the thing is, Mom, Michael is actually in the process of renovating his condo. He's having all of his mail rerouted to a PO box so nothing gets lost in the construction. You should probably just send it to me at my house, and I'll give it to him."

The lie rolls off my tongue fast. So fast I don't even know if it sounds believable—

"He's renovating his condo? I thought you said it was a brand-new building."

Crap.

Keep your lies straight, stupid!

"Well . . . brand new to *him.* The building is actually a few years old. He just wanted to rework the floor plan so he could put in a . . . tasting room."

A tasting room?

What the hell is a tasting room?

"A tasting room?"

"Yeah. For all the things he . . . tastes."

Like a kitchen?!

"A tasting room," she repeats. "Well, that sounds posh, doesn't it?"

I nod over a relieved sigh. Yes, it sounds very posh. My boyfriend, Michael, is *very* posh.

"All right, then, we'll just send it to your house, but make sure that silly old dog doesn't get to it. You know how he's always slobbering on your mail when it comes through the slot—*oh!* The bride is here. Hope, honey, please come over here and tell your sister what we're up to."

Please. That simple little word epitomizes the difference between Hope's relationship with our mother and mine. She always gets a *please* or a *thank-you* served up with her orders; I . . . don't.

"Hey, maid of honor!"

Maid of honor?

I cringe as an image of Molly Ringwald in a flowered headband and pink chiffon dress suddenly flashes through my mind.

"Hi, Hope."

"Isn't this so exciting!"

Sucking back a breath through gritted teeth, I nod. "Yes, it's *so* exciting. Congratulations."

"Aw, thanks, Macaroni. Sorry I haven't called you back. It's just been so crazy telling everybody!"

"Yeah, I bet."

Truth be told, I was grateful she didn't return the message I left her over the weekend. What with the whole Jake Ryan accusation and my search for the perfect wedding date, I've had more than enough to keep me occupied.

"Mom and I are driving down to Chicago to go dress shopping this weekend. You'll come, right?"

"Oh, um . . ."

"Just for *my* dress. We'll do the bridesmaids' dresses the next weekend. Or maybe it's the weekend after that? Ohmygod, I can't remember! I just know we're going to be super pressed for time."

"Yeah, why are you doing this so quickly? What's the rush?"

"Aww, it's because of Whit's grandma. She's just the sweetest old lady, and it's basically her dying wish to see all of her grandchildren get married, and since he's the last one, we just figured, why not, you know?"

Yeah, *why not* just get married . . .

"Of course, Mom is totally freaking out because there is just so much to do—"

"I am not freaking out!" Mom shouts in the background.

Hope laughs.

I roll my eyes.

Her tolerance for our mother has always been *so* much higher than mine.

"But we've got this amazing wedding coordinator, Tammy, who's handling everything. She's fantastic! All we have to do is show up and pick out what we want. We're on our way to the florist right now—"

"And we're going to be late if we don't leave right this second!" Mom hollers. "Mackenzie, we'll see you this weekend. Make sure your house is ready for guests. I don't want to be digging through the hamper for clean towels again!"

Again? It happened once. Maybe twice.

"Yeah, we'll see you this weekend! Oh, here, Dad wants to talk to you. Bye—"

"Hey, Goose."

The sound of my dad's calm voice greeting me with my childhood nickname instantly quells the dithering whirlwind that is Mom and Hope. My shoulders relax, and I take a deep breath.

"Hey, Dad."

"How you been?"

"Pretty good."

"How's the baby business treating you?"

I smile. Dad always asks about work. "Busy, but really good. How about you? How's the retirement business treating you?"

"Great, now that your mom has a wedding to plan."

I laugh. After forty-one years of humbly working his way up the educational chain—middle school teacher to principal to superintendent to his final stint as vice-chair of the State of Michigan Board of Education—my dad finally decided to call it a ball game last fall . . . or so he thought. Little did he know his life's *real* work, surviving my mother 24/7, was still ahead of him.

"Mom's a little preoccupied, huh?"

"Yup. And it's a beautiful thing, Goose."

"So, what do you think about all of this wedding business, anyway? It seems sort of sudden, doesn't it?"

"Yes, but that's your sister. She's never been one for thoughtful contemplation."

I laugh again. "No, she hasn't."

"I think she'll be all right," he goes on in that quiet way of his. "She seems really happy, and he's a nice guy—solid, good head on his shoulders. Although he went to Ohio State—"

"He's a Buckeye?"

I've spent time with Whitman on only two occasions: once just before Christmas and then again in January, when he and Hope were in town for a friend's wedding. I got to know a fair amount about him, but surprisingly his alma mater never came up. Now I know why . . .

"Afraid so," Dad groans over a painful-sounding sigh.

I glance down at the "University of Michigan Alumni" key chain dangling from my ignition and shake my head. A Buckeye in the family. What the hell is Hope thinking?

"I already told your mother to seat us at opposite ends of the table at Thanksgiving dinner."

"Opposite ends of the house would probably be better," I counter.

"Speaking of houses, how's your place coming along? Did you get that front porch squared away?"

A schoolgirl grin tugs on my lips, then flits away just as suddenly as an image of J.T. comes to mind. "Not yet, but I'm working on it. I think I finally found a reliable contractor."

"Well, that's good to hear, but I tell you what. If he ends up being inaccessible, I'll come down after the wedding and do it for you."

Inaccessible. I cringe, because obviously my dad doesn't mean off-limits, as in both morally and ethically. "Oh, Dad, no. You don't have to do that."

"I know I don't *have to.* I want to. I'm pretty good with a hammer and nails, in case you forgot."

"I didn't forget," I say, reflecting on the two-story tree house still wedged perfectly into the crooks of the big elm in their backyard. It was the envy of all the neighborhood kids. "But you're retired. The whole point of being retired is to stop working."

"No, the whole point of being retired is to only do the things I want to do. And I want to work on your porch."

I chuckle. "So, the time away from Mom to come and fix my front porch would just be . . ."

"A little silver lining to the immense joy I'll get in helping my favorite oldest child."

"I'm your only oldest child."

"Which is why you're my favorite."

My heart warms. Same line he's been using on me my whole life and it still makes me feel like the most special person in the world. Not even Jake Ryan could do that . . .

◆ ◆ ◆

There's still a hint of daylight left when I turn onto my street, but rather than enjoy the pretty view of Mrs. Foster's hot-pink hydrangeas, my attention immediately zeroes in on the curb in front of my house. I smile as a stupid little flutter rises in my chest. He's still here . . . I take a quick peek at myself in the rearview, then refocus on the road ahead, my headlights shining directly onto the back of his truck—

The brake lights suddenly ignite, a glaring red glow that instantly squashes my excitement. *He's leaving* . . . I slow my speed and watch from a distance as the big black pickup slowly pulls away from the curb and heads down the road . . . probably off to the flower shop to pick up a Sweetheart's Special for the swimsuit model.

"You're an idiot," I mumble to myself.

My phone chimes from the console beside me. I glance down and see that I've got a new text, from Caroline. I slam my foot on the brake and grab my phone. The message reads:

What's up, hooker?! I've got a wedding date for you! His name's Daniel. We used to work together. He's huge! Part Samoan or Tongan or some shit like that. Wants to meet up w/you tomorrow night. RAWR! I'll forward you his contact info.

I stare down at the text and inhale a deep, motivating breath.

J.T. the Contractor may be off the market, but Daniel the Huge is not.

Jake Ryan complex be damned.

Let's do this.

Chapter 4

A preterm delivery got me racing to the hospital at five twenty this morning, which means I totally avoided seeing J.T. (a good thing, I've decided, because even daydreaming about a married man is still wrong!), and the mother's resulting complications kept me there until nearly six tonight. Thankfully both mom and baby—weighing in at a whopping 5.4 pounds (impressive for a thirty-three-week-old preemie)—are resting comfortably now, but I'm not faring quite so well. I'm supposed to meet Daniel for dinner in twenty minutes, and despite the quick shower I took in the doctors' lounge at the hospital, I'm pretty sure there are chunks of placenta stuck in my hair.

I make a quick pit stop at the clinic (just a few blocks from the restaurant) and change into the emergency outfit I keep stashed in my office. I'd planned on wearing my navy-blue dress but was in such a tizzy getting out of the house this morning that I forgot to grab it. Black pants and the wrinkled, pale-blue blouse that's been stashed in my drawer will have to do. Maybe Daniel the Huge will also be Daniel the Visually Impaired . . .

The clinic has been closed for over an hour, but Andy and Tracy are still here catching up on paperwork. They see me hurrying down the hall and call out to me from the break room, where they're working.

"What?" I lean into the open doorway, visibly out of breath.

"Where are you off to in such a hurry?" Tracy asks.

"I've got a date."

"That's great, Mac," Andy says over a supportive nod.

"With who?" Tracy asks.

I level her with a hard look. "Jake Ryan."

She rolls her eyes.

"His name is Daniel."

"Where'd you meet him?"

"Caroline introduced us."

Her dark eyebrows rise. "Caroline, your patient?"

"Caroline my sort-of friend from high school." The distinction won't matter to Tracy, but it does to me. It feels less pathetic somehow. "She used to work with him and thought we'd be a good fit."

"Really?" Always one for overanalyzing, she sets her pen down on the table and leans back in her chair, arms folded firmly across her petite frame. "You know, I only spoke to her the one time, but she didn't strike me as someone you'd be friends with. She seems really brash and sort of rude."

Andy snort laughs. "Sounds vaguely familiar . . ."

"Shut up." She smacks his arm, prompting him to laugh harder. "She just doesn't seem like the kind of woman you'd personally associate with. I'm surprised you trust her judgment enough to set you up with someone."

Truth be told, I'm not sure that I *do* trust Caroline's judgment, not completely, anyway. She led me down more than one unsavory path the few times we hung out back in school—during my rebellious stage—convincing me to go along with her and the football players to steal our rival's mascot being the most notable. (Despite what anyone tells you, badgers are *not* friendly animals, and you *will* get suspended if you're caught stealing one.) Still, Caroline *is* my friend, and at least she's willing to help me by setting me up. Which is more than I can say for some people . . . "I don't have time for this. I'm late. I'll see you guys tomorrow."

"Have fun!" Andy calls out as I head down the hall toward the front door.

"I will!"

"Don't let him borrow your undies so he can win a bet with his friends!" Tracy taunts, matching my sarcastic *Sixteen Candles* response with one of her own.

I roll my eyes. "His name is *Daniel*, not Farmer Ted!"

The Farmer's Table.

The irony of Daniel's restaurant choice, given my parting words to Tracy, isn't lost on me.

Farmer freaking Ted.

Damn you, Tracy . . .

In a useless effort to smooth out the wrinkles, I drag my palms down the length of my shirt while I scour the busy room for the bar area, where Daniel the Huge said he'd be waiting for me.

Like so many of the new restaurants springing up around this part of town, the industrial look has taken over: polished concrete floors, distressed dining tables, brick walls, naked bulbs dangling from the ceiling—

A gentle tap to my shoulder steals my attention. I quickly turn and—*whoa.*

The man standing in front of me is big. Like a wall. A *really* good-looking wall with brown skin and a clean-shaven head that suddenly has me craving a gumball.

"Are you by chance Mackenzie Huntress? Friend of Caroline?"

I blink hard, captivated by the sultry quality of his deep voice. "Um . . . yes. Hi. You must be Daniel?"

Or Michael . . .

"I am," he says over a brimming smile. "It's great to meet you."

"You too."

"These are for you." He raises a trio of yellow roses.

Not only am I not big on flowers in general, but I hate roses. They remind me of crotchety Aunt Marie's after-bath oil, but the gesture is so sweet that I still bring them to my nose and say, "They're beautiful. Thank you."

"My pleasure. I'm so glad we were able to do this."

"Yeah, me too."

Thank you, Caroline!

"Shall we?"

He presses his big hand gently against my lower back and ushers me through the crowded dining room to a table, where he pulls out my chair before I have the chance to tell him it's not necessary.

Looks like J.T. isn't the only tall, good-looking, *and* chivalrous man in town after all. And this one is accessible. Definitely wedding-date material.

"I'm surprised you were able to meet up on such short notice," he says as I turn to secure my bag on the back of my chair. "When Caroline told me how great you were, I figured I'd have to wait a few weeks before you had room in your schedule."

Room in my schedule . . . ha!

"I'm just glad it all worked out." I turn back and find a red envelope sitting on the table in front of me. My jaw falls slack. I can't remember the last time a man gave me a card for a nonholiday.

And definitely not on a first date.

"Go ahead and open it," he urges with a nod.

Pleasantly surprised, I rip open the envelope and pull out the card. The cover is a picture of a fat orange tabby cat dressed in medical scrubs. The inside simply reads:

Here's to a relaxing meal and good conversation.

—Daniel

Much like my aversion to roses, I am definitely *not* a cat person, but I can still appreciate the cute picture (a gigantic cat in scrubs is sort of funny) and the thoughtful sentiment behind his note. It's flattering to know he was looking forward to spending time with me tonight. Flattering and a little weird, maybe—*no!* No. It's not weird; it's nice. And thoughtful. Daniel is a nice, thoughtful man, and *I* am an open woman who does not set impossibly high standards.

Smiling, I tuck the card back into the envelope and return my attention to him.

"That's really sweet, Daniel. Thank you. It's been a long time since I got a card for something other than my birthday."

"That's because instant gratification is taking over the world," he says over a heavy sigh.

"Instant gratification?"

"Email," he clarifies. "People don't have the patience to write out their feelings onto cards anymore. They just want to spit them out as quickly as possible and then send them on their way."

I nod. I guess I can see that . . .

"There's just no personality to our correspondence anymore," he goes on. "It all feels so . . . disconnected. Like the only way we're willing to engage with people is if there's a 'Delete' key to fix our mistakes and a monitor to hide behind. There's no authenticity or humanity to any of it. It's really very sad."

I'd like to think the heavy frown that's suddenly dragging down his words is some kind of playful joke inspired by our slightly odd conversation, but I don't think it is. He honestly looks sad.

He's sad that people email instead of give cards.

That's . . . sweet.

"Good evening." A twiggy young blonde approaches the table. "Welcome to the Farmer's Table. I'm Ashley. I'll be serving you tonight."

"Hi," I say, and Daniel says, "Good evening, Ashley."

"Can I get either of you started with a drink? We have a limited-time prickly pear margarita that's really tasty."

"Oh, um . . ." I quickly reach for one of the drink menus propped up on the side of the table. Daniel does the same.

"No rush," Ashley says. "Take a look at the menus, and I'll come back in a minute."

Despite my curiosity in any drink with the word *prickly* in its name, I feel my gaze instinctively drift down to the selection of craft beers. A cold beer sounds really refreshing after the crazy day I've had. I set my menu down and—

My eyes snap wide when I see Daniel holding a pale-pink envelope in his hands. "What's that?"

He grins sheepishly. "I can never stop at just one."

I feel the corners of my mouth start to sag.

He got me *another* card?

Two cards on the first date . . .

"This one is a little more from the heart." With the big, hopeful eyes of a kid on Christmas morning, he hands me the envelope. "Go ahead."

Under his intense gaze, I slowly slide my finger beneath the sealed edge and tear the envelope along the top seam. I swallow hard as I pull out the card. This one has an image of two kittens, each donning a winter cap, huddled together beneath a snow-covered pine tree. A seed of unease roots around in my gut as I flip the card open.

Mackenzie,

I can't think of anything more special than spending tonight with you, learning about your hopes and fears, your dreams and desires . . . all the little things that make you the extraordinary woman you are.

Thank you for the opportunity to share this time together.

—Daniel

I blink, hard.

What the . . . Who gives someone a card like this on their first date . . . or *any* date?

"It's all true," he says earnestly. "I meant every word of it."

I swallow against the painful little knot swelling in my throat and slowly raise my head to look at him. *Ohmygod.* His dark eyes are completely glassed over, like he's crying.

Is he . . . crying?

"I love nights like this," he continues, his glistening gaze slowly zeroing in tighter on me. I shift in my seat. "Getting to know someone for the first time is just so, well, it's just so special, don't you think?"

His question hangs in the air like a stink I don't want to acknowledge, let alone try to answer. Thankfully, Ashley returns, saving me the effort of having to.

"Have we decided on anything?"

I stare up into her naive, twenty-year-old eyes and say, "Give me the stiffest drink you've got."

Over the course of the next hour, I drain a couple of gin rickeys while Daniel the Huge reveals his true identity as Daniel the *Freakishly* Sensitive, pouring out his deepest, most heartfelt feelings on every topic under the sun. From the devastation of the disappearing ice caps to his hatred for the cable company's automated phone system—*the intimacy of the provider-consumer relationship should not be overlooked!* He's blinked away so many tears, I'm starting to question my own humanity.

Am I a monster because I don't watch the baby-koala feed on the zoo's website?

Every bone in my body is aching to excuse myself to the bathroom so I can call Claire or Tracy and commiserate over the details of this bizarre night, but I can't. Not only would Tracy gloat about her accurate assessment of Caroline's matchmaking skills, but somehow those two geniuses would qualify Daniel as another casualty in my quest to find the great Jake Ryan.

As if Jake Ryan would *ever* give greeting cards on a first date. Return borrowed undies, absolutely! But never a greeting card . . .

"So, what do you think?" he asks. "Are you up for dessert?"

"You know, I'd love to, but I should probably get going. It's been a really long day."

"Oh, of course it has." I gave Daniel limited details of my busy morning in a pre-date text in the event I was late, so his response isn't entirely unexpected. "I can't begin to imagine how taxing it is to be in your line of work, with people's lives dependent on you. Will you have to check in on that mother and baby again tonight?"

I'd be lying if I said his interest in my career wasn't the one silver lining to this otherwise ridiculous evening. Other than Gia and my dad, no one outside the clinic ever shows much interest in what I do.

"I'll just call to check in on them tonight, but I'll definitely be stopping by the hospital on my way in tomorrow morning. It's nice to see everybody once the dust has settled a bit."

"Yeah, I bet." He drains what's left of his daiquiri. "You know, that must be hard to shift gears like that: one minute you're sound asleep, and the next you're bringing a child into the world under dangerous conditions . . ."

I nod. It is hard. Sometimes it's *very* hard.

Thanks for noticing, Daniel.

"Do you come from a long line of doctors?"

"Not very long. Just my grandpa. He was a pediatrician."

"Was?"

"He died about fifteen years ago."

"Aw . . ." Daniel's chin starts to tremble, again, which means he's about to cry, again. Strangely, though, this time I don't find it irritating. I'm glad that he recognizes the importance of grandparents. "I'm really sorry to hear that."

"It's okay. He was ninety-two years old and lived a very long, happy life . . ." I surprise myself with a little laugh as a memory of my last conversation with Grandpa Harold suddenly comes to mind. "He was the one who helped me decide to go into obstetrics instead of geriatrics, which is what I was leaning toward."

"Really?"

Lost in the sweet memory, I nod absently. "He told me that dealing with brand-new people who *want* to be alive is a hell of a lot easier than dealing with old ones who don't."

Daniel bellows out a laugh, jarring me from the memory and back to the present, where I start laughing along with him.

"Sounds like sage advice," he says, his dark eyes now sparkling with the same pleasant ease our conversation has taken.

An unexpected smile steals my expression. When he's not crying in his margarita, Daniel is actually really nice to talk to.

He may be viable Michael material after all . . .

"So, did we save room for dessert?" Ashley returns, a dessert menu in one hand and our check in the other.

"No, I think we'll just take the check," Daniel says.

"All righty." She sets the check down on the table. "It's been a pleasure serving you tonight. Have a great rest of the evening."

"You know, I'd really like to do this again," Daniel says as he reaches into his back pocket for his wallet. "Maybe we could try that new Korean place over on the West Side? I've heard great things about it."

An hour ago, I wouldn't have even considered another meal with Daniel as a possibility, but now, with the clock ticking on my date deadline and still no reply email from Skip, the one man on *my* list, I'm not sure I have a lot of options. And Lord knows Mom would drop an egg to see a big hunky guy like Daniel crying at her—I mean *Hope's*—wedding . . .

"Yeah, that would be nice."

Smiling at my response, Daniel lays his credit card inside the little leather folder, while I reach for my bag. "I'm just going to use the restroom before we leave. I've got a bit of a drive ahead of me."

"Sure, take your time. I'll wait for you here."

With a surprising amount of hope in my stride, I set off for the ladies' room. Thankfully there's no wait, so I'm heading back into the dining room within a couple of minutes—

Ohmygod.

My stomach lurches as I approach the table and see Daniel hunched over writing . . . inside a card!

"What are you doing?"

"Just leaving a note for Ashley," he says, smiling up at me. "Isn't this perfect?" He closes the card to show me the front cover. I cringe. It's another damn cat, this one wearing a chef's hat and an apron. "Monetary tips are so impersonal"—he reopens the card so I can see that it's filled cover to cover with his neat handwriting—"so I share my experience with the waitstaff instead. It gives them an opportunity to hear firsthand where they're excelling and what things could use a little improvement. Overall, I thought Ashley did a good job, don't you?" I'm too dumbfounded to answer, so I just nod.

The card is her tip . . . oh no.

No, Daniel. No!

Don't ruin greeting cards for her.

She's just a baby.

She's got her whole life ahead of her!

He signs his name at the bottom, adds hers to the front of the envelope, and then props the finished product up against the salt-and-pepper caddy so she can't possibly miss it.

"You know, I should probably use the restroom before we head out too." He stands, looking perfectly pleased with himself. "Shall I just meet you out front?"

"Sure."

I hang back at the table until he's out of sight and then quickly trade out all the cash in my wallet for the card. I shove it into my bag and head for the door.

Dammit, Daniel!

Why couldn't you just have asked to borrow my undies . . .

Chapter 5

The next morning
Thirty-eight days until the freaking wedding

I stagger into the kitchen, glaring at the wilting roses and the pile of ridiculous cat cards lying on the counter. I'm all for a man who's in touch with his feelings, but there's no way I could take Daniel to the wedding. He'd be sniveling before we even pulled into the church parking lot.

I take the whole mess, including Ashley's unopened card (I couldn't bear to read it), toss it into the trash, and then grab my phone and thump out a quick text to Daniel that I hope conveys *my* feelings without hurting his:

> Thanks again for a nice evening and the offer for another date, but I'm going to pass. Work is keeping me too busy for a social life, but don't worry—that's the way I want it. Please don't waste any tears on me. Take care.

Rerun slowly hoists himself off the pillow in the living room while I load the coffee maker up with some Colombian roast, then head off to my office to check email. I'm beyond grateful to see that Skip has replied to my message.

Hi Mac,

Great to hear from you! Yes, I'm still in Chicago but at my own clinic in Evanston now. Would definitely like to meet up. How about the Cubs game Friday night?

—Skip

Short and sweet and without a hint of emotion.

Ladies and gentlemen, we have ourselves a potential wedding date. And he likes the Cubbies—bonus!

"Hey, Skip"—I'm speaking the words aloud as I type them—"a game sounds great. Just let me know when and where. Mac."

I'm just about to hit the "Send" button when there's a rap on the back door.

Woof!

Rerun's gruff bark startles me more than the knock.

"Who's there, bud? Is that Gia? Did she run out of coffee again?"

Rerun takes off to investigate while I follow behind, cinching my robe up tighter. Gia is the only person who would be knocking on my door at six in the morning . . . I round the hallway that leads back into the kitchen and see Rerun's tail wagging—

Ohmygod.

I gasp, and my feet turn to concrete.

It's J.T.

He waves at me through the door's paned window, his top teeth sinking into his plump bottom lip. My breath catches beneath a sudden flurry of nervous, excited energy. He has a bottom-lip bite?!

"Morning," he calls. "I'm sorry to bother you so early." His already deep voice is muffled by the dual panes of glass, making it sound huskier and . . . sexier than it did the last time I saw him. "Should I come back later?"

I swallow hard. "No, it's okay. You're fine."

Yeah, *you're fine*, all right . . .

As subtly as possible, I rake my fingers through my mess of hair and head toward the door. Rerun now has his snout pressed against it, his entire body wiggling in anticipation. Silly dog, not that I can blame him. If I had a tail, it would definitely be wagging right now.

I open the door, and Rerun barrels out to greet him. "I'm sorry. He's got no manners when it comes to visitors."

"That's okay. We're old friends, aren't we, Rerun?" J.T. kneels and gives him a scratch on the head, eliciting multiple licks on the cheek in return. "You like keeping me company when I work, don't you, old man?" It's slight, but I pick up a hint of doggy baby talk. *Heaven help me.* "Yeah, you do . . ."

"I hope he's not in your way. He's perfectly fine being in the yard on his own, but if there's a person nearby, that's where he wants to be."

"Nah, he's no trouble. I like having him around. He reminds me of my dog."

"What kind of dog do you have?"

"*Did* have." He glances up at me, a painfully endearing expression steeling his face. "He was a mutt. A pit-shepherd mix, but he had a thick tail just like this guy, so I think there was some Lab in there too. I had to put him down last summer."

"Oh, I'm so sorry to hear that. How old was he?"

"Fourteen."

"Gosh, that must have been hard. But that's a nice long life for a dog."

He nods while slowly returning his attention to Rerun. "Yeah. He was a good dog. We went through a lot together . . ."

I have no way of knowing what experiences he's referring to, but based on the way his words just trailed off, like a song that suddenly lost its melody, they must have been pretty meaningful.

A gust of chilly spring air sweeps in through the open door. I quickly back away, saying, "Come inside. I was just about to pour some coffee."

"What, no cocoa?"

My cheeks flush at his playful reminder. "No. No cocoa."

Rerun stays glued to J.T.'s side as he shuts the door and makes his way over to the far side of the butcher block island.

I head for the cupboard to get some mugs. "So, what's got you out and about so early?" I cast a quick glance over my shoulder and, to my surprise, find his attention focused intently on me. His brown eyes snap wide for a split second before he quickly shifts his gaze down to his hands.

"Oh, um . . ." He clears his throat, cheeks reddening beneath his morning stubble. "I just wanted to make sure I got to talk to you about how things have been going, since we haven't had a chance to reconnect."

The awkwardness in his response sends a little tingle dancing across my skin. *Was he checking me out?* The thought no sooner crosses my mind than I catch a glimpse of my terrifying reflection in the microwave's glass door. If he *was* looking at me, it wasn't because he liked what he saw.

I clear my head with a quick shake and reach for the coffeepot. "Yeah, sorry about that. I think I just missed you on Monday, and yesterday turned out to be sort of"—an image of a blubbering Daniel flashes through my mind—"crazy." And monumentally disappointing. The only way Daniel would have ever told me about his dead dog would be in a card. A card with a stupid cat on the front . . .

"That's okay. Gia said that you work a lot. You're a doctor, right?"

"Mm-hmm. An obstetrician."

"Wow. That's impressive. That must be really fulfilling work."

"Most of the time."

"Most of the time?"

I sigh. "Well, pregnant women can be a little . . ."

"Scary?"

"You sound like you're speaking from experience."

"My sister has a couple of kids," he explains, and I can't help but think that means that he doesn't have kids yet. No doubt his super-model wife wants them—probably twins that she can dress up in matching outfits so they can parade around the mall looking like a walking Pottery Barn advertisement. "She pretty much turned into that little girl from *The Exorcist* when she was pregnant. She got really mean and yelled at everybody all the time." He chuckles. "It was like she was possessed. Nobody could do anything right."

I can't help but laugh too. Demonic possession is a very common side effect during pregnancy.

I fill the mugs while he continues, "I remember my poor brother-in-law used to hang out at our house all weekend because he was too scared to go home. Especially during football season. If her team lost, oh man, she would lose her mind."

"Well, now, that actually sounds reasonable." I set the mug down in front of him, a steely look in my eye. "You can't fault a girl for being loyal to her team."

"Even if it's the Raiders?"

The Raiders?

I gasp, horrified.

"Don't ask me." He raises his hands, absolving himself of any association. "Sometimes I wonder if we were even raised by the same people."

"The Raiders. That's just . . . un-American."

He offers me an amused grin and then raises the mug to his mouth. The rising steam acts as a sexy little curtain, veiling his lips from my sight. Those full, supple lips that are just begging to be touched—

"I need some creamer." I quickly head to the refrigerator and grab the carton from the shelf, pausing long enough for the cold air to settle my heart rate and redirect my thoughts to more appropriate, rational places.

He's married, Mac. Despite the easy conversation and equally easy view, he is committed to someone else. And just because he's looking at you doesn't mean he's interested in you. He's just here to talk about the plumbing. You're just having a hard time assimilating to normal male behavior after what happened with Daniel. That's all this is. Just relax and focus on the nice conversation with the nice married man.

Mostly convinced, I inhale a deep breath and head back to my coffee. I add a hearty dose of the hazelnut creamer and then offer some to him.

"No thanks. I take it black."

For some reason this doesn't come as a surprise. With his calloused hands and that rugged salt-and-pepper stubble working his jawline, J.T. *looks* like the kind of guy who takes his coffee black. He probably eats his steak rare too. And sleeps without a pillow.

Or clothes.

My mouth starts to water.

Yeah, he definitely sleeps naked—

"So, everything's been going really well here," he says, thankfully stealing me back to the present. I quickly raise the mug and take a drink, hoping to hide the heat flushing across my cheeks. "Some roots from that big elm tree in the corner of your yard got tangled around the main line, but I was able to clear them and replace the bad piping. All I need to do today is install the new drywall, put on a little paint, and you'll be good to go."

"Oh thank god. I thought for sure you were going to tell me you unearthed a dead body or something."

"No. No dead bodies. Not human anyway." He grins.

"With this house it wouldn't surprise me," I mumble and take another drink. "So, is that tree going to continue to be a problem? I hate to cut it down. It gives such great shade in the summer."

"No, we don't need to take it down. It'll definitely cause problems again at some point—those roots are massive—but not anytime soon. And when it does happen, we'll just deal with it the same way."

I smile. I like how he says *we'll*.

"So, I also wanted to talk to you about your front porch," he goes on, pausing to take another drink. "Would it be okay with you if I started this weekend, say Sunday afternoon?"

My eyes grow wide. "You work on the weekends?"

It's slight, but I catch another glimpse of that flush I saw earlier. He drops his head slightly and says, "On occasion. For the right client."

His flirtatious tone stupidly sets my heart to racing again. I raise the mug up to my mouth and, over a budding grin, say, "So only your most *pathetic* clients earn weekend status . . ."

He raises his head, offering another glimpse of that delicious bottom-lip bite I saw earlier.

"Not pathetic. Charming."

Charming?

His gaze stays steady on mine for a split second, long enough that I can *feel* my heart hammering against my sternum before he blinks hard and abruptly shifts his attention back down to the mug.

"Yeah, so . . . I should probably head out back and finish things up. I'm sure I'll be gone by the time you get home tonight, so I'll just plan on seeing you again on Sunday."

I swallow hard. "Okay."

He takes one last drink of coffee and then offers me an awkward smile before he makes a quick beeline for the door. I'm not surprised to see that Rerun is hot on his heels.

"Okay if my partner tags along?"

I nod absently, too confused by what's just happened to give his question much thought.

We had a moment, right?

That wasn't just me . . . Something happened there . . .

Like they've been friends for years, the two disappear out the door and head across the backyard toward Gia's place, while I'm left to try to reconcile what just happened.

I'm quite certain that I just had a *moment* with the hot contractor. And I'm 100 percent certain that I liked it. I really, really liked it.

But the hot contractor is married, which is really, *really* bad.

Not just because that ring means he's officially off-limits, but because *he* had a moment with *me* even though he's got a hot super-model wife at home. And being attracted to a guy like that is even worse than *not* being attracted to a man who cries at the drop of a hat.

Dammit, Jake Ryan. Where are you when I need you?

It's Claire's volunteer day at the boys' school, so I'm surprised to see her van in the parking lot when I arrive at the clinic. I'm even more surprised when I find her walking down the hallway wearing a business suit and nylons. *Nylons!*

"What's wrong? Who died?" I ask, eyeing her with caution.

"No one. I've got that woman coming in to interview today."

"Oh right." I've been so caught up in all the J.T.—er, *Michael*—drama that I forgot we were looking for Claire's replacement as office manager.

"So, I heard you had a date last night with one of Caroline's friends." She waggles her eyebrows. "How'd it go?"

Even though I know Claire would have been as turned off by Daniel as I was, I decide to keep the details of my time with Mr. Sensitive to myself. I'll fill her in once I've nailed things down with Skip.

"So . . . ," she prods, her blue eyes growing wide with curiosity.

"It was . . . fine."

She makes a sour face. "*Fine* doesn't sound like wedding-date material."

I shrug. "It just wasn't a good fit."

"Why? What was wrong with him?"

The fact that she just assumes I would find something wrong with Daniel is annoying. Not because she's proving her ridiculous Jake Ryan theory to be true, but because she's implying that I didn't give him a chance before I decided it wasn't going to work, and that's simply not the case, as evidenced by the heap of cat cards sitting in my garbage.

"Nothing was wrong with him."

"Oh come on." She levels me with a hard look. "What was it? Does he wear his pants too tight? Does he drink beer from a straw?"

I scowl.

Who would ever drink beer from a straw?

"I'm just wondering what the deal breaker was, because you're going to have to start looking past the shortcomings, or you're not going to have a *Michael* in time for the wedding."

"Yes, I'm very aware that I don't have a lot of time," I counter. And crying over the negative portrayal of snakes in the media is *not* a shortcoming. It's a flipping freak show! "But I'm not worried. I already have plans with someone else Friday night, and I know this guy's going to be a better fit."

"Really?"

I nod.

"Who is it?"

I'd like to tell her that his name is J.T., the lip-biting, dog-loving contractor who thinks I'm *charming*, but I can't. So instead I respond with the real answer: "His name's Skip Overstreet."

"Skip Overstreet . . ." Her lips twist in thought. "Why does that sound familiar? Have I met him?"

"I don't think so. He's an OB over at General, or he was until he opened up a private practice last year." Of course, Andy and Tracy know Skip because our paths all crossed at the hospital, but I can't imagine a situation where Claire ever would have met him.

She considers him for a moment longer before she lets her thought go with an easy shrug. "Okay, well . . . I hope it goes as well as you expect it to."

"Oh, it will." I nod confidently. "Skip's a really good guy. He'll make a perfect wedding date."

Chapter 6

Friday: date night with Skip
Five short weeks until the freaking wedding

I take the Red Line from downtown out to Addison station, then make the short walk to Wrigley Field. Parking at the commuter lot and catching the train was a bit of a challenge, given my busy day, but it's worth the hassle not to deal with game-night traffic. And, obviously, landing myself a worthwhile wedding date is worth any amount of extra effort.

It's no surprise to find the iconic red-bricked courtyard outside the ballpark littered with people. Like me, most are sporting their Cubbies ball caps or white-and-blue pinstriped jerseys, but there are a handful of brave purple-wearing Rockies fans mixed in too.

The spring air is cool and breathes thick with the promise of rain, but there's been no production from the low-hanging clouds yet. Not that a little rain could detour the die-hard Cubs fans like me from cheering on our boys.

Eager to get this evening underway and secure myself an acceptable wedding date, I raise the zipper on my jacket and head toward the Marquee Gate.

As promised, Skip is there waiting for me.

My mouth pulls up into a pleased smile.

He's just as I remembered: exactly my height with a stocky, athletic build, a news anchor smile, and a right-cheek dimple so deep you could get lost in it.

He's going to look great in a tux.

With the first pitch just minutes away, we're forced to limit our greetings.

"Hey, stranger," I say, and we exchange a friendly hug. His plaid shirt feels warm and comfy against my hands. Not as soft as J.T.'s shirt but still . . . snuggly. "It's so good to see you!"

"Yeah, you too." He steps back from me, his blue eyes sparkling beneath his blond brow. *Oh yeah, really good in a tux.* "I'm so glad you emailed. How's everything?"

"Great. Busy but . . . you know, good—"

A woman suddenly crashes into my shoulder. "Sorry," she mutters, then disappears into the moving crowd.

I motion toward the turnstiles. "Should we . . ."

"For our own safety I think we better."

The seductive smell of concession food steals my attention as soon as we enter the ballpark, reminding me that the last thing I ate was the doughnut I shared with Rerun this morning. Today was volunteer day at the free clinic, which always means back-to-back appointments. There's never time to eat.

"Okay if we grab something before we sit down?" I motion to the concession booth.

"Absolutely. Eating's one of my favorite hobbies."

Because Skip took care of the tickets, I insist on paying for dinner: two ballpark dogs with sides of onion rings and beers. We stop at the condiment bar to load up our dogs, extra mustard and relish for him, and then head to our seats. The announcer has just invited a local Girl Scout troop to the mound to perform the national anthem when we finally sit down: fifth row, field level, just behind the third-base line.

"Very impressive, Dr. Overstreet," I say, nodding to the coveted view in front of us. I pop an onion ring into my mouth and then stash the rest of my food under my seat until we're done with the anthem.

"Yeah, unfortunately I can't take credit for them. One of my patients works in the Cubs' front office, so she hooks me up with seats whenever I want."

I scowl. Skip's patients land him prime seating, while mine set me up with emotionally unstable men. Something's *very* wrong with the world.

"Ladies and gentlemen, please rise for the national anthem."

We stand, ball caps pressed over our hearts, and direct our attention to the pitcher's mound, where the scouts are lined up like fidgety little soldiers in their matching knee socks and green hair bows.

"Poor kid." Over a stifled laugh, Skip nods toward the smallest of the troop. She's been bestowed the honor of holding the flag, but with the way the pole is bobbing, she won't be holding it much longer; it's way too heavy for her. I grin. Not at her obvious discomfort but at Skip's teasing response to it. Daniel would be halfway through a box of Kleenex by now.

By some miracle, the little scout manages to keep the flag from hitting the ground through the entire out-of-tune performance, but the moment her troop leader emerges from the dugout, she throws it to the ground and runs off the field, screaming.

Skip raises his beer and says, "Here's to *that* kid for holding out as long as she did."

I raise my beer. "To *that* kid."

I keep a cautious eye on him as he presses the plastic cup against his lips. There you go, big boy. Two long drinks, no straws. *Suck it, Claire!*

The players take the field, and we settle into our seats.

"So, how's private practice treating you?" I ask while strategically arranging my dinner on my lap. "I mean, aside from the great seats you can have *anytime you want.*"

He grins. "That's a hard one for you, isn't it?"

"The only gift a patient's ever given me was some chocolate at her six-week postdelivery appointment once—"

"Chocolate's always good—"

"Not when it's regifted from Christmas, and it's July. There was a reindeer gift tag on the bottom of the box addressed to someone named Phyllis."

He barks out a laugh while giving my arm a flirtatious nudge. "You didn't even make the chocolate list."

"Right?" Laughing myself, I tuck a small piece of onion ring into my mouth while shaking my head. "And that was a breech delivery too. I earned my *own* box of chocolate, dammit."

"So, what did you do with them?"

"Oh, I still ate them."

"There ya go! You always eat the chocolate." This time he raises his beer in my honor.

Good at toasts. That'll come in handy.

"Seriously, though, private practice is a lot more difficult than I thought it would be," he goes on, an earnest expression settling in. "I mean, I love setting my own hours and having more face time with my patients, but the business side of things is really tough. What the hell do I know about hiring receptionists?"

"I hear ya." I take another pull off my beer. "We're looking for a new office manager right now, and it's proving to be really difficult."

"I thought Andy's wife . . ."

"Claire?"

"Yeah, Claire. I thought she was your office manager."

"She is, but their kids are keeping her too busy, so she's having to step back. How do you know her?"

"We sat at the same table at a fundraising event a while ago." So Claire was right. They have met before. "The Humane Society, I think. Or was it the Rotary . . ."

Skip's lost in thought, his lips slowly starting to twist over to one side of his mouth. It's obviously an involuntary act on his part, but it's sort of sexy. Not lip-bite sexy, but kind of hot nonetheless.

"I don't remember where—" he goes on, clearing his thoughts with a little shake of his head. "But I do know with all certainty that Andy was wearing a tiara and a pink boa."

I laugh. "That was the Rotary event. He and Tracy had a bet about one of our patients' due dates, and he lost. That was the payoff."

"Ah . . . yeah, okay. I vaguely remember hearing something about that." He takes another drink. "But, yeah, going back to the Claire thing. I totally feel you. It's hard to find good, reliable staff. Would you believe in the six months since I've taken over the practice, I've gone through *three* different receptionists? How hard is it to answer the phone and schedule appointments?"

An image of Daisy suddenly flashes through my mind. I roll my eyes. *Very* hard, apparently.

"I guess it just takes a lot of trial and error, huh?"

"Yep," I say. "And a lot of patience. But you'll be fine. A year from now you'll be an old pro."

"Well, I don't know about that, but I appreciate your optimism." He nudges my arm again. "Attaboys sound a lot better coming from you than my mom."

An excited grin stretches across my face as I pop the rest of the onion ring into my mouth. I knew this was going to be a good night, but I never expected it to be *this* good. Skip is great! He's smart and funny and easy to talk to. I don't feel quite as relaxed around him as I do around J.T. . . . but it's still going really well. He's everything I could possibly want in a wedding date. Or, dare I think it, maybe even a boyfrie—

A revolting sloshing sound suddenly steals my hopeful train of thought. I look to Skip and—

Eeewwww.

Bun bits—

Slosh. Slosh. Slosh.

Stringy onion parts—

Slosh. Slosh. Slosh.

Fleshy chunks of ballpark dog—

Slosh. Slosh. Slosssshhhhh.

I shake my head, willing myself to turn away, but I can't.

I can't!

Why can't I turn away—

Deep-fried batter balls lumping and clumping in the corners of his mouth—

My gag reflex kicks in. I raise my hand over my mouth.

No.

NO!

This is *not* happening.

Perfect-wedding-date Skip does *not* chew with his mouth open—

Slosh. Slosh.

GOD!

I pinch my eyes shut, willing the vile sound to go away, but it's too loud. It's like he's *inside* my head—

Slosh. Slosh. Slosh.

"Hey!" He suddenly nudges my arm, prompting me to pry my eyes open to look at him. My gaze immediately zeroes in on a little pool of brown liquid that's gathering in the corner of his mouth. A disgusted shudder rattles through my body. *How are you a doctor? How do you even function in society?*

"Look!" Nodding excitedly, he points toward the outfield. "Issh ussh!"

It's us?

Cringing, I slowly turn my attention to center field—

Oh. No.

It *is* us—on the freaking jumbotron—our pixelated faces framed inside a pink heart with the words *Kiss Cam* dancing across the screen.

"Thish isshh sho cool!"

His words come out smothered beneath his half-chewed, spit-soaked bites, but I'm still able to make out what he's saying. And contrary to what he thinks, this is definitely *not* so cool. It's horrifying! I cower back against my seat, shaking my head, while our neighbors on all sides chant, *"Kiss, kiss, kiss . . ."*

No. No. No!

"We gotta do it!" Motivated by the crowd, Skip places one hand on the armrest between our seats and starts leaning in closer. Thankfully he's swallowed most of his food, but the little brown mouth puddle is quickly evolving into a stream that's now trickling down his chin.

My stomach wrenches, and I turn away from him just as his greasy lips press against my cheek.

The crowd whistles and hoots. The man beside me grouses, "Robbed! He was robbed!" while Skip pulls away from me, grinning with delight.

"I can't believe that just happened," he crows. "I've never been on the jumbotron before. Have you?"

I raise my hand to my cheek, feeling dirty and violated. No, Skip, I have never been on the damn jumbotron before.

I excuse myself to the bathroom, returning only after I've scrubbed my cheek raw and I'm sure that Skip has had ample time to finish his meal. My stomach is still growling for food, but I leave mine sitting under the seat. My brain has eliminated the possibility of eating any-time soon. Probably ever.

Because it's a tight game, I'm able to keep my attention focused on the field without appearing obvious about my inability to look at him—*I can never look at him again*—and our conversation is limited to play-related mumbles, which is good, because every time he opens his mouth, all I hear is that revolting sound: *Slosh. Slosh. Slosh.* I seriously don't know how he's managed to survive this long, unless I'm the only person he's ever encountered who isn't deaf and blind.

We're just heading into the bottom of the fifth, and I'm thinking I might be able to survive this night without crawling out of my skin, when Skip spots a food vendor climbing the stairs in the next section over. My lungs vise around my breath, fearful for what's about to happen.

No. No, no, no . . .

"Nachos sound good, don't they?"

I whimper.

Nope.

No way.

Without a better plan, I grab my phone from my bag. "Sorry," I say, staring down at the blank screen. "Patient emergency. Gotta go. But thanks for the game, it was . . . fun." I bolt out of my seat and make a beeline for the aisle, stumbling and tripping on my neighbors' legs along the way.

"We don't have to get nachos!" a confused Skip calls out after me. "We can get something else. Do you want something else?"

I toss a quick glance over my shoulder and nod. Yes, Skip, I *definitely* want something else.

◆ ◆ ◆

I've never been big on pity parties, but after the week I've had, I'm throwing myself one.

I swing by Chicago Joe's—a family-owned deli / bar / liquor store not too far from my house—and head toward the aisle where he keeps the jugs of premade margaritas. Obviously drowning my frustrations in booze isn't going to solve my wedding-date dilemma, but at least it will dull them for a while.

It's no surprise that the deli area is buzzing with activity. Besides Joe's to-die-for Italian beef sandwiches, there's always a game airing on the big flat screen that's mounted to the wall, and tonight's no different. It's the Cubs game I just escaped.

I set the bottle down on the counter by the register, my attention focused on the TV in the dining area to my left. It's the bottom of the eighth now, and the score is tied. *Holy crap!* We might actually win . . .

"Anything else for you, Doc?" Manny, Joe's nephew who basically runs the place, asks me.

Despite the savory smell of the sandwiches, I still can't stomach the thought of eating. But watching the rest of the game with some other fans—fans who aren't massacring their food and then slobbering the remnants all over my face—sounds kind of nice. Like a little reward for the hell I just endured.

"Yeah, actually, I think I'll have a beer."

Since all the tables are taken, I settle in with my longneck at the small bar. The two seats on my left—in the direction of the TV—are occupied by an older couple I recognize from the dog park. We've never spoken, but Rerun's always very interested in their border collie . . . or specific parts of their border collie. The stool on my right is empty, though with the way this place is filling up to watch the game, I doubt it will stay that way for long.

"Here we go, Cubbies, here we go!" a man chants from one of the tables as the commercial comes to an end and our boys in stripes take to the outfield.

"Let's go, Cubs!" someone else yells.

Their cries are contagious, inciting the rest of the patrons to join in with their own cheers and yelps.

"Come on, boys," the old man beside me says earnestly. He turns his ball cap backward on his head, then raises his pinched fingers to his lips, kisses them, and makes the sign of the cross on his chest.

I grin. This is just what I needed.

"Let's go, Cubbies!" I shout, then follow his lead by turning my own cap backward. He offers me an approving nod and turns back to the game.

The Rockies get two base hits and a double, earning them another run as we head into the bottom of the ninth. Even though we're down by one, Chicago Joe's is still alive with hopeful energy. Die-hard as we are, Cubs fans aren't often given a reason to celebrate—we have to capitalize on every opportunity we get.

"Come on, Cubs—you got this! You got this!" My scream is lost among the sea of other yelps and superstitious cries, but it's still invigorating. I take another pull off my beer, my gaze fixed intently on the screen above me when a touch to my right shoulder steals my attention.

I turn back and—

Ohmygod.

I slap my hand over my mouth just as a sputter of amber bubbles starts to erupt from my lips. Thankfully, I'm able to contain it, but not before J.T., in all his unexpected glory, raises his hands up in a mock shield over his face.

"You really need to work on your drinking skills." He laughs, that damn adorable grin peeking out at me from behind his veil of fingers.

I snort while dragging the back of my hand across my mouth.

"I'm so sorry." I chuckle. "I swear I don't have a hole in my lip." His amused gaze darts to my mouth, prompting a frustrating tickle to stir in my chest. *Oh dear . . .* I shake off the sensation with a clear of the throat, then say, "So, what, um—what are you doing here?"

"Just picking up some food," he says. "I'd ask you the same, but I think it's pretty obvious." He taps at the bill of my hat with his finger. "Pretty sure I heard you from the parking lot."

My cheeks flush, though it's not because I'm embarrassed. (I'm proud of my loyalty!) It's because of the way he's looking at me: sort of skittish, like he was the other morning, but also a bit . . . enthralled. Like learning I'm a Cubs fan has thrown him for a loop.

"You're pretty hard-core, aren't you?" he asks.

"Well, yeah." I raise my palms. "It's the Cubs—you gotta support your team. Plus"—I thumb toward the TV behind me—"do you see what's happening here? We're only down by one. We can totally pull this off."

He shakes his head. "Eh, I don't know. The Rockies have a really solid closer this year." He settles easily onto the stool beside me, his delicious brown gaze shifting to the TV. "He hasn't lost them a game all season."

"Yeah, well, that's 'cause this is the first time they've played us."

His grin deepens, and he turns his attention back to me. We lock eyes for a pulse-pounding beat before the distinct sound of a cracking bat draws our attention back to the TV.

"Go, go, go!" I scream, springing to my feet along with J.T. and the rest of the patrons. We're all yelling and waving our arms frantically, as if we can somehow help propel the ball over the ivy-covered outfield wall—

"No!"

"Son of a bitch!"

"Dammit all!"

The Rockies' freakishly quick center fielder snags the ball out of the air just inches from the wall.

"Ugh, so close," I groan, flopping back onto the stool. "He almost had it."

He gives my arm a consoling pat. "It's okay. We've still got two more at bats. Anything can happen."

His optimism is nothing short of endearing, as is his company. This night is proving to be pretty good after all—

"Here you go, brother." Manny suddenly appears, dropping a to-go bag on the bar top in front of J.T. "Two Italian beefs with a large side of slaw. You need anything else?"

Two Italian beef sandwiches.

Two.

Because he's not eating alone.

My heart wrenches.

Of course he's not—

"Uh—no, that's everything. Thanks." He stares at the food for a moment before he turns back to me and says, "Well . . . I, um, I should probably get going."

Despite the unwarranted disappointment stirring in my bones, I force a smile and say, "You're not going to stay and see how the game ends?"

He frowns. "Nah. I can't."

"Okay. Well, it was fun running into you."

He finds my eyes again. "Yeah," he says. "It was. And we're still good for Sunday, right?"

I nod. "Yep. We're still good for Sunday."

I wish it were just the disappointment of the Cubs losing that's got me whimpering in my car on the way home, but it's not. It's the fact that J.T. is undoubtedly eating the world's best sandwich in the company of the world's most beautiful woman right now. And that I wasted three hours of my life on a human garbage disposal. And that Hope's stupid wedding is going to be here before I know it—

"Dammit, Chicago!" I pound my fist against the steering wheel. "There are over a million men in this city. I just need one. Just one!"

I turn down my street, my stomach twisting when I see a familiar silver sedan parked in front of my house.

Mom.

Why is she—*oh god.* A snippet of our last conversation comes to mind. I grip the steering wheel tighter. Mom *and* Hope are here to shop for dresses.

I crank the wheel hard right, slamming on the brakes in front of Mr. Feldspar's house, just four doors down from mine. I cut the engine and reach for the bottle of margaritas. No way I'm going in there sober . . .

Thirty minutes later, when the bottle is half-drained and I'm feeling a bit fuzzy around the edges, I decide it's time to face my audience. I climb out of the car and walk to my house. Gia is stationed in front of an easel at the top of the driveway. I don't ask what she's working on, but at first glance it appears that naked Steve is taking a moonlight stroll on the beach. She must be out here for inspiration.

"The dynamic duo got here a few hours ago," she says, her gaze shifting between the canvas and the cloud-covered moon. "Your mom seemed sort of pissed that you weren't here to greet them."

"Not surprising," I grumble.

"What crawled up your ass?" She turns to look at me and grins when she spots the bottle in my hand. "Wild night, huh?"

"Horrible night is more like it." I raise the bottle and take another drink.

"What happened? Here, hit me with a spot." She motions for the bottle, which I reluctantly hand over. She takes a pull—"*Gah!* How can you drink this shit warm?"

I snatch the bottle back from her. "Desperate times call for desperate measures."

"What are you desperate for?"

I sigh. "A decent date for Hope's wedding. The two guys I went out with this week were horrible."

"Horrible *how?*"

Despite my inebriated state, her emphasis on the word *how* isn't lost on me. In fact, it carries a similar tone to the one Claire and Tracy used when they dropped their asinine Jake Ryan bomb. Lucky for her, I'm too tired to set her straight. Besides, once she hears my reasoning, she'll understand.

"One was like a fucking Hallmark commercial. I swear, he cried about everything." I raise the bottle for another drink. *Ugh.* She's right.

This should be cold. "And the other one"—I swipe at the residual dribble from my lip—"the guy I went out with tonight, was like some sort of fucking first-world Neanderthal. He's super smart and funny, and he *looked* really good, but once he started to eat—it was just—the food . . ." I gag as images of that poor ballpark dog come to mind. "It was just so fucking gross."

"Wow. Three f-bombs in thirty seconds. Somebody's drunk."

I scowl but can't argue with her snide observation. I tend to go vulgar when I'm boozing. I'll have to watch that when I face my mom. *My mom. Fuck, my mom is here . . .*

"So just find someone who isn't so *horrible.*"

"Easier said than done," I mutter. "The only *non*horrible guy I'm interested in is fu—*fuhreaking* married. He *is* married, right? You're positive he's married?"

Her eyes narrow. "Who are you talking about?"

"J.T."

"Ahhh . . . yeah, okay. I can totally get on board with that."

"Hey!" I lurch toward her. "I'm the one who gets to board him, not you." That comes out different than intended. I shake my head. "I mean, yeah. He's hot. But he's also *really* sweet and charming, and I *need* to know for sure if he's married, because I am *not* a home-wrecker. So is he?"

"You're the one who saw his ring."

"Yeah, but . . . maybe his wife died, and he's just too sad to take it off. That could happen, right?"

This ridiculous scenario came to me while I was chugging in my car, and I really like it. Not the his-wife-dying part but him not *actually* being married anymore. Maybe he bought two sandwiches because he was taking one to her grave site . . . like a tribute or something. People do weird stuff like that, right?

"Yep. That could totally happen—if you're in a Hallmark movie."

"I hate you."

She shrugs. "I don't know what you want me to tell you. All I know is he comes into the shop and buys the Sweetheart's Special at least twice a month. I don't look to see who he addresses the card to."

My shoulders sag, and I raise the bottle for another drink. I'm sure there's no costumed cat on the front of those cards, but the fact that J.T. actually takes the time to write out a message says he's committed to someone.

"See, I'm totally screwed," I grumble. "All the single ones are horrible."

"Well, I told you Carlos said he'd be up to hang out with you, and he's definitely not horrible."

My eyes snap wide. "Carlos? Who's Carlos? You didn't tell me about anyone named Carlos."

Her eyes narrow beneath her retro frames. "I didn't?"

"No."

"Oh." She shrugs. "Okay, well, Carlos is a guy I know from the studio who said he'd be up for meeting you."

"When?"

If I were in a sober state of mind, there's no way I'd be this excited to meet one of Gia's artist friends. I've seen enough of them over the years to know they're not really my type. And that's not because they drive Priuses instead of red Porsches. It's because our lifestyles don't really mesh. But right now, when I'm half-drunk and 100 percent desperate, the prospect of *any* date is exciting.

"I don't know. He didn't say for sure."

"Well, can you text him or call him or something?"

"Damn, you really are desperate, aren't you?"

"Yes. I told you I was. I've only got like five weeks until the wedding, and I *have* to find a decent Michael to bring with me."

"*Michael?* Who's Michael?"

I blow out a big breath. "Michael is the imaginary man my mom thinks I've been dating for the last few months."

She bursts out laughing. "You have a fictitious boyfriend?"

Again, my compromised state is diluting reality to more tolerable levels. Levels that make it somehow acceptable to confess that I, a thirty-nine-year-old professional, invented a make-believe boyfriend because I'm too scared of being publicly shamed and verbally assaulted by my mother to tell her the truth.

"Yup." I take a pull off the bottle. "I made up a boyfriend."

"Why? Is she *that* bad?"

She no sooner asks the question than the familiar squeak of the back door sounds, and then a biting tone cries out, "Mackenzie Rose, is that you?"

Shit.

I instantly revert to my teenage self and tuck the bottle behind my back. "Hi, Mom!"

"Where have you been? Did you forget that your sister and I were coming down this weekend?"

I hear Gia snickering behind me. I guess she's getting the answer to her *Is she that bad?* question.

"No, I didn't forget. I just had plans. I'll be there in a minute."

"Well, don't be too long. It's going to rain."

As soon as she disappears into the house, I turn back to Gia. "*Please* get ahold of Carlos. Whenever he's available, I'll make it work."

"Should I let him know he'll need to change his name to Michael?"

"Shut up." I take one last pull from the bottle, then hand it over to her. "Wish me luck."

I'm not surprised to find that my house smells of pizza. Picking up a deep dish from Giordano's is always my family's first priority when they come to visit. Even though I'm still turned off by the thought of eating, I grab a slice. I need something to help soak up some of my buzz.

I take a few bites, then head into the living room, where I can hear the two of them watching TV.

"Hello . . ."

"Macaroni!" Hope springs off the love seat and greets me with a big hug.

"Hey, kiddo. Good to see you." She feels a little thicker around the middle than she did when I last saw her three months ago. That's typical for Hope. She flits between a 10 and a 14, always making either size, and the one in between, look good. "Congratulations."

"Well, thaaank you!" Her words come out with their usual dramatic flair as she pulls away from me, her left hand splayed wide in front of her so I can admire her new accessory. It's very big. And very sparkly. "Isn't it pretty?"

I nod.

"It sure is, sweetie," Mom adds with a pleased smile, then gives me one of her don't-wrinkle-me hugs. Contrary to my sister, she feels thinner than she did the last time I saw her. Along with Barbie-blonde hair and naturally straight teeth (some of us were in braces for four years), she and Hope also share the same yo-yo body-weight gene. "Where have you been? I assumed you'd be here waiting for us—"

"Yeah, sorry—"

"That Gia person had to let us in."

"I know, Mom. I'm sorry—"

"Are you aware of the mountain of wood lying on your front lawn?" She points a manicured nail toward the window that overlooks the front yard. "It looks like a construction site out there."

I sigh. "Yes, Mom. I'm very aware of it. That's the rotted-out porch. I've told you about it." She shakes her head, disgusted by the notion. "The contractor is coming on Sunday to start replacing it."

"Well, I should hope so. It's unsightly. What must your poor neighbors think?"

"I'm sure they hate me—"

"And you're sure this contractor is reliable? He's not going to run off with all your money, is he?"

The dig is an obvious reference to Brian, the thief. She likes throwing that one out whenever she can.

"So, where were you?" Hope wisely, *thankfully*, intercedes.

"At the Cubs game."

"Oooooh, with Michael?"

Hope's flirty question catches me by surprise, though it shouldn't. Of course she'd assume I was out with my boyfriend. That's what women in relationships do—they go out with their boyfriends.

"Uhh . . . yep. I was with Michael . . . my boyfriend . . . at the Cubs game . . ."

My cheeks ignite beneath the bumbled lie, so I quickly make my way over to the corner where Rerun is lying belly-up on his pillow, waiting for me to greet him.

"Will we get to meet him this weekend?" Hope questions while plopping back down on the love seat.

"Oh. Um . . ." Kneeling down beside him, I keep a steady scratch on Rerun as I try to formulate the least bullshit-sounding response I can. I'm not used to lying to Hope. *Dammit!* This would be so much easier if I were sober. "No. He's on call at the hospital all weekend, so . . ."

"Well, surely he can still have dinner with us," Mom says through a pinched expression. "On-call doctors still get to eat, don't they?"

I force out a snorty-sounding laugh that's meant to cover up the panic that's suddenly rising in my chest. "Yes, he can still eat," I answer while internally kicking myself for not having the wherewithal to tell a more specific lie. *Damn margaritas!* "What I meant to say is that he's on call at a hospital up in . . . Milwaukee, so he's actually driving up there early tomorrow morning."

Milwaukee?

Where the hell did that come from?

"Milwaukee?" Hope's brows scrunch together. "As in Wisconsin?"

I nod slowly.

. . . Yes.

He is in Milwaukee, Wisconsin.

My boyfriend is working in Milwaukee, Wisconsin, this weekend.

"Why does he have to go way up there?"

My throat instantly swells shut.

I don't know, Hope.

I have no idea why Michael has to go all the way up there.

No one would ever drive two hours, out of state, to be on call at another hospital.

That's just stupid.

I blink hard, desperate to somehow salvage this ridiculous lie, but my thoughts are so saturated in tequila and triple sec I can't get a grasp on anything. *Fuuuuuck!* Think, Mackenzie, think! Why is Michael on call at a hospital two hours away—

"Well, it must be for that volunteer group he works for, right?" Mom offers up, unknowingly saving me from my own demise. "Didn't you say they travel all over the world?"

"Yes!" I shout so loud Rerun jerks beneath my hand. "That's exactly what it is, Mom. And they do travel all over the world. Even here in our world—I mean"—I give my head a quick shake—"here in our country. It's not just trips to Africa anymore. They do a lot of stuff in the States too."

"Awww, that is so sweet," Hope says, easily buying into the idea.

"Yeah, he's really sweet. He's a *really* good guy."

"Well, he certainly sounds like it." Mom nods with approval, a rarely seen sight. "In fact, from what you've told us, he reminds me a bit of your grandfather. He helped out with the Red Cross Disaster Relief group for a long time. Did you know that?"

I nod. Of course I know that. Grandpa was the blueprint I used when creating Michael's personality.

"You should consider volunteering for something like that," Mom says. "I'm sure there are women all over the world in need of medical care during pregnancy."

My jaw falls slack.

Is she actually taking an interest in my work?

"Well, yeah. I already do. Every other Friday we spend the day volunteering at a women's clinic on the South Side. That's where I was today."

"Really?"

I nod happily. Even though I've told her about the free clinic at least a dozen times, it feels good to know she's finally listening to me.

"Well, good for you. It's important to help the less fortunate. I'm glad to see that your grandfather's influence has worn off on you."

"Yeah, that's really great, Mackie poodle," Hope chimes in over one of her cherubic smiles. It must be the booze, but even her cheeks look fuller to me. "You know what you should do?" She suddenly drops her feet to the floor and leans forward off the love seat, her blue eyes sparkling with excitement. "You should join the volunteer group Michael works with! Then you two can travel the world together! *Ohmygod!*" She clutches a throw pillow against her chest and collapses dramatically against the cushions. "That would be so romantic! Two important doctors, jet-setting around the world to save lives. It'd be like a movie or something!"

In the history of my life, Hope's exclamation points have never had any effect on me . . . until right this second. A fat smile erupts across my face, and despite the obvious impossibility of this scenario, I start to nod. "Maybe. That *would* be really romantic."

"Michael would love that, wouldn't he?"

I'm so drunk on the mere idea I can't stop nodding. "Of course he would!"

"You know, I remember my mother tagging along with my father on a few of his volunteer trips," Mom cuts in, a foreign, playful grin settling on her lips. "She always said she was there to help prepare meals for the volunteers, but I suspect it was more for some alone time with Grandpa."

Hope gasps. *"Really?"*

"Mm-hmm. I'm pretty sure Uncle Steve is a product of a couple of those *cooking* trips."

I burst out laughing. Not at the mention of my grandparents' sex life—good for them—but at my mother's playful tone. I can't remember the last time I heard her like this.

"Oh my god, that's precious!" Hope cries.

"It really is, isn't it?" Mom agrees, now chuckling herself. "Those two always had so much fun together. You could really tell they enjoyed the other's company—like best friends. Just like you and Whitman." She smiles at Hope. "And I imagine you and Michael." She turns to me. "You *enjoy* being with him, don't you?"

It suddenly dawns on me that the only reason my mom is being so gosh darn likable tonight is because she thinks I'm in a relationship. Without *Michael* in the picture, she'd be as disinterested in me as she always is.

FUCK.

I swallow hard. "Yeah. Of course I do."

"Well, I'm very glad to hear that."

"Me too," Hope adds. "I'm so happy you finally met someone!"

I force a smile.

"He's not on call every weekend, is he?"

Without thought I shake my head. "No. Just once a month."

"Oh good! Then we can meet him when we come back in a few weeks. We can *all* go out for dinner."

"Wait—*what?*" I sit up straighter. "Why are you coming back in a few weeks?"

"For the bridesmaids' dresses," Mom answers curtly, then reaches for a white, lace-covered binder sitting on the couch beside her. The front of it says, *Hope and Whitman, A Day to Remember*. With obvious familiarity, she flips it open to a tab marked ATTIRE and then turns the book around to show me the page. There are images of four pink

dresses on it. Bubblegum pink with my auburn hair and freckles . . .
ugh. "We've got it narrowed down to these four selections, but we need
to see how everyone looks in them. That Harper has been known to
pack it on if she's not careful."

"I know, Mom," Hope says. "She's renewing her Weight Watchers
membership as we speak."

"Well, I sure hope so. Because one heavy bridesmaid can throw off
the whole balance."

Hope turns back to me, sighing. "Speaking of Harper and Meghan,
is it okay if they stay here too? I don't want to put you out, but I hate
the idea of them staying in a hotel when it's supposed to be like a fun
girls' weekend—"

"Of course it's okay," Mom cuts in with a flippant wave.
"Mackenzie's got plenty of room for everyone. It's not like she's got a
husband and kids to contend with."

I nod absently because my inebriated brain cells are too busy trying to catch up to what's just been revealed: they're coming back, and
they're expecting to meet Michael when they do because I said he would
be around.

So now I have *three* weeks to find an acceptable date instead of five.

Twenty-one days instead of thirty-five.

The mother of all f-bombs starts to rumble in the pit of my stomach, but before it has a chance to formulate, I quickly stand up and
head for the kitchen.

"Where are you going?" Mom calls after me.

I don't answer.

I can't answer.

I push open the back door and stalk across the yard to where Gia is
still busy painting. She glances up from the easel but thankfully doesn't
say anything. Clearly, she recognizes a horrified expression when she
sees one. I snag the bottle of margaritas from where it sits on the ground
beside her, raise it to my mouth, and start to chug.

Chapter 7

Thirty-five days until the wedding
Twenty days until Mom and Hope come back . . . and meet
Michael
Seven thousand wedding gowns tried on
Three Motrin, two glasses of complimentary champagne, and one
very greasy breakfast burrito rolling around in my stomach

Every square inch of Christoph's Bridal is a decadent wash of white: from the satin curtains draping the individual dressing rooms to the sprays of orchids climbing the walls, the entire building screams *wedding!*—which is why I've excused myself half a dozen times for a breath of fresh air. All this *wedding* business is a bit suffocating.

"You need to avoid halters altogether," Mom calls out to Hope while she jots down more notes in her book. She's taking pictures of every dress with her phone and then writing detailed descriptions about each one so they can review the options with the wedding coordinator when they get home. "You're just too curvy. We don't want your girls popping out while you're walking down the aisle. And that color. What was that, vanilla?" She makes a sour face over a question she doesn't want answered. "Vanilla would look awful against Whitman's tuxedo. You need to be more sensible when choosing colors, Hope."

I sink back into the velvet chair cushion behind me and sigh. Who knew scrutinizing your child over free champagne would be so much fun . . .

"Mac Daddy!" Hope suddenly pops her head out from behind the curtain of her private dressing room. Her full cheeks are flushed the shade of strawberries, like she's winded. "Can you come help me?"

Chelsea, our *bridal specialist*, had to attend to a customer out in the showroom, so Hope was left on her own to try to navigate her way into the latest dress. Apparently that hasn't been as easy a task as she thought it would be.

"Absolutely," I answer, grateful to get away from Mom for a few minutes. I hurry across the carpeted room and duck behind the curtain. "Wow."

"You like?"

I nod at her reflection in the mirror. "Yes. It's . . . *wow*. Hope, you look beautiful." Truth be told, I think she looked beautiful in every dress so far—even the ones where her boobs were falling out—but this one . . . this one is really something.

She grins. "Thanks. I think this might be it, but I can't tell for sure until I get the back laced up."

While the front of the ivory dress is somewhat simple—a flowing empire waist with a delicately beaded bodice that perfectly displays her enviable D cups—the corseted back and train are a little more complicated. No wonder she needed help.

I drop down onto my knees and start cinching up the pretty ribbon.

"Do you think you and Michael will get married?"

A sour taste starts to well in my mouth. "It's way too early for that."

"But would you? I mean, if like a year from now he asked you?"

"I don't know. It's impossible to know what our relationship would be like."

Fictional, Mac.

A year from now your relationship with Michael would *still* be fictional . . .

"Okay, so let's say it's going great. You absolutely adore him, and you couldn't imagine your life without him. Would you do it?"

"Yeah, I guess."

"So you're not opposed to the idea of marriage?"

I shake my head. "Not at all. Why? Did Mom say I was?"

She doesn't answer, so I glance around the miles of organza cascading at her feet and look at her in the mirror. She flashes me a toothy grin. I roll my eyes.

"Just because I *haven't* gotten married doesn't mean I never would. I just haven't met the right guy yet . . ."

For some frustrating reason, an image of J.T. suddenly flashes through my mind. My heart starts to race. He must have looked *so* good on his wedding day . . .

"Well, maybe Michael is your Mr. Right."

I clear my throat. "Yeah, maybe."

The corset ribbon is delicate, so I take my time gently tugging each length a little tighter while Hope continues to shift from side to side, taking in all angles of herself in the mirror.

"What about kids?" she goes on.

"What about them?"

"Do you want them?"

Had she asked me that question ten, or even five, years ago, the answer would have been an easy *yes!* But now that I'm staring down the barrel of the big four-oh, I'm not so sure. Besides the fact that I don't have a partner to have a baby with (some days Rerun feels like a ton of work—there's no way I could ever go it alone), I've seen how difficult pregnancy can be for women my age. And while I'm more than happy to help my patients achieve their dreams of being parents, I can honestly say I've never *wanted* it the same way they do.

"I sort of think that ship has sailed." From the corner of my eye, I see her bottom lip roll out into a pout. "But I'm fine with that," I add firmly. "Not everybody's supposed to be a parent. Some of us are just destined to be really awesome aunties."

I'm thinking of all the fun times I've had with Claire and Andy's boys over the years: watching their Little League games, attending Christmas recitals, going to the movies, or riding go-karts . . . Aside from the one hellish weekend I spent babysitting them when all four came down with strep throat, I feel like I've had the pleasure of enjoying kids without actually *having* them. Being an aunt is really the best of both worlds.

"Well, I'm glad to know you feel that way," Hope goes on. "Because you're going to be one before too long."

My mouth pulls up into a smile. "You and Whitman plan to start trying right away, huh?"

"Not exactly . . ."

Her cryptic response steals my attention. I glance up at her reflection and find her smiling back at me, blue eyes glistening with emotion. My jaw falls slack, and my gaze instinctively drops to her belly.

"Are you . . . ?"

She nods quickly.

I blink hard, shocked and thrilled.

"Oh my god, Hope!" I quickly stand and pull her in for a hug, mindful not to smoosh the dress. "Congratulations. That's so exciting!" And it explains why they're getting married so quickly—and why she looks a little fuller. She must be a few months already. "I'm so happy for you!"

"Thank you. We're really excited too."

"When are you due?"

She takes a step back, hands caressing her belly in that tender way all moms-to-be do. "June twenty-eighth."

My eyes snap wide. *"June?"*

91

"Yep. I'm going to have a little summer baby to dress in bikinis or tiny little swim trunks. Ohmygod, it's going to be so much fun!" She raises her hands up to her mouth and starts giggling like a child. It's a very sweet sight, and at some point I'm sure I'll be able to reflect on it as a wonderful memory, but for now I can't enjoy it because all I'm focused on is the fact that she's—I quickly do the math in my head—thirty-one weeks and not even showing!

"Your doctor has confirmed your dates?" The physician in me takes over. "Not just by your menstrual cycle but by an ultrasound? They've been doing tests?"

She nods.

"And the baby is measuring normally? Because it should be at least three pounds by now."

"The baby is totally fine," she says, her expression softening a bit to accommodate my obvious concern. "Dr. Tan says it's growing right on schedule and that I am a poster child for a good pregnancy . . . except for the fact that my uterus is tipping the wrong way."

"Retroverted," I say over a relieved sigh. "A retroverted uterus tips toward the rectum instead of the belly. Which explains why you're not showing."

"I know, it's crazy, right? I didn't even know I was pregnant until a month ago. My boobs weren't sore or swollen or anything, and I was still having a light period . . ."

I nod in understanding. That happens sometimes. And, of course, those women are hated by the masses, but it *does* happen.

"Well, the tipped uterus shouldn't cause any problems with your pregnancy," I say. "And there are exercises you can do to help with positioning before delivery, too, if that becomes an issue."

"I know. My doctor told me all of that. Everything's good, Mac. I promise."

Tears start to swell in my eyes as my concern for the situation starts to pass and the joy I felt moments ago reclaims its hold on my heart. My little sister is going to have a baby!

"This is so great, Hope. You're going to be such a good mom."

She sniffles on her own tears. "Thanks. We thought about waiting until after the baby was born to get married, but Whitman's sort of old fashioned and thought it was better to be married *before* the baby actually gets here."

I laugh. "I'm sure Mom appreciated that. Her mah-jongg group would probably revoke her membership if she has a grandbaby born out of wedlock."

Hope's smile quickly gives way to a grimace. "Yeah, well, the thing is . . . she doesn't exactly know . . ."

"What?"

She shakes her head and crunches her nose up like a bunny, the way she did when she was little and got caught doing something naughty.

"You haven't told her?"

"I wanted to, but . . . I don't know. I got sort of scared. You know how she is . . ."

I nod because, *yeah!* I know *exactly* how she is. But until this moment, I never realized that Hope knows how she is too. She's always been Mom's little golden girl—all smiles and ribbons, impressed by the unimportant things in life just like Mom—but now . . . *ohmygod.* Is it possible that Hope's been padding their relationship with some tall tales too?

"So, she just thinks you guys are getting married right away because of Whitman's grandma? That same story you told me the other day?"

She nods sheepishly. "She doesn't have a clue. I guess my tilted uterus served me well, huh?"

I laugh. "Yeah, I guess it did. But, oh man, she is going to lose her mind when she finds out. She's wanted a grandbaby forever. Not telling her isn't going to go over well."

She sighs. "I know. But we didn't want any extra drama to go along with the wedding. I mean, look at her." She pulls the satin curtain away from the wall so we can see out into the viewing area. Mom's scribbling notes so furiously I'm surprised there's not a little plume of smoke wafting up from the paper. "She's already going psycho over all of these wedding plans. Can you imagine how crazy she'd be if she knew there was a baby in the mix too?"

I nod over a heavy sigh of my own. She's absolutely right. Mom can only tackle one life event at a time, which means not only do I have to help keep this baby situation under wraps, but my need to secure a wedding date has just been ratcheted up a notch. No way I'm going to shortchange Hope of her perfect day, knowing what's in store for her once the wedding's over . . .

Chapter 8

Thirty-four days to find an acceptable date
. . . and roughly six hours until J.T. comes to work on the porch

The one upside to having a mother who strives to keep up with appearances is that she maintains this standard even when there's no one around to impress. Case in point: the elaborate breakfast she insisted on *whipping together* even though Hope and I assured her we were fine with the day-old doughnuts in the pantry.

For the *three* of us, she's prepared a red-pepper-and-goat-cheese frittata, a mountain of crispy, skin-on potato wedges, about four pounds of sausage links, country biscuits with homemade honey butter, an enormous bowl of precisely cut fruit, and a pitcher of mimosas. It's an obnoxious amount of food, but it also provides me with a week's worth of leftovers. Considering my cooking skills, I'll gladly take it.

We sit down at my never-used dining table, where Mom proceeds to load up our plates—and our glasses. Hope casts me a wary glance, aware that *not* drinking in front of Mom would tip her baby hand. Because Mom's mimosas are notoriously weak, I make a subtle pinching gesture with my fingers, indicating that a little bit will be okay. She smiles gratefully and takes a tiny sip. Since I'm not pregnant, I take a big one.

"We need to find someone to babysit Aunt Ginn during the ceremony," Mom says. She's picking at a biscuit with her fingers, popping only bird-size portions into her mouth. This is what she does. She makes gobs of food and forces it on everyone else but hardly touches any herself. "Nobody in the family wants to be responsible for her, but I don't see how I can pawn her off on any of your other guests . . ."

"She needs a muzzle," Hope whimpers over a forkful of frittata. "Why do we even have to invite her? She ruined Amanda's wedding."

Aunt Ginn is my dad's oldest sister. At eighty-two she's still in great shape physically, but her mental health—specifically her inability to refrain from yelling out whatever random thought crosses her mind—has been known to cause a fair amount of tension within the family. In her defense, she's not entirely aware of what she's saying, but screaming out, *"I thought only the virgins got to wear white!"* as my cousin Amanda walked down the aisle last summer definitely didn't earn her much love.

"I know she did, dear, but she's family. We *have* to invite her."

"Fine." She stabs at a piece of sausage, her bottom lip rolling out into one of her signature pouts. I swallow a sigh and then take another long pull off my mimosa. Baby lie aside, she's still a lot more like Mom than I am. "How about David?" she offers up. "He's always gotten along well with her."

Mom fires her a pointed look. "Have you forgotten that David will be bringing *Phillip* to the wedding?"

David is our cousin on Mom's side, and *Phillip*, the name she can say only in a whisper, is his partner. Until about ten months ago, David was married to Heidi, but now they're divorced, and he's with *Phillip*. For the most part the family has been very accepting of this revelation (David watches a lot of HGTV—it wasn't really much of a surprise), but a few of the older family members are having a harder time adapting. When Aunt Ginn saw the two of them sneaking a kiss under the mistletoe last Christmas, she screamed, *"Which one of them does the pitching?"* If she were to be seated anywhere near them at the wedding, there's no telling what she'd say.

"Ugh, that's right," Hope groans. "Well, I guess we could ask someone in Whit's family—"

"Absolutely not. We need to keep her as far away from the Gentrys as possible. They don't need to witness all our dirty laundry. What would they think?" Grimacing, Mom pops another bird bite into her mouth while her blue eyes narrow in concentration. Hope and I exchange a quick, knowing glance. There's no way she could handle baby drama right now . . . A few minutes pass, and I'm just taking in a forkful of potatoes when Mom cries out, "I've got it!" and smacks her hand against the table. "Michael can do it."

The unchewed potatoes catapult straight into the back of my throat, forcing me to cough as I say, *"Wh-what?"*

"Your Michael is the perfect solution. He's only there as your guest, so he won't feel put out if he's having to pay more attention to Ginn than the wedding."

Anxiety creeps up my spine, and I start to shake my head while still trying to swallow my food. No. No, no, no—

"Ohmygod, that's totally perfect." Hope reaches across the table and grabs my hand, her eyes wide with relief. "She'll feel special because she gets to sit with your hunky doctor boyfriend, but really he'll just be babysitting her—"

"No. It's not a good idea—"

"Oh, of course it is." Mom disregards me with a flippant wave. "This is what boyfriends do for their girlfriends—"

"Mom, *no*—"

"They will sit in the back," she continues, talking right over me, "and if she starts getting unruly, he can just usher her out one of the side doors."

"Actually, there's only one entrance into the chapel," Hope offers. "But everybody will be facing the front, so that won't be an issue. He won't mind, will he? You yourself said how sweet he is. I'm sure he'll be glad he can help me on my special day—"

Woof!

Rerun's unexpected bark instantly stifles the conversation.

Woof! Woof!

He takes off running toward the back door, tail swaying.

Mom scowls. "What on earth has gotten into him?"

My heart starts to race expectantly, hopefully.

Is that J. T.?

Did he decide to come by this morning instead?

I sit up straighter while tucking some flyaways behind my ear.

"Helloooo!"

My shoulders sag at the sound of Gia's familiar call.

"Yo, Mac, where you at?"

"We're in the dining room," I holler back to her.

"Where you at?" Mom mutters, disgusted.

Hope rolls her eyes, proving she's not as ignorant to Mom's arrogance as I've always thought she was.

"Damn, that is a lot of food." With her platinum hair spiked up into a mohawk, Gia enters the dining room. Mom's seen her plenty of times but never with her hair fully erect. Her jaw practically dislocates. "What's the occasion?"

"No occasion. This is just what my mom does on Sunday mornings."

"Mackenzie . . ." Mom grouses, her appalled expression quickly transforming to one of annoyance.

"Well, it looks amazing, Mrs. Huntress," Gia goes on, very visibly eyeing the selection. "Like the centerfold of a Martha Stewart magazine."

Martha Stewart?

Good god, why not just compare her to Jesus himself . . .

"Well, aren't you sweet," Mom says, easily trading out her scrutiny for the compliment. "It's just a little something I whipped up, since

Mackenzie would rather wear rubber gloves than oven mitts. Sit down and join us," she orders, motioning to the empty chair. "There's plenty to go around."

"Don't mind if I do."

Mom heads to the kitchen for an extra plate, while Gia takes her designated seat across from me.

"Martha Stewart, really?" I mutter.

"Starving artist," she mutters back.

"All right, dear, let's get you started . . ."

Mom loads the plate: a scoop of potatoes, a fat slice of frittata, three sausage—

"Nope. No meat." Gia throws her hand out in front of Mom, prohibiting her from depositing the offending links onto the plate.

"Pardon me?"

"I don't eat meat."

Mom's nose wrinkles. "What do you mean you don't eat meat? Who doesn't eat meat?"

My mother knows damn well what a vegetarian is, but to her ears, it's as if Gia's just professed that she's a card-carrying member of ISIS.

"I don't," Gia says, unmoved. "But you can go ahead and hit me with another spot of potatoes . . ."

Hope kicks me under the table, and I roll my lips together to keep from laughing.

A long, uncomfortable moment passes before Mom says, "All right. I'll *hit* you . . ."

She plops another helping onto Gia's plate, then sits back down and starts working on her mimosa.

"So, Carlos said you should come by the studio this afternoon," Gia says to me, unfettered by the tension in the air.

My eyes snap wide. *No! Don't talk about Carlos here—*

"Who's Carlos?" Hope asks.

My chest cinches around my breath. I fire a nasty glare at Gia.

She smirks and then, over a casual shrug, says, "Oh, he's this artist I know who *really* wants to meet Mac."

I clamp my teeth together and intensify my stare.

Don't you dare say anything.

"Why does he *really* want to meet you?" Mom questions, shifting her narrowed gaze between Gia and me.

A knot suddenly swells in my throat, making it even harder to breathe. I grab my mimosa and quickly swallow it down.

"Because your amazing daughter has decided that bringing real live human beings into the world isn't impressive enough, so now she wants to learn how to paint," Gia replies over a bite of potatoes, then gives me a wink that does little to ease my angst. "He's teaching a beginning class this afternoon and said it would be the perfect opportunity for you to come by."

"Oh, how fun!" Hope crows. "What kind of painting?"

"Watercolor," Gia answers.

"Aww . . . I love watercolors!"

"Oh, Mackenzie," Mom mutters. "Do you really think taking a painting class is the best use of your time? Michael's coming back later today. Surely you want to spruce up so you're ready to see him. Wash your hair or . . . something."

Despite my annoyance at Gia for bringing up Carlos at the most inopportune moment imaginable, I'm more irritated, and frankly disappointed, with my mother. *If* there were a real Michael in my life, I surely wouldn't revolve my life around his. And he damn well wouldn't expect my hair to look good on a Sunday afternoon.

"Actually, Michael and I both think it's healthy to have separate interests," I say, chin raised in a small show of defiance. "He's very supportive of me pursuing . . . art." The lie hangs like a rotten stink in the air, but thankfully Gia's the only one who's aware of it, and this time she keeps her mouth shut. "What time is the class?" I ask her.

"Three o'clock at the art center over on Liberty Road. Room C."

A wave of disappointment rolls through my gut, knowing that attending the class will interfere with my plans to see J.T. when he comes to work on the porch.

J.T., who is still as off-limits to me today as he was sitting on the stool beside me Friday night . . .

I inhale a deep breath and, on the exhale, say, "Great. I'm really looking forward to it."

◆ ◆ ◆

I check the clock.

Dammit.

It's two forty-five and there's still no sign of J.T.

I *really* want to see him, but if I wait any longer, I'll be late for watercolor class.

Watercolor class.

This is how low I've had to stoop to find a respectable man . . . Sighing, I give Rerun a parting pet and then head outside. The same dark clouds that have been threatening rain all weekend are finally starting to deliver. A few dime-size drops land on my windshield as I start backing down the driveway. I'm just a few yards from the street when, through the backup camera, I see J.T.'s truck pull up to the curb.

I slam on the brakes and quickly press the button to lower my window. Through the side-view mirror, I watch intently as he climbs out of the truck and makes his way up the driveway. My pulse spikes as I take in his long, loping stride; it's somehow accentuated by the perfect fit of his well-worn jeans, making him look even sexier than usual—

"Hey there," he calls out, now just steps from my door.

I quickly clear my throat and lean out the window, only to be caught short when I see—*"What happened?"*

There's an abrasion, roughly an inch long, just above his left eyebrow. It's not actively bleeding, so it shouldn't need stitches, but it's still bloody and a bit swollen, which suggests it's a fresh injury.

"It's nothing." He raises his hand to the wound, wincing as he grazes it with his fingers. "One of the boards just slipped when I was loading them into the truck."

I glance back at his pickup and see a stack of long two-by-fours piled up in the bed. I know from helping my dad with projects as a kid that each of those weighs at least ten pounds—not necessarily a burden to carry, but I'd imagine pretty painful if it slams into your head.

"We need to close that up so it doesn't get infected."

I reach for the door handle, but he quickly shakes his head, saying, "No, it's fine. It happens all the time. Just a hazard of the job."

"Yeah, well, a hazard of *my* job is that I'm bound by law to help people who are injured. So, unless you want me to go to jail, you need to let me help you."

He chuckles at my ridiculous explanation but concedes just the same. "Well, if it's a matter of jail time, then I can't possibly object."

Mindful of the time, I race up the driveway and into the house. After a quick handwashing, I grab the first aid kit and a bottle of water, then head back outside.

"Go ahead and lean up against the driver's seat," I instruct him as I lay my supplies out on the Jeep's hood.

He does as he's told while I dampen a gauze pad with some water. I round the open door so I'm standing directly in front of him.

"Okay, this might sting a little . . ."

I lean forward, very aware of our close proximity, and gently press the gauze against his skin. He winces and slams his eyes shut.

"Sorry."

"It's okay . . . ," he says through clenched teeth.

"Did you catch the end of the game the other night?" I ask, hoping to keep his mind off the pain.

Still grimacing, he says, "Yeah. It was a heartbreaker for sure."

I clean the area as quickly as possible, doing my best to focus on the wound rather than the way his warm breath keeps tickling my neck.

Dear god, that feels good—

"How's it looking?"

Oh! I quickly clear my throat—and my thoughts. "Good. It's not bad at all."

Swallowing hard, I reach for the NEOSPORIN, dab a tiny bit onto the wound, and then cover it with a Steri-Strip. "All done. Just keep it dry for the next day or so, and you'll be good to go."

I quickly back away from him and gather my things.

"Thanks," he says, slowly stepping away from the car so I can resume my place inside it. He shuts the door for me, his strong hands pressed against the open window jamb. "I can't remember the last time someone made a fuss over one of my little accidents. I'm going to have to hurt myself more often."

My stomach somersaults at the playfulness of his words, but as I catch another glimpse of his wedding band, I'm reminded that someone else *should* be making a fuss over him. Someone else, according to Gia, whom he was fighting with outside the flower shop . . . *Is it possible that the swimsuit model has a rotten bedside manner?*

"So, you're headed out, huh?"

"Yeah," I say, shrugging off my train of thought. "I have this . . . thing."

He grins. "A *thing*?"

I nod. Yes, a *thing* that will hopefully distract me from thinking about you . . .

"What time do you think you'll be back?"

"I'm not really sure." My guess is that a beginner's painting class lasts no more than an hour, but I sort of assumed we'd go out for a cup of coffee or something after to get to know each other in a more private setting. Which is what I need to do. I *need* to get to know Carlos to determine whether he's wedding-date material, not lose myself in J.T.'s big soulful eyes. "How long do you think you'll be here?"

"Well, I'd like to get all the debris cleared today so I can start building the frame for the new porch tomorrow." He turns to look at the woodpile sitting in the yard while I keep my eyes fixed on the sexy wrinkles kissing his temple. "But I suppose some of that will depend on the weather—"

A dangerously tempting image of a rain-soaked J.T. suddenly flashes through my mind: his charcoal thermal pressed up tight and slick against his chest, eyelashes blinking back salted raindrops that trail down the length of his jaw and over his plump lips—

"It feels more like a movie-in-front-of-the-fire than a work-outside kind of day, don't you think?" he goes on, oblivious to my train of thought.

He returns his attention to me, a hopeful expression stealing what little breath is still circulating through my lungs. Our eyes lock for a quick, pulse-pounding beat before I force my gaze away from him and to the steering wheel, reminding myself that he is off-limits. For movies, for playing in the rain, *for anything*! So long as there's a ring on his finger, J.T. is the forbidden fruit I'm not allowed to eat, no matter how unhappy his marriage appears to be . . . or how badly I want to taste—

"Are you okay?"

I feel his hand press against my arm. It tickles every nerve ending in my body and sends a flood of blood racing to body parts I nearly forgot existed—

He's married, Mac!

You may be a lot of things, but you're not a home-wrecker!

"Yeah, I'm . . ." I pinch my eyes shut and inhale a deep breath in an attempt to regain myself. "I'm fine," I go on and slowly brave a look up at him. "I just have to hit the road, or I'm going to be late. I'm taking a painting class, so . . ."

I glance at his hand, wishing it were an invitation for him to tighten his embrace, but he recognizes it for what it is. A request to let me go. Disappointment steals his smile, and he slowly pulls his hand away.

"Painting, huh? Well, that'll be fun."

"Yeah. Hopefully."

"All right, then." He forces a smile he clearly doesn't feel. "You have a fun day painting, and I'll just plan on seeing you sometime tomorrow night then. And thanks again for fixing me up." He taps his head and smiles.

"Any time."

Silently cursing myself—and my damned integrity!—I throw the car into reverse and take off toward watercolor class.

Carlos, you better be a freaking prince . . .

Chapter 9

Twenty minutes later . . .

A steady, messy mist is falling by the time I pull into the art center's parking lot. I'm ten minutes late for class thanks to my heartbreaking run-in with J.T. I hate that I left him feeling like his touch wasn't welcome when it most definitely was—*my god it was!*—but it shouldn't have been.

Dammit, it shouldn't have been!

Resolved to focus on the task in front of me, I climb out of the car and run across the wet parking lot toward the old bricked building.

Originally a law firm, it was one of a handful of downtown Naperville locations that were renovated as part of a citywide arts initiative. Along with the art center, there's also a community theater, a library, and a small museum dedicated to the history of Naperville. During the summer months, local artists are invited to showcase their work there; Gia's already secured a week in July to display her *Guttenberg: Man, Myth, God* collection. To my surprise, it's already sold out.

Given that it's a Sunday afternoon, I'm not surprised that no one is manning the information desk. Unsure where to go, I decide the hallway on my left is the best option, as the one on the right is completely dark. I peel off my wet jacket and head down the hall. I pass a few unhelpfully unmarked doors before I come upon a half dozen or so people sitting outside another unmarked door. Most have their attention focused on a device, but a couple of women are talking to each other, so I decide they might be open for a question.

"Excuse me." They pause their conversation to look at me. "Do you know where room C is? The beginners' watercolor class?"

"This is it," one of the women says, thumbing over her shoulder to the nearest door.

"Oh good." I wait for a moment, then rock back on my heels. "Are we waiting for the teacher to arrive or . . ."

The other woman shakes her head. "No. He's in there. Class started a few minutes ago."

"Oh. Okay. So you're not in the class then . . ."

The first woman laughs, while the second woman shakes her head and says, "Oh goodness, no," over an amused smile.

My eyes narrow.

That's funny?

Suddenly feeling a bit uneasy, I run my hands over my damp hair and inhale a deep, hopeful breath.

All right, Carlos, it's time for you to sweep me off my feet . . . I open the door, step into the brightly lit studio, and immediately notice that it's filled with children, none of them more than five or six years of age.

A painting class for kids . . . Oh, Gia . . .

"Well hello. You must be Mac."

The slowly delivered greeting emanating from the back corner of the room steals my attention. I turn and feel my eyes snap wide at the sight that awaits me. With olive-toned skin and a mane of thick, raven-black curls cascading over his shoulders and down to the middle of his back, the man staring at me could very easily be posing for the cover of a romance novel, sans the acid-washed jeans or unbuttoned pirate shirt that shows off a bare chest and unnaturally purple-hued nipples. *Please, god, don't have purple nipples . . .* My cheeks flush hot, though it's not that same kind of impassioned heat that overcomes me when I see J.T.

In fact, it has nothing to do with my libido at all. It's because every pint-size face in the room is now staring at me too. Over the years, I've given talks in front of hundreds of doctors and other medical professionals without batting an eye, but put me at center stage in front of a bunch of children, and I turn into a self-conscious mess. Something about those wide, wondering eyes intimidates the hell out of me.

Tightening my grip on my jacket, I swallow hard. "Hi. Yes. Sorry I'm late."

He waves off my apology. "Not a problem." Once again his words come out slowly, like he's savoring the way every syllable feels crossing his tongue. "I'm just happy you were able to make it—and that Gia thought to introduce us. I'm Mr. Carlos."

Mr. Carlos.

Okay, so long as that's *just* for the kids.

"Please, take a seat in front of one of the empty easels."

His dragged-out instruction makes me feel less like painting than it does hiding under a blanket . . . or . . . or maybe *snuggling* under a blanket . . . What did J.T. say? *It feels more like a movie-in-front-of-the-fire than a work-outside kind of day, don't you think?*

My breath flutters, and I start to smile—

No! I quickly shake off the frustrating memory. *I'm here for Fabio—er, Carlos. Stay focused on Carlos!*

I sit down in front of the nearest empty easel; on one side sits a tiny towheaded boy, and on the other a girl who could easily pass as one of Claire and Andy's kids: orange hair, piercing blue eyes, freckles dusting every square inch of her pale skin—it's a good thing Claire's not here. One look at her and we'd have an Amber Alert on our hands.

The little boy sticks his tongue out at me and then returns to swirling his brush in the puddle of green paint in front of him, while the little girl says, "You're really old."

In another situation I'd beg to differ, but . . . "Yeah, I know."

"Whatth your name?"

Three missing baby teeth force her to lisp.

"Mac. What's yours?"

"Thamantha."

"Samantha?"

She nods.

"That's a very pretty name."

"Thank you. My mom named me after thomeone from her favorite movie."

"Oh really—"

"Remember, your muse does its best work when we're quiet . . ." Carlos doesn't address us by name, but it's clear that his interruption— still delivered as slow as molasses on a winter morning—was directed at us.

Samantha covers her mouth with a pudgy hand while I fight the grin that's spreading across my lips.

"Uh-oh," I whisper to her. "We better be quiet."

She nods quickly and turns back to her painting.

"As a reminder, today's theme is the beach," Carlos goes on, clearly for my benefit, as he continues to meander through the room, checking in with his students along the way.

It's been a long time since I painted something other than my living room walls, but the concept of watercolors isn't lost on me. I dip my brush into the provided cup of water, then begin to swirl it around in the blue paint sitting on the tray in front of me. I drag a thick line across the gleaming white canvas.

"Try to imagine all the things you'd see at the beach: waves, or sand, or maybe some beautiful fish . . ."

The slow cadence of his speech is really starting to grate on my nerves, but I admit that it does make it easier to picture myself at the beach.

"Think about all of the beautiful colors you'd see: red umbrellas, orange sand buckets, white clouds . . ."

I slap more and more blue onto the canvas and can almost feel the warm sand creeping in between my toes, taste the salt water against my lips, smell the sweetness of coconut-scented sunscreen wafting on the breeze. My eyes instinctively drift shut as a delicious image of J.T. starts to unfold in my mind's naughty eye: he's lying on the beach, shirtless, his taut skin glistening beneath a layer of tanning oil—

Ouch!

A sudden poke to my right arm shatters the illicit daydream. I turn to my right and find my little neighbor boy scowling at me, the butt end of his paintbrush still poised like a weapon.

"It's not nap time."

"I wasn't sleeping." I rub my arm. "I was just . . . thinking about the beach."

His scowl deepens. "That doesn't look like the beach."

I turn back to my painting. Unfortunately, he's right. It's just a mess of blue lines without any kind of form or shape to it.

"Well, it's my first class," I explain to the six-year-old. "And I haven't painted in a *really* long time."

He blinks.

"You know what? I'm a doctor. I deliver little babies into the world every day. That's a really important job . . ."

The little cherub rolls his eyes, unimpressed, and turns back to his easel.

"Heeth got anger-control itthewth," Samantha whispers.

"Yeah, I can tell," I whisper back to her. And his parents need to lock that down with professional help, or they're going to be buried in lawsuits before he hits the third grade . . . but for the moment I'm actually grateful the little turd poked me. It stole me away from my dangerous daydream and brought me back to the present, which is exactly where my brain needs to be.

We're here for a wedding date, Mac.

Stay focused.

I redirect my attention to Carlos, who's now wandering toward my side of the room. Like his diction, his progress is unhurried. He lingers behind each student, studying their picture and offering up slow-spoken observations before he moves on to the next.

As he continues to inch his way closer, I'm better able to appreciate his build. He's tall, at least six feet, and is definitely packing some muscles under that tunic-style shirt. He would more than fill out a tux . . . but for some reason my mind's not able to grasp the image. Probably because of the hair. It's *so* pretty that it's almost distracting. Maybe if it were pulled back from his face, I could visualize a tuxedo better—

"The brush is your master. It will determine how much force you should apply . . ."

I cringe.

Nope.

The beautiful hair's not the problem—

"You are only the willing vessel meant to guide it with your hands—"

What the hell—

"Let the brush determine your strokes—"

Ohmygod.

Logically, I know that he's talking about paintbrushes and not penises, but my brain has just officially gone there.

"Feel the movement of the brush beneath your hand. Grip it gently with your fingers . . ."

I clench my teeth against the sour taste that's suddenly welling in my gut and shove the paintbrush into the first color I come upon. It's red, which is probably fitting, as I'm sure my ears are about to start bleeding . . . I slather a heaping glob onto the canvas.

"Use gentle strokes," he goes on, the word *stroke* stretched out over the course of a mile. "Long, gentle strokes—"

I wince.

Is this why those moms were laughing? Did they know my ears were about to be violated—

"Or for more color, deep, heavy strokes—"

Strokes.

Strokes.

Stroooooooooooooooooookes.

The word reverberates like X-rated shrapnel against my bones. I quickly slap my hand over my mouth to keep from gagging. If this is art-class speak, then pillow talk would warrant a felony!

No way.

I'm tapping out—

He comes to a stop right behind sweet little Samantha. I swallow hard, bracing myself for the next assault.

"What's wrong?" he asks.

I cast a cautious glance to my left and see that Samantha is furiously rubbing at her eye. "There'th thomething in my eye."

He kneels down in front of her for a better look. "Ah, it's just an eyelash. Hold still and I'll get it." He delicately pinches the rogue lash between his fingers and then holds it out for her to examine. "You see, that's all it was. Just a silly eyelash."

She stares down at it and smiles.

"Now you get to make a wish," he says.

"Huh?"

"That's what you do when you catch a fallen eyelash. You close your eyes, make a wish, and then blow it away so the eyelash fairies can take it back to their castle and make your wish come true."

"Really?"

He nods and raises his hand. "Go ahead, Samantha. Make a wish."

Go ahead, Samantha. Make a wish.

Make a wish . . .

Though still tainted by his icky, slow delivery, there's something so delightfully endearing about his instruction that I can't help but wonder if I'm being too critical of him. Maybe being a seductive slow talker isn't the *worst* thing in the world . . . I no sooner have the thought than he says, "Sweetie, you're going to have to blow a lot harder than that if you want to make it move."

◆ ◆ ◆

I'm riding that fine line between laughter and tears, sanity and strait-jacket, as I pull the Jeep to a grinding halt at the top of the driveway, windshield wipers working overtime to keep up with the torrential downpour. I'm not sure what vile acts I committed in my former life, but they must've been *really* bad to deserve the flaming shit-arrows Cupid's been firing at me for the last week. *What the hell was Gia thinking?* I could *never* take Carlos to Hope's wedding. With every slow-spoken word dripping with seductive undertones, my mother would think he was trying to talk her out of her SPANX upon introductions.

UGH! This is all so unbelievably unfair! I pound the steering wheel with my fist, again.

"I'm a nice, normal woman!" I scream. "Why can't I find a nice, normal man who isn't married? Is that really so much to ask?"

A whimper swells in my throat as I glance over my shoulder toward the front yard. Through the rain-slick window, I see that J.T. somehow managed to clear all the rotted wood before the heavy rain hit, but sadly the improved curb appeal does little to ease my disappointment. I was really hoping he'd still be here—

"Screw you, Cupid!" I give the wheel one last punch, then climb out of the car and sprint through the rain for the safety of the house.

I trade out my wet clothes for some flannel pajamas, turn on the TV, and then head into the kitchen to bury my feelings with leftovers. Rerun's supportive tail wags earn him a sausage link, but I keep the rest for myself. It's going to take a lot of calories to numb this pain.

113

I ram a heaping spoonful of cold frittata into my mouth and am just about to go for the potatoes when a familiar voice emerges from the living room.

"Ohmuuhgod," I sputter, sending frittata bits flying. Is this on right now?

Rerun tends to the crumbs while I bolt for the living room, loaded-up dish in hand. I can't remember the last time I saw *Sixteen Candles*, but just the sound of Molly Ringwald's character, Samantha, evaluating her small boobs instantly transports me back to that lazy summer when Amanda babysat us and introduced us to him, to Jake Ryan. Beautiful Jake Ryan . . .

An unexpected surge of excitement hums through my body as I plop down on the couch and stare intently at the screen.

God, I love this movie!

Grinning like an idiot, I settle deeper into the cushions, savoring the richness of the food and the familiarity of the dialogue.

"You guys are insane," I mutter, my thoughts momentarily turning to Claire and Tracy. I don't have a Jake Ryan complex. I just know a damn good movie when I see it.

My own disappointing love life slowly starts to fade as the movie moves forward and we delve deeper into Samantha's. I shake my fists in frustration and grumble, "Nooo! Do *not* look back at him," when she's answering the sex test during independent study and gets to the *Who would you do it with?* question, then immediately burst into giggles as we get our first look at Jake. Oh, Jake . . . Why don't more men wear crew cuts?

Just like when I was a teenager, my limbs stiffen when Samantha naively scribbles *Jake Ryan* down on the wide-ruled page, and then my heart turns to Silly Putty when he practically falls out of his desk trying to steal the note with a stretch of his long leg. Damn, those boots are sexy, all worn out and rugged looking. They remind me of the work boots J.T. wears . . . My protective instinct kicks in when we get a glimpse of Jake in the arms of that snooty Caroline Mulford at the school dance.

"She only likes you because you're rich and popular!" I scream helplessly at the TV. "She's going to ruin your parents' house! Kids are going to park all over the lawn, and that track girl with *huge* boobs is going to drop dumbbells through the floor; champagne's going to explode everywhere!"

Despite my concern for his future well-being, I can't help but notice that Jake's red-and-blue plaid shirt bears a striking resemblance to the one Skip wore on our date. *He's got no manners, but at least he has good taste in clothes . . .* Anticipation swells through my veins as Samantha finally musters up enough courage to talk to Jake. I hug the throw pillow tight against my chest, bracing myself for the moment when he says, "Hi," and then—*there it is!* THE LIP BITE!

"Ohmygod!" I collapse against the cushions, squirming with delight, and watch through a screen of fingers as he drags his front teeth over his bottom lip. My god, he looks *just* like J.T. . . . From the nerds in night vision goggles to the Chinese exchange student's front-yard stupor, every character, every scene, holds my attention as tightly as the one before, but none can hold a candle to what's unfolding in front of me right now.

Samantha has just explained to the church organist that her sister forgot her veil, and now she's hurrying to return it before they leave for the reception, but she's too late. Everyone's leaving, and they don't even realize she's not with them. Sadness falls over her, and she turns her attention down to the veil in her hands. She thinks she's been forgotten, again, but then that dreamy background music picks up, and we see him, Jake Ryan, standing in front of his sexy red Porsche, waiting for her! Samantha slowly raises her head, and then—

I gasp.

He gives her a little wave. A sheepish little wave that sings louder than a thousand love songs. But she can't believe it's directed at her, so she looks over her shoulder to make sure he wasn't greeting someone else, then turns back and says, "Me?" And he grins like she's the cutest thing he's ever seen and then says—

"Yeah, you!" I scream the line out for him, then press the pillow against my face and collapse against the cushions, giggling. Nearly forty years old and I *still* turn to mush!

Rerun nuzzles my arm with a wet snout.

"It's okay, bud," I say, slowly sitting back up. "I'm not possessed. I'm just enjoying a little escape from reality."

Still smiling, I return my attention to the screen just in time to watch the final scene.

Jake and Samantha are sitting in front of a beautiful birthday cake that he bought her, having this deliciously awkward conversation, and then he tells her to make a wish—

I blink hard.

Make a wish.

Samantha, make a wish . . .

The familiar words hit me square in the gut, forcing my jaw to drop.

That's exactly what Carlos said to my toothless neighbor during art class . . . the one moment when I thought there *might* be a chance for him . . . the one moment when he sounded like him, like Jake Ryan.

An unexpected and unwelcome truth starts to rattle my bones as the movie scenes I dismissed as coincidental likenesses to my dates suddenly unfold in a much different light: Daniel showing a respect for elders, *just like Jake to Samantha's grandparents*. Skip dressing in plaid shirts, *just like Jake*. Even Brian, the thief, drove a red Porsche (which was repossessed, but still!). They weren't snippets of appreciation for *them*. They were glimpses of likenesses to *him* . . . to Jake Ryan.

And then there's everything I love about J.T. . . .

The boots, the lip bite, *his* plaid shirt, and the complete obliviousness to how incredibly *hot* he is . . . my heart starts to hammer.

Holy shit.

Claire and Tracy were right. Jake Ryan has been hijacking my love life for twenty years and counting . . .

Chapter 10

Thirty-three days until the wedding
Day one of my new reality . . .

"I've got the Jake Ryan complex!" I burst into the break room, adrenaline from last night's revelation still pumping hard through my veins. Claire and Tracy both look up from where they're sitting at the table. "You guys were right! I measure up every guy I've ever dated to Jake Ryan. I didn't even realize I was doing it—but I was! *Every guy!* All of them. But I think I may have actually found—"

"Sweetie, we're sort of in the middle of something . . ." Using her restrained mom voice, Claire glances at the fiftyish woman sitting opposite them.

"This is Helen Strider," Tracy says over a wry grin. "She's interviewing for the office manager position."

My eyes snap wide.

Tracy laughs.

Claire glares at her.

"I'm sorry." I offer Helen an apologetic look. "I don't usually run into rooms screaming. It's just that I had this monumental epiphany about my love life last night, and I had to tell them."

"Oh, that's okay." Her green eyes light up with excitement. "I love girl talk."

"Surely it can wait until we're done here," Claire suggests.

"Oh no it can't," Tracy says. "Sit down and tell us everything."

She motions to the empty chair beside Helen, who is quick to join in with an encouraging nod. Claire sighs and says, "Okay, tell us what happened. Helen, this is Mac Huntress, by the way. She's the other doctor in the office. She's usually *very* professional . . ."

"I am. Hi. Nice to meet you." I give her hand a quick shake, then drop down into the chair.

"So, you finally saw the Jake Ryan light, eh?"

"Yes. I did," I answer, ignoring Tracy's smug tone. "Last night. I just got home from a *horrible* sort-of date with this X-rated slow talker, and I started watching *Sixteen Candles*, and it all just hit me—"

"Oh, I just love that movie," Helen mutters wistfully.

I glance at her and nod. Of course you do, Helen. You're a smart, sensible woman!

"Everything you guys told me was true! Even though all these guys I've been dating really *are* horrible, I've been measuring them up against an impossible standard—or what *seemed* like an impossible standard—until I met—"

"Wait, wait, wait. X-rated slow talker?" Claire interrupts, too focused on getting the details from the bad dates to let me finish telling her about J.T. "Are you talking about Skip Overstreet?"

"You went out with Skip Overstreet?" Tracy cuts in.

I shake my head. "No. I mean . . . yes. I did go out with Skip Overstreet, but he wasn't the X-rated slow talker. That was Mr. Carlos—"

"Mr. Carlos?" Tracy questions.

"He's this artist guy that Gia set me up with."

"You let *Gia* set you up with someone?"

The disapproval in Tracy's voice mirrors her expression.

"I know, I know. Stupid move, but I was desperate."

"I guess so," she groans.

"So, wait, what happened with Skip?" Claire persists.

"Skip is a pig who can't keep his food in his mouth—"

"Oh my gosh, yes!" She smacks the table with her palm. "*That's* how I knew his name. Andy and I sat at a fundraising dinner with him once. He was so gross." She turns to Tracy, chuckling over a sour expression. "He spewed pieces of prime rib all over the table—"

"Eww. He used to cover our patients for us at the hospital," Tracy grouses.

"I can't believe you went out with him," Claire finishes, turning back to me.

"Yeah, well, I did. And he ate a hot dog and onion rings, so you can imagine how fun that was."

"What happened with the guy Caroline set you up with?" Tracy asks, still unwilling to let me get to the most crucial development in my epiphany.

"He has an unnatural obsession with the Hallmark store."

"Say what?"

"He was an emotional basket case. He cried through half our date!" Tracy and Claire exchange a glance but don't expound upon it, which is good, because I'm in no mood to try to defend myself. Jake Ryan complex or not, Daniel was a train wreck. "Look, the bad dates aren't what's important here. What I'm trying to tell you is that I feel like I might have found *my* Jake Ryan."

"*You have?*" Claire says at the same time Tracy says, "*Who is he?*"

"His name is J.T. He's the contractor who's fixing my porch."

"Ooh, handymen are so sexy," Helen offers.

Another insightful comment by Helen. We should hire her.

"So, what's the problem?" Tracy asks. "Why do you look like someone just punched you in the face?"

My shoulders sag, and I swallow a humiliated little whimper before I say, "Because he's married."

"Married?" Claire asks.

I nod.

"Married?" Tracy chimes in.

"Yes, married," I say. "Jeez."

"Well, that's not going to work," Tracy grumbles.

"Yeah. I know."

"So, what is it about him that makes you think he's *your* Jake Ryan?" Claire asks.

Even though I've already come to terms with the answer to that question, hearing my rationale aloud, with other people present, makes me feel more than a little stupid. Still, I tell them everything, and by the time I'm done, my breath is fluttering, and I'm smiling so hard my cheeks are about to split.

"Damn, lip bites are really hot," Tracy says over a sigh.

Claire nods. "Yeah, they are . . ."

"And you know what else?" I go on, grateful for the camaraderie. "The actor who plays Jake Ryan is named *Michael* in real life—"

"No way!" Tracy grunts.

"Michael Schoeffling," Helen confirms with a nod, unaware of the relevance the name *Michael* has to this story.

"Seriously?" Claire asks.

I nod. "*And* he's some kind of carpenter slash handyman now. It's uncanny, you guys! It's like the whole damn universe is pointing me in this direction, telling me that *this* is my guy, but then he's got that stupid ring on his finger and . . . *ugh*—" Disappointment steals my words, and I slump down in the chair. "I finally find my Jake Ryan, and he's fucking off-limits. Sorry, Helen. I usually only swear when I'm drunk."

"Oh, that's okay. I'm the same way. One shot of tequila and I'm dropping f-bombs all over town."

"Maybe he's not actually off-limits," Claire goes on with a surprising show of optimism. "Maybe there's more going on with him than you know."

"Wait a second. Are *you*, Mrs. Happily Married, telling me to pursue a married man?"

"Pursue? No." She levels me with a pointed look. "Confirm what his situation is? Yes."

"I second that," Helen offers. "If you've been searching for this guy your whole life, you owe it to yourself to find out the truth about him."

"You really do, Mac," Tracy agrees earnestly.

I'm more than grateful for their support, but in all honesty, I'm a bit taken aback by it. "Shouldn't you guys be insisting that I get therapy or something?" I raise my palms as if inviting them to fit me for a straitjacket. "I'm a grown woman who's basically been pining over a fictional character for twenty-five years—a character who, according to the internet, some people consider a misogynist—"

"Oh, please . . . ," Tracy groans.

"Actually, he was kind of a jerk to Caroline the night of his party," Claire counters over a half shrug.

"Oh, stop with all that," Helen replies, her tone now more maternal than girlfriend. "Was he perfect? No. But what seventeen-year-old boy with keys to a Rolls and an open liquor cabinet is? The point is, you know darn well why you were attracted to him: despite some of his immature actions, he was sweet, and thoughtful, and—good Lord—*so* handsome." She fans herself with her hand. "There is absolutely no way a woman who is capable enough to bring human beings into the world isn't equally as capable of knowing when she's found a *grown* man who embodies all those good traits. Now stop second-guessing everything, and go see if this is your guy."

I blink hard, startled by her pointed instructions, even though I really appreciate them.

"Well, you heard the woman," Tracy says. "Go get your man!"

◆ ◆ ◆

"Suck that, Molly Ringwald!" Helen's little pep talk has me screaming with pride as I take my exit off the interstate. Thanks to some bold driving (that earned me a few angry honks and one *very* aggressive middle-finger salute), I made the forty-mile drive from the clinic back to Naperville in under thirty minutes, all because I'm determined to square things away with J.T. before he packs up his tools for the day. "All you had to deal with was some missing undies." I smirk. "That's child's play compared to the lengths I'll go to get my Jake Ryan . . ."

I speed into town, through my neighborhood, and finally make the left onto my street—

Ugh . . . No!

The hopefulness that propelled me home in record time disappears as I pull up to the house and see that he's not here. *Dammit.* I glance at the dashboard clock and sigh. It's barely four o'clock. I thought for sure I'd given myself enough time. Although if he's avoiding me after the way I left him yesterday, there may never be enough time . . . I put the car to rest at the top of the driveway, then open the side gate and call for Rerun to join me as I head out to the front yard to observe the work J.T. got in today.

To the average passerby the wooden frame jettisoning off the front of my house might not appear all that impressive, but to me it's like looking at a rainbow after forty days of flooding.

Nice work, sir.

I run my hands along the thick wooden anchor beams cemented into the ground and smile. I'm going to have a porch again. A beautiful, sturdy front porch with a cliché "Welcome Friends" doormat and some obnoxiously big flowerpots that overflow with color: red poinsettias in the winter and hot-pink geraniums in the summer. And I'll buy some wicker patio furniture too—a couple of rockers centered right in front of the living room window. And I'll get one of those indoor-outdoor pillows for Rerun to lie on—

Where is he anyway?

"Come here, boy!"

I expect to hear the familiar jingle of his dog tags as he comes lumbering down the driveway, but I don't hear anything.

"Rerun!"

I wait for a moment.

Still nothing.

I glance back at the living room window.

If Gia had left him inside, he'd have his nose pressed firmly against the glass by now. His old bones may be creaking, but his hearing is still sharp as a tack.

An uneasiness niggles my spine as I head toward the backyard. As expected, Gia's flat is dark. She works at the flower shop on Monday afternoons, and she never leaves Rerun alone at her place anyway. Not since the day he made a meal out of one of her Steve sketches. I take a quick turn through the rest of the yard, calling out his name, but don't see any sign of him.

Where are you, old man? I head for the house but stop short when I see a piece of cardboard propped up against the back door. It's a haggardly written note scrawled out in pencil.

Mac,

Something's wrong with Rerun—I think he had a seizure.

Not sure what vet you use, so I'm taking him where I used to take Angus.

Hidden Trails Vet Clinic on West Maple.

Call me when you get this. 555-0142

—J.T.

Ohmygod.

My heart twists over a broken, terrified breath.

Rerun!

Without thought, I throw the sheet of cardboard to the ground and sprint for the car. I know exactly where the clinic is. It's not our usual vet, but I've driven by it a thousand times. It's on the way to Claire and Andy's.

Disregarding all traffic laws, I race back through the neighborhood and toward the South Side of town. I'm several miles into the trip by the time I have the presence of mind to call J.T. *Shit!* I didn't bring the stupid note with his number.

I tighten my grip on the steering wheel. "I'm coming, buddy. I'm coming . . ."

My knuckles are running white by the time I finally tear into the parking lot nearly fifteen minutes later. I park right beside J.T.'s truck and run inside.

"I'm here for Rerun!" My cry, sounding as desperate as I feel, startles the woman sitting behind the front desk. She jolts out of her chair.

"I'm sorry, you're here for who—"

"Mac."

I turn to my left and see J.T. rising from the long, padded bench that runs the length of the wall. Worry lines peek out from beneath his Steri-Strip, forcing my throat to swell with emotion.

I swallow hard. "What happened?"

"It looked like a seizure."

"A seizure?"

He nods. "Has that happened before?"

I do my best to recall every second of the nine joyful years Rerun's been in my life. There's been some limping, plenty of middle-of-the-night puking, and even some stitches thanks to that raccoon that was stupidly snooping through the trash last summer, but never a seizure.

A seizure?

My chin trembles as I shake my head in response.

"Okay. That's probably a good sign then. Here, let's sit you down." J.T. throws a stabilizing arm around me and gently ushers me over to the bench. "Can I get you some water or something?"

I smile weakly. "No. Thank you."

He sits down close beside me, easily transitioning his hand to that tender spot between my neck and shoulder. The warmth and pressure of his touch feel good, comforting . . . calming.

I take a few deep breaths, then turn to him. "So, what happened? Was he acting weird or . . ."

"Not at all. Gia took him for a long walk before she went to work this morning, and then he was hanging out with me all afternoon. He seemed totally fine. I had just loaded up my tools and was getting ready to play ball with him, and then he just sort of fell down and started convulsing—"

My chest tightens over a whimper. My poor baby . . .

"It didn't last that long." He gives my shoulder a reassuring squeeze. "And according to the internet, he wasn't aware of what was happening."

"You looked it up?"

He smiles sheepishly. "I know you doctors hate when we google things, but I felt sort of helpless just sitting here."

Despite the circumstances, my heart warms. What a good guy . . . "How was he when you brought him here?"

"Pretty disoriented. I had to carry him in. Of course, his tail was still wagging."

A small grin breaks across my lips. "Of course."

"I'm really sorry about the note. I tried to get ahold of Gia to get your number, but she didn't pick up—"

"Oh, no, it's fine." I lay a reassuring hand on his knee. The contact prompts his Adam's apple to bob and my pulse to quicken, all concern for his marital status suddenly nonexistent. "I'm just . . ." I swallow hard myself. "I'm so grateful you were there."

He nods slowly, gaze locked in on mine. "Me too."

"Excuse me, Rerun's mom?"

I quickly pull my hand back, returning my attention to the woman at the front desk. "Yes?"

"Dr. Massey is still running a few tests, but she wanted me to let you know that Rerun's vitals all look good and that he's resting comfortably."

"Oh, thank god."

"She'll be out to talk to you in a little while."

"Okay. Thank you." I turn back to J.T. and, over a relieved sigh, say, "Well, that's a step in the right direction."

He smiles. "Yeah, it sure is."

Taken verbatim, his words are upbeat, but to the ear, they sound sort of sad. Considering the good news we just got, it's a little concerning.

"Is everything okay?" I ask.

He's quick to nod, but still his gaze drops away from me. "Yeah. I, um, I just ran into someone earlier I wasn't expecting to see, and it sort of threw me off, I guess."

I can't help but notice that he's rubbing his wedding band with the pad of his right thumb, an absent motion, like he's not even aware he's doing it. My stomach twists. He's feeling conflicted about *us* too.

"But I'm fine," he goes on, raising his head to reveal a brighter expression. "How was the rest of your day? Besides all of this."

"Oh, um . . ." Despite the elephant in the room, his inquiry is sweet and brings a flush of warmth to my cheeks as I think back on the events of the day—the events of the last twenty-four hours—that led me to being here right now. Events that motivated me to reschedule my last two appointments so I could get home early enough to see him.

I turn slightly, allowing my shoulder-length hair to veil the blush on my cheeks. "It was pretty good. Busy, but good. How was yours? I mean, aside from the run-in with the unexpected person. It looks like you made some good progress on the porch."

"Yeah, we did, but not as much as I hoped." He sighs and scratches the back of his head. "Jeff's daughter had some sort of recital at school, so he had to take off a little early. There's only so much one person can do."

"Jeff?"

"An old high school buddy of mine. He's been out of work for a while, so he helps me out whenever I need an extra set of hands."

"That's nice. Do you keep in touch with a lot of your friends from high school?"

"Nah. Just a couple guys. How about you?"

"Just one girl. She's actually a patient of mine."

"Really? Is that weird at all?"

I shrug. "I could see how you'd think that, but I'm actually pretty good at compartmentalizing: work is work; personal is personal."

The words come out with stone-cold confidence, but the truth is other than Caroline, who is definitely *not* a typical patient, or friend, I've never been in a position where I've had to separate personal affiliations from patient involvement. I can't even imagine a scenario where that would come into play—

"And how was the painting class? Am I sitting beside the next da Vinci?"

I roll my eyes. "Hardly. We were supposed to be painting a restful beach scene. Mine looked more like the aftermath of a shark attack."

He laughs and gives my leg a playful nudge with his knuckle. "Nah, I'm sure it was good. You're just being hard on yourself."

"No, really, it was terrible," I go on, returning his delicious touch by shouldering into his side. "The six-year-old kid beside me called me out multiple times for how bad it was."

"Ouch."

"Yeah. Speaking of ouch, how's your head?"

I gently graze my thumb along the spot in question, prompting him to grin and say, "Much better, thanks to my favorite doctor."

We carry on with our light, flirtatious banter for a while before an elderly husband-and-wife team comes in to pick up their equally old poodle, and I'm reminded that it's getting late and that J.T. most likely has somewhere else he needs to be. Or, at the very least, some*one* else he needs to be with.

A knot of worry starts to tangle in my chest.

It's now or never.

Time to see if you're *my* Jake Ryan or not . . .

"I really appreciate you sitting here with me," I say, voice wavering with trepidation, "but it's fine if you need to go. There's no way of knowing how long the doctor's going to take and, well, I'm sure your wife is expecting you."

His brows furrow. "My wife?"

My heart thunders against my chest, and I nod while motioning toward his left hand.

It takes him a second to catch up, but when he does, his eyes grow impossibly wide, and he starts to shake his head. "*Oh, no.* No, I'm not married—"

"You're not?"

"No. *Shit.* No. I'm not—"

"But what about the Sweetheart's Special?" I blurt out the question louder and with more urgency than I'd ever imagined asking it.

Startled, he jerks back. "*The what?*"

"The Sweetheart's Special. The flowers you buy from Gia's store. She said you're in there buying them all the time. If they're not for your wife, then who are you buying them for?"

His eyes narrow for a split second before recognition sets in, and he starts to shake his head. "Oh, no. No. The flowers . . . they're for my mom."

"Your *mom?*"

He nods quickly. "Yeah. She's got dementia and doesn't remember much of anything anymore, but there are a few things she can't shake:

one of them is that my dad always bought her flowers from Mancato's Flower Shop. He passed a few years ago, but I keep sending her the flowers as if they were from him."

Delivered from another man, it might sound like a well-crafted line to get himself out of trouble, but the earnestness in his voice assures me it's the truth.

"I swear," he goes on, "the only woman I'm buying flowers for is my mom. You can ask anybody—ask my sister. We fight about it all the time. She thinks it's mean to lie to her, but I don't think of it that way. I'm not trying to fool her. I'm just trying to keep the few good memories she has alive for as long as possible."

His sister.

His sister is the swimsuit model Gia saw him fighting with.

And he recognizes that sometimes a little lie is necessary if it keeps your mom happy . . .

"That's about the sweetest thing I've ever heard," I say, beyond relieved, and utterly enamored. "What other memories are you keeping alive?"

"Well, it's not exactly a memory. It's more of a familiar routine." The softest flush crosses his cheeks, and he drops his head slightly. "She loves the Cubs, even more than you. She and my dad actually met at a game in 1952—"

"Seriously?"

"Yeah. They were sitting two rows apart, and my dad was cheering for the other team—the Cardinals," he adds, which, of course, prompts me to scowl. He grins. "Apparently they got into a pretty serious disagreement about a call on the field, were asked to leave the ballpark to settle their dispute, and then one thing led to another and they were married three months later."

"Aww . . ." I press my palm over my heart. Falling in love at a Cubs game. How perfect!

129

"Dad never fully converted, but he did become a pretty loyal fan," he goes on. "They had season tickets for close to fifty years, and if it was an away game, they watched from home, always with Italian beef subs from Chicago Joe's. It was their thing." He shrugs adorably. "So now I record all the games for her and, when I can, drive down and watch them with her. That's where I was going the other night when I ran into you at the deli."

The extra sandwich was for his mom.

His mom, who loves the Cubs more than I do . . .

"Look, Mac, I promise the only reason I've even been wearing the ring was to keep women away." My jaw drops and my eyes snap wide. *"Not you,"* he quickly clarifies and reaches for my hand. "I wasn't trying to keep *you* away. It's just . . ."

I could easily spend a lifetime gazing at the beautiful sight of his long, strong fingers blanketed over my hand, but the sound of his rapid breathing prompts me to turn to him.

He smiles timidly. "I found that when I *wasn't* wearing it, I got a lot of attention that I didn't really want or wasn't ready for." He gives his head a little shake, like he's haunted by a memory of something he *wasn't ready for.* "I put it back on with the intention of taking it off once I knew I was ready for something—"

His attention suddenly darts away from me, over my shoulder.

Something?

Something . . . what?

"Hi there," a soft, feminine voice says. "Sorry to keep you waiting. I'm Dr. Massey. You must be Rerun's mom?"

Her timing is nothing short of terrible, but of course I'm still grateful to hear her voice.

Rerun is our focus, not the beautiful SINGLE man sitting in front of you who was just about to confirm whether or not he's your Jake Ryan!

I clear my throat and reluctantly pull my hand away from J.T. so I can offer it to her.

"Hi, yes. I'm Mac Huntress. How's he doing?"

She sighs. "Well, he had a rough afternoon, as I'm sure you've heard, but he's looking pretty good now." J.T. gives my shoulder a tender squeeze. "He came in a little dehydrated, so we're giving him some fluids, but otherwise he's just a sweet, happy old guy who's taking it all in."

A tear pricks the back of my eye, and I smile.

Sweet old Rerun . . .

"I ran a few basic neurological tests, which he passed with flying colors," she goes on, her kind eyes staying fixed on mine, "so I think we can rule out a stroke and assume it was a seizure. Does he have a history of them?"

I shake my head. "Not that I know of."

"Okay. Well, it's possible that it was just a one-off, but hereditary epilepsy isn't totally uncommon in Labs, so we'll want to keep an eye on that. Is there any chance he came into contact with toxic chemicals in the last few days?"

"I don't think so. I haven't used anything new around the house, and Gia only uses environmentally safe paints. You don't use anything toxic, do you?" I turn to J.T., who is already shaking his head.

"No, never."

Dr. Massey smiles. "Okay, then it may have just been a fluky thing, or even a sudden change in brain activity. Sometimes if a dog goes from restfulness to excitement too quickly, it can be jarring to their systems, especially in an older dog like Rerun."

Considering how excited Rerun is whenever J.T.'s around, I'm surprised he isn't convulsing more often.

"If it's okay with you, I'd like to keep him overnight so we can run a tox panel just to make sure his liver and kidney functions are okay. The tests are a little pricey, but—"

"No, that's fine. Definitely do the tests."

"Does he have any food restrictions we need to be aware of?"

"Uh, no."

She chuckles. "A true Lab, then, huh?"

"Oh yeah. He'll eat anything you put in front of him."

"All right, well, he's in good hands here, getting lots of love from the staff, so you go get some rest, and we'll touch base with you tomorrow."

I leave my credit card and contact information with the woman at the front desk, then head out to the parking lot, where J.T. is leaning against the passenger side of his truck, waiting for me. I really should be thinking about my sweet old dog right now, but the sight of J.T.'s long, muscular frame silhouetted by the dim fluorescence of the overhead security lights is too delicious to ignore, as is the conversation we started and desperately need to finish.

"Get everything squared away?" He stands tall as I approach our cars, hands shoved into his front jeans' pockets like a timid schoolboy uncertain what to say.

My breath hitches on a hopeful beat, and I answer, "Yep. We're all set."

"She tends to be a little overcautious." His words thrum with the same jittery energy I'm feeling. "But I think that's good. Better safe than sorry, right?"

"Definitely."

Our gazes lock for a long, tenuous beat before my attention shifts down to his black T-shirt. I can see his chest rising and falling beneath deep, rapid breaths.

My pulse quickens.

He's as nervous as I am.

He steps closer.

"If you want, I can pick him up tomorrow, since I'm already in the neighborhood . . ."

My stomach flip-flops, both at his sweet offering and his proximity. I can smell him now, that same delicious peppermint scent I've savored before, but now it's coupled with the ruggedness of fresh-cut wood and the headiness that comes from a long day's work.

I swallow hard.

"That would actually be really helpful. I have an induction scheduled early tomorrow morning. It's her third, so hopefully once she's dilated it won't take too long, but you never know . . ."

Anticipation building, I take a step forward, narrowing the space between us to less than a foot. Despite the cool evening air, the brimming tension is hot and is slowly stealing what little oxygen is still circulating through my lungs.

His gaze softens slightly, and with a delicate touch, he brushes a wisp of hair from my face, his ring finger no longer bound by the shiny golden band.

"Before Dr. Massey came out, I wanted to tell you that, well . . . I'm not perfect. My last relationship ended pretty badly, and there's some residual stuff that sneaks up on me from time to time. Nothing big, but it's there." He doesn't spell it out, but it's pretty clear that the *stuff* he's referring to resurfaced today during his unexpected run-in. His vulnerability makes my chest swell with affection. *Sweet man . . .* we've all got our stuff. "But the thing is, Mac"—he settles his palm against my cheek, eyes focused intently on me—"I told myself I wasn't going to take that ring off again until I was sure I was ready to move on to something new—to *someone* new. And I am now. I'm ready to move on."

A delighted ache swells in my throat. "With me?"

He grins, amused by the unexpected squeak in my voice. "Yeah, you."

Yeah, you. Just like Jake said to Samantha on the church steps. Except that this is *my* Jake, and this is so much better than a movie. With slow, deliberate movements he strokes my cheekbone with a graze of his calloused thumb, then leans forward and kisses me. My eyelids flutter in time with my heartbeat, overwhelmed by the tenderness of his touch and the warmth of his breath against my skin.

Good god in heaven . . .

Moving on instincts I've long thought dormant, I cinch my arms tight around his waist and pull him closer, parting my lips and allowing a surge of that decadent peppermint taste to flood my mouth with a sweep of his tongue. It tickles and teases my taste buds and demands every nerve ending in my body to rise to attention.

Flutters electrify like currents through my limbs as he rakes his long fingers through my hair, gripping and searching through the tangles for a way to deepen our connection. Propelled by the same desire, I press my palms firm against his back, seeking out his corded muscles with my fingertips in hopes of finding some leverage to deepen the kiss . . . to lose myself completely to his touch.

Memories of that damn lip bite begin to tease and taunt me with every shared breath, prompting me to take a little nibble on his bottom lip. A pleasured groan escapes him, demanding I bite harder. He whimpers softly, and I feel his lips pull up into a smile.

"You've got a thing for lips, don't you?"

Over labored, hungry breaths, I mutter, "You have no idea . . ."

Chapter 11

Mmm . . . day one with my yummy guy
Thirty . . . something days until the wedding

He asked me to wake him so he could say goodbye before I left, but as I gaze at him now—sound asleep, naked and tangled up in *my* bedsheets—there's no way I'm going to disrupt this image. It's too damn delicious. Besides, if I woke him, we'd just end up doing what we did countless times last night, and I *really* have to get to the hospital, no matter how badly I want to stay here.

I lick my lips but wince as I'm immediately reminded of how much kissing we did last night. I swallow a giggle. If I were watching my life play out on a big screen, I'd tsk the main character for hopping into bed and going googly over a man so quickly, but this isn't a movie. By some divine twist of fate, this is *my* life. Finally, I get to be Samantha Baker . . .

I'm still grinning like a happy, sated fool by the time I emerge from the delivery room nearly seven hours later. Much to my surprise, Jackie Tremont's third baby wasn't as eager to enter the world as her previous two. Still, baby Charles, weighing in at a whopping nine pounds and four ounces with a headful of jet-black curls, finally emerged after the Pitocin worked its magic, and now he's resting comfortably with his proud parents, and I'm finally able to take some time for myself.

I check my phone. A spray of schoolgirl tingles erupts from the tips of my toes, tickling every bone in my body. As anticipated, there's a text message from J.T. sent at eight o'clock this morning, along with three others sent shortly after: one from Claire, one from the vet, and the last from my patient-friend Caroline. Of course I open J.T.'s first:

Good morning.

You were supposed to wake me up so I could give you a proper goodbye.

Guess now I'll just have to suffer through this day until I can give you a proper hello instead.

A decadent shudder unexpectedly surges through my body, prompting me to cover my mouth before I start moaning. *The things that man can do with his hands . . .*

I'll work on the porch until it's time to get Rerun. I'm sure he'll have plenty of kisses for you when you get home. That'll make two of us.

I quickly thump out my response:

I look forward to a proper greeting.

I should be home by 3.

Next, the vet's message:

Hi, it's Gina from Hidden Trails. Rerun's tox tests came back clean! He had a good night and will be ready for pickup around 2. We got your message last night, so we'll call Mr. Walsh to come pick him up. Dr. Massey will call you in a few days to check on him. The total charge to your credit card is $518.77.

Ordinarily, a $500 vet bill would have my stomach wrenching, but today it doesn't even faze me. In fact, I consider it money *more* than well spent. Had Rerun not ended up at the vet yesterday afternoon (a tragedy I, of course, *never* wanted to happen), J.T. may not have ended up in my bed last night. A true silver lining if ever there was one . . .

Claire's message:

Hello?!??! WHAT THE HELL HAPPENED WITH THE HANDYMAN? We're DYING over here. CALL US! Hope all goes well with Tremont baby. And let me know who's on duty so I can update the file.

I grin, already eager to witness their expressions when I fill them in on all the details.

Tremont baby is good. Just finished up. I'll be heading home soon. Stanco is doc on duty. All is well with the handyman. He's definitely NOT MARRIED but is indeed VERY handy . . . And if you haven't already, hire Helen!

Finally, I open Caroline's message:

What's up, hooker?! I'm back from Seattle. Tired but feel ok. How was Daniel? Wedding date material? Quickie in the closet material? He's big, right?! Will fill out a tux (and a condom) nicely I bet ;)

I cringe, disgusted by the mere suggestion of sex with Daniel. He'd be crying before he even got undressed . . .

> Glad you're feeling well. Daniel was very nice, but I won't be seeing him again to know how he fits into anything. O_O

> I met someone else—he's perfect! I'll fill you in when I see you at your appointment in a few weeks.

I no sooner hit "Send" than a new message from J.T. arrives. I quickly tap on the screen, bringing the message up. *Ohmygod.* I gasp, covering my chapped lips with my fingers. It's a selfie of J.T. and Rerun, both boasting big, happy smiles that are accentuated by their matching salt-and-pepper facial hair.

> Just a couple of old guys waiting for you to get home . . .

My heart softens as I tap out my response:

> I'll be there as soon as humanly possible.

Unfortunately, what's *humanly possible* can't compete with hospital paperwork and an accident on the interstate that slows traffic to a near standstill. It's well after five by the time I finally make it home, but my guys don't seem any worse for the wait. They're playing ball in the backyard when I pull up the driveway.

I climb out of the Jeep, my thundering heart suddenly in a state of confusion: Which one do I kiss first? Rerun bounds up to the gate, his entire body swaying in anticipation. I laugh. I guess that answers my question. I push open the gate and drop down to my knees.

"There's my old man. Hello, buddy." He leans into me, groaning happily from behind his tennis ball while I hug his neck and scratch the sweet spot behind his ears. "I missed you, sir. Yes I did. I missed you . . ."

"I don't have a tail to wag, but I promise I'm as happy to see you as he is."

I glance up and see a grinning J.T. calling out to me from the back patio.

"I don't know, he's *pretty* happy . . ."

His grin widens, and he slowly starts to make his way across the yard toward me, but rather than just walking, he's making ridiculously cute, and painfully awkward, shimmying movements with his shoulders and hips.

I burst out laughing, my heart overflowing with delight. "Oh my god." I quickly stand in anticipation of receiving him. "You *are* happy to see me."

"I told you."

Fighting his own laughter, he finally reaches me and immediately plants a warm, hungry kiss on my mouth. The pressure against my sore lips seems to elevate my sensitivity, inviting the same heavenly sensations that stole my inhibitions last night to pulse through my veins once again. I moan softly as his tongue searches out the nuances of my mouth, his hands traveling with familiarity along my lower back and over my thigh—

Woof!

Rerun nuzzles his way between us, killing the romantic mood.

"Do you think he's jealous?"

"I have no idea," I chuckle while dabbing at the moisture on my lips.

"What's the matter, Rerun?" J.T. bends down and gives him a pat. "I thought we were buddies. I thought you liked having me around. You're supposed to be my wingman."

Rerun licks his cheek as if acknowledging his concern.

"What's wrong? Can't I give your mom a kiss?"

139

He barks again and then starts turning in a circle, the way he does when he's hungry.

"You don't seriously think it upset him that I was kissing you, do you?"

I can't help but grin at his worry. "No. He's just hungry. And come to think of it, so am I. I haven't eaten anything since this morning."

He glances up at me, top teeth grazing his bottom lip. "Well, then we better find you something to eat, because you're going to need your energy tonight."

That same tingle I felt moments ago returns full force as flashbacks of *last* night's energy-stealing activities start cycling through my mind. I smile.

Indeed, let's find something to eat . . .

◆ ◆ ◆

Rerun enjoys his kibble, along with the last bits of Mom's frittata, while J.T. and I feast on the rest of the leftovers. We're sitting in the living room, he in the corner of the love seat and I in the corner of the couch, where the two pieces of furniture meet up at a point; this way we can more easily face each other while we eat. The TV is on but turned down so low the newscaster's voice is almost inaudible. Each of us has a beer nestled between the cushion we're sitting on and the one beside it, and I'm shifting from having my bare feet tucked up under me or resting on the edge of the coffee table. It's a comfy, casual, relaxing dinner . . . and with my current company, it may be the best meal I've ever eaten.

"Tell me again why you have all this food?" He motions to the collection of serving dishes sitting on the coffee table in front of us. "I know you told me last night, but I had more important things on my mind."

I grin. Didn't we all . . .

It was close to midnight by the time we ventured out of my bed-room in search of some much-needed sustenance. (And water. Lots and lots of water. It turns out that earth-shattering sex leaves a girl a bit parched.) We stood at the island in the kitchen and attacked the left-overs for a solid fifteen minutes before we made our way back upstairs to resume our activities.

"My mom and sister were in town for the weekend," I say while tucking a chunk of biscuit into my mouth. "Mom tends to go a little overboard with Sunday brunch." And just about everything else . . .

"She made all of this for you and your sister?"

"Well, Gia ate some, too, but yes." I take a swig of beer. "My mother functions as if the queen of England is on her way over. Everything has to be *just* right all the time; tablecloths should always be pressed and starched, floors swept and polished, and smiles forced and presentable to the world." I flash him a toothy grin. "She's always been very caught up in the appearances of life."

"That must have been fun growing up."

"It wasn't always pretty," I admit, glancing at the box of Kleenex sitting on the table in the front entryway. "But I figured out early on how to make it work." One B cup at a time . . .

"So, is it safe to say you're more like your dad then?"

I nod. "Definitely." Though if I'm being honest, Hope's the one who got the lion's share of his go-with-the-flow disposition.

"Same here."

"Ooh. Was your dad a hot contractor with exceptional taste in women too?"

He smirks from behind the lip of his beer bottle. "Well, I can't speak to the *hot* factor, but yes on the women—and on being a contrac-tor." He takes a swig, then continues, "He loved his job, building things, getting his hands dirty . . ."

My heart aches at the heaviness weighing down his voice. I can't imagine how hard it would be to lose my dad.

I set my empty plate down next to his on the coffee table, then pull my knees up against my chest and settle deeper into the couch. "How long ago did he pass?"

"Two years. My mom had just been diagnosed with dementia, and he was trying to keep an eye on her while still maintaining the business. It just got to be too much for him. He had a heart attack on a jobsite and died in the ambulance on the way to the hospital."

"Oh my god." I reach over the arm of the couch and give his hand a gentle squeeze. "I'm so sorry."

"Yeah, it wasn't fun. And it happened at the worst possible time . . ." His attention slowly wanders down to the beer bottle he's gripping in his other hand. He stares at it for a long beat before he starts scratching at the corner of the label with his thumbnail. In a softer voice he says, "I'd just found out that I was never legally married to my wife, because she was already married to someone else."

I gasp and cry out, *"What?"*

Despite the seriousness of the conversation, he chuckles at my obvious confusion and raises his head.

"What do you mean your wife was married to someone else?"

He smiles weakly. "I mean that for almost three years she allowed me to believe that the private wedding she arranged for us on the beach in Hawaii was real, but it wasn't. The pastor was actually a bartender, wannabe actor who worked at our hotel, and the marriage license itself was a fake, just some template she printed off the internet. The whole thing was a sham—all of it. I was just her dirty little secret that nobody knew about."

I blink hard, trying to wrap my brain around what he's saying.

"I'm sorry. I'm still not getting this. How—I mean, why would she do that?"

"Because I wasn't good enough for her."

"You weren't good enough for her?" Now I'm not only confused. I'm angry. "How are *you* not good enough for anyone?"

142

He shrugs too easily. "Her dad is a big-shot investment guy—vacation houses, private jets, all that kind of stuff, and when he found out I'd proposed, he said he'd disown her if she said yes; apparently my blue-collar background wouldn't provide an adequate lifestyle for his precious daughter."

The matter-of-factness in his tone pricks at my heart like a thousand little needles, prompting me to graze my thumb along the sexy calluses that line the inside of his palm. How anyone could think this beautiful, hardworking man wasn't good enough for their daughter is beyond me. Though I could totally see my own mother having a similar opinion on his profession. Wretched woman.

"She never really got along with her parents," he continues, "so she made it seem like it was a no-brainer; all that was important to her was being happy. So, she said yes to me, and we got married a few months later. As far as I knew, she hadn't talked to her parents in almost three years."

"But she had?"

"Oh yeah. Turns out she never cut ties with them. After her dad gave her the ultimatum, she told him that *we* broke up, and then she started dating an old friend of the family—someone her father approved of. They ended up getting married a month before we did—"

"Oh my god . . ."

"I thought she was away on another one of her business trips, but it turns out she was actually on her honeymoon with him. It all seems so obvious now." He chuckles again, though this time it's propelled not by my confusion but apparently by his own hindsight. "She was never home for an entire weekend and always had to travel over major holidays, but I never thought anything of it—that's just how it was. We lived in Rockford, which is where my business was, and she rented a little studio in Chicago, where she worked. She commuted back and forth. I offered to move my business there so we could be together, but I was really established. I was working just off referrals and had a waiting list of clients. It didn't make sense to scrap it and start over. It wasn't ideal, but we made it work. And we had my family around, so . . . yeah."

He gives his head a slow shake, suggesting his family was as affected by her betrayal as he was. Of course they were. She lied to them too. And not the benign, nobody-gets-hurt kind of lies like J.T. and I tell our moms. It was a big fat selfish ruin-your-life kind of lie that should shame her.

"That was literally like three weeks before my dad passed," he continues, "so needless to say it wasn't a real good time for me."

I sigh and give my head a disgusted, heartsick shake of my own. "I don't even know what to say."

"There's not much to say." He shrugs. "I was just a total idiot."

"No you weren't. You were in love—you trusted her."

He hangs his head, clearly still haunted by the warning signs he missed.

"Did she ever tell her parents, or the other husband, the truth?"

"Nah—well, I mean, I don't know for sure, but I doubt it. She had no reason to tell them anything. As far as they were concerned, she was just on *business trips*"—he frees his hands so he can air quote the words—"when she was at home with me, so eliminating that *inadequate* part of her life probably wasn't that big of a deal."

The heaviness in his voice makes my throat feel thick and achy.

Even though it's not a much happier direction, I decide to reroute the conversation away from his horrific ex.

"And so that's when you moved down here to take care of your mom?"

"Yep. Me and Angus, my dog. I finished the job I was working on, packed up my tools, and moved into my parents' place to take care of her. I had a nurse come by during the day while I worked on Dad's contracting jobs, and then I took care of her at night. But within a couple of months, it became clear she needed full-time care, so we moved her into a facility down in Joliet, right by my sister's house." His sister, the swimsuit model. "I drive down a lot—to visit with her and watch the games, and, of course, I send the flowers . . ."

He winks at me, forcing my chest to swell with an even deeper affection for him than I already felt.

"You're the perfect child."

He barks out a laugh. "Trust me, if my folks were here, they'd convince you otherwise."

"I'm serious." I give his hand a little swat. "Not all kids would pack up their lives and do what you did, especially considering what happened with your ex. I'm sure your dad would be really proud of you for taking all of this on."

"Yeah, he would. Although I'm not so sure he'd like me changing the direction of his business. Which is what I'm going to do."

"What do you mean? What are you going to do?"

"I want to get out of residential work and move on to bigger jobs—office buildings and strip malls, that kind of thing. It's harder for sure and will probably take some time to establish myself, but I feel like I'm up for the challenge."

"I have no doubt you are," I say with confidence. "And I'm sure your dad would approve. He'd want you to do what makes you happy."

"You sound just like my sister."

"Yeah, well, she's a smart woman. Except for the whole Raiders thing."

He smiles, then takes another drink of his beer. "Speaking of football, this probably isn't the best time to tell you that I went to Ohio State, is it?"

My breath catches on a stifled cry. "Please tell me you're kidding."

He holds a straight face for a painfully long beat before he finally cracks. "Yes, I'm kidding. I did a couple years at Northwestern before I left and got my contracting license. I'm not the enemy, I swear."

I sigh, more relieved than he could ever know.

"That's not funny, mister." I grab the throw pillow out from under my arm and chuck it at him. He catches it and starts to laugh. "Our family is about to be infiltrated by one of those awful Buckeyes."

"Oh no, really?"

"Yeah. My sister's getting married to one of those heathens. That's why she and my mom were in town, by the way. They were shopping for her wedding dress." He nods with interest, but I continue on with my rant. "Dad and I are already strategizing seating arrangements for major holidays. It's going to get ugly."

"Damn, I thought Cubs fans were committed, but you Michigan people are cutthroat."

"You bet your sweet ass we are." I give my head a firm nod, then take a long, proud pull off my beer. Go Blue!

"So, when's the wedding?"

It suddenly dawns on me that I haven't thought about the stupid wedding, or my need for a date, in the last twenty-four hours. Clearly my mind has been more happily occupied . . . "I guess we're down to . . . I don't even know. It's over Memorial weekend."

"Wow. That's coming up fast."

I nod. Don't I know it.

"Is it safe to assume that your mom has a hand in it?"

I smirk, impressed with his astuteness. "More like her entire body. I'm sure at the end of the day it will be a beautiful event, but the lead-up is proving to be pretty torturous. I don't suppose you'd have any interest in going with me?"

The question rolls off my tongue without thought or any consideration for the fact that I already have a wedding date—made up as he is . . . A twinge of embarrassment nips at my spine. I guess now's as good a time as any to tell him about Michael—

"You want me to meet your family?"

It's not so much his question that catches me by surprise but rather the way his eyes are quickly expanding to the size of dinner plates.

Oh shit.

"It's too soon, isn't it?" I blurt out. Not exactly what I was thinking about, but a reasonable response nonetheless. "I'm sorry. I knew it was too soon—"

"No, no. It's not too soon." He gives my hand a reassuring squeeze. "I just wasn't expecting you to ask. But I'm flattered. And I'd be honored to go with you."

"Really?"

"Absolutely. You'll just have to make sure I'm up to speed on all the quirky family dynamics, so I don't get myself into any trouble."

Relief swells deep inside me, prompting me to exhale the breath I've been holding since I got Hope's *I'm getting married!* message.

I've got my date. And he's perfect!

"Okay . . . well." I swallow hard. "Um . . . other than my crazy mother, my homophobic, foulmouthed aunt that you'll likely have to babysit, and my secretly pregnant, bride-to-be sister, I can't think of any other quirks you'd need to be aware of . . ."

"Your sister is secretly pregnant?"

I nod. "Yep. Eight months. And I'm the only person who knows. My mom is going to lose her mind when she finds out."

"Your mom doesn't even know?"

I shake my head, a blooming smirk tickling my lips. Surely, he'll appreciate Hope's motivation. *Gotta keep the mom happy . . .*

"Nope," I say. "My sister's keeping it from her so she doesn't freak out before the wedding. She's already stressing out, but knowing her first grandchild's on the way would send her straight over the edge. That's the last thing we need."

I expect him to start laughing—or at the very least smile—but he doesn't. Instead he adopts a sort of wary expression that makes his forehead crease in a way I've not seen before. Not judgmental, more like . . . disappointed.

Like mom lies should be reserved for acts of compassion rather than self-preservation . . . *Uh-oh.*

I shift against the cushions.

"So, how about you?" Oblivious to my internal discomfort, he leans forward and grabs the last sausage link off his plate, then pops it into his mouth. "Did you ever want kids?"

I swallow hard, stifling my restless thoughts with a quick shake of the head. "Uh—yeah, maybe at one point. But not to the degree that I would have worked real hard to make it happen. If I had had the right partner—someone to help with the burden of my busy career, then yeah, I think so. But I'm actually pretty happy with the way things worked out. I love the idea of being an aunt. Plus, it's not like I'm without any dependents . . ." I nod toward Rerun, who's now snoring contentedly on his pillow. "And I've got Gia, who sometimes feels like a child, so my hands are pretty full."

"I like Gia. She's fun."

I level him with a hard look. "You mean wacko. You saw her Steve Guttenberg paintings, didn't you?"

"Oh yeah. I saw a whole lot of Steve."

I drain what's left of my beer, then volley the same question back to him. "What about you? Were kids ever on your radar?"

"Yeah, I guess when we first got married, but she was *traveling* so much that we decided it wasn't a good idea. She is pregnant now, though."

My eyes grow wide. "She is?"

He nods. "I ran into her the other day at a lumber store in Joliet. She and her husband were shopping for wood for a custom-made baby crib."

My heart wrenches at the memory of him at the vet's office, just after he'd *run into* someone unexpectedly.

"I'm sorry. That must've been really hard."

"Yeah, it was," he admits over a slow nod. "But not because of seeing them together or even because of the baby. It was because it was a reminder of what she did and why she did it." He sighs. "Knowing that I didn't measure up to her standards would have been hard to hear, but at least I would have known the truth and been able to deal with it instead of being kept in the dark all that time. You know what I mean?"

A lump of Michael guilt is lodging itself in my throat, making it hard to talk, so I nod instead.

"I think that was the hardest part of it all," he goes on, shaking his head. "She didn't have enough respect for me to be honest with me. It's just not right to lie when someone's feelings are involved."

Obviously, his statement isn't directed at me, or even at Hope, but the venom in his tone still stings and assures me that he doesn't have much tolerance for lies . . . I swallow hard and say, "It probably took a long time to work through all of those feelings, huh?"

He nods. "Yeah. And it still rears its ugly head every now and then," he admits, while offering me a broken smile that confirms what I already know: he's not sad at the loss of *her* but rather the idea of what he thought they had. "But I've been pretty well over it for a while now. Since last December fourth, to be exact."

"Well, that's fairly specific . . ."

He smirks. "That was her fortieth birthday. She always said she was going to kill herself the day she turned forty, so I tried to embrace the thought, even though I knew she was just being dramatic."

I chuckle. "That seems fitting."

He nods while an unexpected flush slowly starts to appear on his cheeks.

"What?"

He drops his head. "Nothing. It's . . ." He sighs. "It's embarrassing."

"Okay . . ."

He drags his hand through his hair, then looks up at me with an adorably pained expression. Over a heavy sigh he says, "Remember how

I told you I was still wearing my wedding ring because I got attention I wasn't ready for when I didn't wear it?" I nod, though after tonight it's pretty obvious the ring represented more than a "No Vacancy" sign. "Well, the night I took it off for the first time was *that* night, December fourth. A couple of my buddies took me out for beers to celebrate my newfound freedom, and there was this woman who sort of knew one of my friends, and she seemed really nice, but . . . god." He shakes his head, looking positively tortured by what he's about to say. "Let's just say I drank way too much, and when I woke up the next morning, she was definitely *not* as charming as I remembered her being."

The regret and embarrassment dragging down his confession are nothing short of heartbreaking, if not slightly endearing. Fighting the urge to smile, I climb off the couch and snuggle up beside him on the love seat.

"After everything you went through, a regretful one-night stand is sort of understandable."

"Not for me. Aside from believing I was married when I wasn't, that was hands down the stupidest thing I've ever done."

I'd like to argue that a one-night stand isn't stupid—it is—but reiterating what he already knows isn't going to help the situation.

"Yeah, well, we all do stupid things sometimes," I say.

"Whoa, sounds like somebody's got a few skeletons in her own closet," he teases, nudging my ribs with his knuckle. "Tell me, Dr. Huntress, what horrible secrets are you hiding?"

His question comes out with all the playfulness of a child on the jungle gym but still rocks me straight to the core. He's just set me up with the perfect pitch: a hanging breaking ball right over home plate. The perfect opportunity to come clean about Michael—a lie that doesn't really affect him but could still change the way he feels about me. *God, I don't want to change the way he feels about me!* But I want to be honest with him. If anyone deserves an honest relationship, it's him.

Shit.

I drop my head and heave a deep, motivating breath. "Actually, there is something I've been meaning to tell you . . ."

"Oh yeah?"

I slowly return my gaze to his and feel my heart wrench at the trust—the vulnerability—welling in his eyes.

I can't do this.

I can't run the risk of losing him.

Not now—not when I just got him!

I'll tell him later, after I tell Mom we've broken up.

I'll tell him Michael was just one of the guys I dated before—it doesn't have to be a big deal.

If I handle it right, he'll never be any the wiser—

"It's that bad?" he prods, amusement waning.

Resolved to handle this behind the scenes, I force out a laugh. "No, not bad, just . . . embarrassing." His brows rise curiously, and I sigh. The Michael thing is nothing—better to gnaw on a little humiliation than choke on a bone of contention. "Have you ever seen *Sixteen Candles*?"

"The movie?"

I nod.

"Yeah. I mean, I don't think I ever sat down and watched it straight through, but my sister and her friends were obsessed with it, so I'm sure I've seen most of it."

"Okay, so then you know who Jake Ryan is?"

His head tips in consideration. "Is he the dude with the Porsche?"

Leave it to a guy to only know Jake Ryan by his car. Ugh.

"Yeah. That's him. And like your sister, I loved that movie growing up, but I especially loved that character. For me he was like the perfect guy. I wanted Jake Ryan to be *my* boyfriend." J.T. nods, like he's not totally shocked by what I'm saying. I swallow hard. Just wait, buddy . . . "But the thing is . . . well, it turns out that it wasn't just a teenage crush. It was something I carried over into my adult life."

His eyes slowly start to narrow, like he's not sure whether I'm being serious or need a refill on my meds. I scratch my brow, suddenly wishing I'd been brave enough to unload the Michael lie. Being a liar has to be better than being crazy . . .

He nudges my leg, urging me to continue.

Despite my building humiliation, I inhale a deep breath and blurt out the rest. "It was recently brought to my attention that I use Jake Ryan as the standard for the men in my life, which is why I've never been able to find one that I'll be happy with . . . until you. I'm pretty sure that *you're* my real-life Jake Ryan."

"Really?"

Amusement lingers on his question—and on his lips; they're twitching like he's working hard not to laugh.

Ohmygod.

What have I done?

Mortified, I cover my face with my hands and cry out, "I know, I'm a total freak! There is something very wrong with me . . ."

"No, there's nothing wrong with you."

Finally giving way to his stifled laughter, he throws his arm around me and pulls me against his chest. It shudders in time with my own laugh.

"If it makes you feel any better, when I was in seventh grade, my buddies and I stole a copy of *Weird Science* from a Blockbuster video," he groans. "Kelly LeBrock owes me like a hundred pair of tube socks."

My lungs erupt beneath an explosion of laughter that forces me to roll away from his chest so I can catch a breath. Now my head is resting on his lap, and I'm looking up at him. Despite the happy tears blurring my vision, this is the most beautiful sight I've ever seen.

He looks down at me, and as his laughter slowly starts to fade, he strokes my hair away from my forehead and says, "I'm honored to be your Jake Ryan."

I swipe at my eyes, all uncertainty about keeping my secret vanishing beneath the sound of his beautiful words. "Really?"

He nods, then leans down close and says, "If you want, I'll take you upstairs and show you just how honored I am."

"Okay!"

I quickly roll off him and onto the floor but knock my knee against the coffee table in the process. *Ouch!* The sound startles Rerun, and he starts to bark.

Grimacing against the pain, I drop back onto the couch, whimpering, "Dammit. Now he's awake. He won't go back to sleep without going potty."

Chuckling, J.T. gives my back a quick rub and says, "I'll take him out. You get yourself squared away, and then we'll meet upstairs in a couple of minutes."

"You sure? I can do it . . ."

"Yeah, I'm sure. Jake Ryan would take the dog out for a bathroom break, wouldn't he?"

I glance up to find him smirking.

"You *do* think I'm a freak, don't you?"

He shakes his head, then strangely pulls his wallet out of his back pocket and removes his driver's license. He sets it faceup on the coffee table in front of me.

"Like I said, I'm honored to be your Jake Ryan . . ."

I wait until he and Rerun are out of the room before I lean forward and peek at his license.

Oh. My. God.

My heart melts in utter disbelief as I stare down at the name in front of me:

JAKE THOMAS WALSH

My J.T. is a Jake.

I've got my Jake!

Holy shit.

Chapter 12

Fourteen days until the blessed event
One day until I introduce Mom to the real man in my life: my Jake
(who will always be J.T. to me)

"The next time I have the brilliant idea to have four children, put a bullet in my head first—this is ridiculous!"

I laugh. Poor Claire. She's just picked up Carson from Pop Warner practice and is now heading out to Grant Park, where Noah's finishing up his baseball clinic. From there they'll swing through the McDonald's drive-through on the way to Mrs. Roberson's house, where Ben is taking piano lessons, before she loops back around to the South Side YMCA, where Aidan's in the finals of a three-on-three basketball tournament. At some point, she's hoping to sneak in a bathroom break, but the odds aren't in her favor.

This is the story of Claire's life these days, and the very reason why she's yet to meet J.T., even though she's dying to.

"Tell me again what it's like to be young and in love," she whimpers into her Bluetooth speaker. "But keep it PG, 'cause I've got little ears in the car—"

"Hey, I'm not a baby!" I hear Carson cry out from the back seat.

"Stop it! Play with your phone. I'm talking to Auntie Mac. Okay," she reroutes back to me. "Lay it on me. What are you two kids doing tonight? And there better be rose petals and champagne involved, or I'm hanging up."

Grinning, I glance down at the extra-large pizza sitting on the passenger seat beside me. "I hate to burst your bubble, but we don't live the romantic, fairy-tale life you think we do."

"Are *you* stuck driving four stinky heathens around in a minivan?"

"I'm not stinky!" Carson wails.

I laugh. "No."

"All right, then, shut up and give me the details."

"Well, I would, but I'm actually pulling into my driveway right now—oh wow!"

"What? What's happening? Is J.T. running through the yard in his boxer shorts?"

"*What?* No!" I laugh again as I take in the impressive structure to my left. J.T. has been working hard to finish the front porch renovation before Mom, Hope, and the other bridesmaids arrive tomorrow night. Based on the sight in front of me, he's nearly done. "J.T.'s just about done with the porch. It looks so good."

"Oh hallelujah! One less thing for your mom to nag you about this weekend."

"Exactly."

"So, what's your plan for introducing them?"

I come to a slow stop at the top of the driveway, not surprised to find my two guys playing ball in the backyard. Like takeout, after-dinner walks, and toe-tingling sex that lasts late into the night, it's one of the many happy little routines we've adopted over the last couple of weeks.

I guess my life *is* a little more romantic than Claire's . . .

"*Hello?*" she calls out, reclaiming my attention. "What's your plan?"

"Oh right, sorry. I'm just going to keep it short and sweet. I'll tell her that Michael and I broke up but that someone even better—someone absolutely perfect—has come along instead. My hope is that once she meets him and sees how good we are together, she'll completely forget about the whole successful neurologist son-in-law dream."

Claire snorts. "Yeah, that sounds like your mom. She's not big on neurologist sons-in-law. She'd much rather brag to her snooty pals about how you dumped the doctor to shack up with the handyman."

I sigh. She's got her pegged pretty well . . .

"And what about said handyman? When are you going to tell *him* about Michael?"

Claire is well aware that in the very early days of our relationship I really struggled with not coming clean to J.T.—and that since then I've been too blissfully happy to even think about it. But it's time to pay the piper . . . I sigh. "I don't know. Sometime before they get here. There's no way I'm going to send him into the lion's den unprepared."

As always, Rerun is first to greet me at the gate, with J.T. following a few steps behind.

"Somebody was very productive today." I smile up at him from where I'm kneeling beside Rerun. "The porch looks fantastic. I can't believe you're almost done."

"Yeah, it's coming together pretty nicely."

I tip my head. Something's off about his voice. It sounds sort of flat. Almost like it did that day at the vet's office.

"Are you okay?"

He's quick to nod.

"You sure? No unexpected run-ins at the lumber mill?"

"No, definitely not," he assures me. "I'm just tired. And ready for my welcome-home kiss."

Mmm . . . Welcome-home kisses. Yet another of our happy routines.

I hop to my feet and plant a hot, hungry kiss on his mouth, but rather than return my affection in the usual way—wandering hands all over my body—he cuts the kiss short and says, "Can I bring anything in from the car?"

I blink hard, startled and confused.

Since when don't his hands wander . . .

"Um, yeah. I got pizza."

"From Giordano's?"

I nod.

"Damn, you're the perfect woman, you know that?"

I smile, though I'm not sure I'm feeling it.

"How about I get dinner together, and you get us something to drink? I picked up a bottle of that merlot you like when I ran out this afternoon."

"Yeah, okay," I answer.

He gives me a quick peck and then makes his way out to the car while I'm left to wonder if he's really just tired or if something else is bothering him . . . For the most part, our dinner conversation is as easy and comfortable as it always is, but every now and then, he seems to get distracted by his own thoughts and momentarily disappears from the conversation. Never for long, but it's noticeable enough that I'm starting to worry.

I don't say anything until we're back from our walk and getting ready for bed. I've just slipped into the slinky, floor-length nightie Tracy convinced me to buy, while he's standing at the bathroom sink brushing his teeth with his new toothbrush. (Considering how often he stays over—not only for the amazing sex but also for the convenience of rolling out of bed and working on the porch—he decided he needed a toothbrush that lives at my house, along with a stick of deodorant, a razor, a tube of his *super* peppermint toothpaste, some extra clothes, and a steady supply of Fruity Pebbles; he eats like a twelve-year-old boy.)

I sidle up behind him, link my arms around his waist, and lean into his back, saying, "Are you sure everything's okay? You seem a little bit distracted tonight."

He nods, his mouth too full of toothpaste to answer.

"You're sure?"

I release my grip on him as he leans farther forward and spits. "Yep," he answers, still facing the sink as he gives his mouth a quick rinse with a handful of water. "I'm just really tired."

Again, the flatness in his tone contradicts his assuring words, leaving my intuition even more restless than before. Despite what he says, he's not acting like himself. Since his past is already out in the open, there's no reason he wouldn't tell me if he had run into his ex. I guess it's possible that he's just tired, like he says. Maybe he's one of those people who sort of shuts down when he's overly tired. I had a couple of friends like that in medical school—they didn't last beyond the first week of residency.

He wipes his mouth with a hand towel, then finally raises his head. Through the reflection in the mirror, I see his eyes grow wide as he takes in the sight of me in my long, lacy nightie.

My pulse spikes with a deliciously familiar rhythm.

"I don't think I've seen that before . . ."

I shake my head, heart thrumming at the way his lips are starting to pull up into a grin.

He tosses the towel to the floor, then slowly turns around to face me. His gaze tracks me from tip to toe before it finally settles back on my eyes.

"I like it."

"Good. But I bet you'll like it a lot more when it's lying in a heap on the floor . . ."

With a playful grin, I backpedal toward the bed, urging him toward me with a crook of my finger. As hoped, his top teeth plunge into his bottom lip, an involuntary response I've come to learn presents itself when he's feeling either nervous or, as is the case now, excited. He heeds my call and starts following me toward the bed, his wanton gaze speaking the words he's not verbalizing himself.

I drop down onto the bed while tugging on the nightie's thin black strap at my shoulder.

"I think you're going to have to help me take this off . . ."

His lip bite gives way to an adorable little grin. "Oh, I'm happy to help. But . . ." He suddenly stops his progress, feet cementing to the rug at his feet. "I think we should save it for tomorrow, when I'm not so tired."

My jaw drops. "You're too tired . . ."

"I'm sorry." He drops his head. "It's not you. You look amazing. You're . . ." He refocuses his attention on me. He sighs. "You're perfect, Mac. It's me. I'm just *really*—"

"Tired. Right, I know."

My response comes out clipped, like I'm angry, or like my feelings are hurt by his rejection, but the truth is right now I'm feeling more concerned than anything. It's been obvious all night that something's bothering him, and while every *Cosmo* article would tell me otherwise, I feel confident that it has nothing to do with how he feels about me . . . yet he still insists on keeping it to himself.

"Is there anything you want to talk about?"

A big knot slides down his throat before he gives his head a shake and says, "No. Not just yet."

"Okay," I concede over a broken smile. At least an explanation sounds like it's on the horizon. "Then let's go to bed."

I pull back the covers and settle into my side of the bed, on my right side so I'm facing the door. He stays still, unmoving, for a tenuous beat before he finally crosses the room and turns out the light. The mattress shifts as he drops down onto the bed, then slides under the covers beside me.

My heart beats hard and hopefully as he settles into his usual sleeping position: spooning me from behind, his chest pressed firmly against my back, arm resting with familiar ease over my hip. As always, the heat radiating from his body is intoxicating and beckons me to nestle deeper against his embrace . . . but I don't. I can't.

Despite my earlier concession, I *do* feel a little rejected.

And hurt.

159

J.T.'s warm, slow breaths tickle the back of my neck, alerting me awake. Blurry eyed, I glance at the clock on my nightstand: 5:13, less than an hour since the last time I looked.

I carefully untangle myself from his arms and slide out of bed. He snuffs at the disruption but thankfully doesn't wake up.

My heart softens as I stare down at him. He looks so at ease now. Peaceful. A stark contrast to the tossing and turning he struggled against all night. Whatever conflict he's wrestling, it didn't afford him any of the extra sleep he claimed to have needed, and I didn't fare much better.

Yawning, I grab some clothes from the closet, then quietly make my way to the guest bathroom to shower. Technically, it's a "non-patient" Friday at the clinic, but my patient load is so heavy right now that I scheduled a few appointments this afternoon anyway, including one with Caroline. I hadn't planned on starting my day this early, but some extra time at the office will do me good—I'm years behind on paper-work. And a little alone time would probably be good for J.T.—and me.

I get Rerun squared away with breakfast and a trip to the bathroom, then head out to the car. Much to my surprise, Gia's already up and heading out herself.

"Where are you off to so early?" I ask, taking in her ensemble with a raised brow. She's in head-to-toe black: beanie, sweatshirt, leggings, combat boots, even fingerless gloves. All black. Like an old-timey bank robber.

"I corral the Zig Zags on Fridays."

"Corral the . . . *what*?"

"The Zig Zag *scooters*," she clarifies while tugging the beanie down tighter over her ears.

I shrug, and she sighs.

"The little electric scooters you see around town? People rent them for as long as they need them and then just leave them on the sidewalk or wherever for someone else to rent—"

"Oh, sure. Okay. I've seen those around." I've never tried one myself, but they seem pretty popular. Though they are kind of an eyesore.

"We go out and find the ones people have ditched and put them back into circulation."

"How do you know where to find them?"

She gives me a tired look. "They have GPSs on them."

"Oh. Right. Of course." I give my head a quick shake. I'm going to need serious amounts of caffeine to get through this day. "How long have you been doing that?"

"A few weeks now."

"I thought you started at Wicked Brews a few weeks ago."

"I did, but the customers were assholes, so I quit."

"Okay." She wouldn't last a day tending to pregnant women.

"So, did I hear right?" she goes on, fishing her car keys out of her hoodie's front pocket. "Is the wedding Nazi coming into town again?"

The wedding Nazi. Mom would *love* that.

"Yes, she is. Tonight, actually. Hope and her bridesmaids too. We're getting fitted for our dresses tomorrow."

"And the wedding's in two weeks?"

"Yep."

"Well, at least you've got a date now." She nods toward my bedroom window, which overlooks the backyard. "Unless you were planning on asking Carlos to go with you?"

Ignoring the waggle of her pierced brow, I cross my arms over my chest and say, "Not funny. I'm still considering raising your rent for that one."

"Hey, I was just trying to help." She smirks. "A lot of moms book *private* lessons with Misssssssster Carlos. I just figured you might want to get in on some of the action too."

I cast a sad glance back toward my window and shake my head. No, I'm getting plenty of action with someone else. At least, I was . . .

"Will your mom be cooking again?"

What makes the menu isn't my main concern for the weekend; it's peeling off the Michael Band-Aid gently enough so that nobody gets hurt in the process. I turn back to her, shrugging. "I don't know. Maybe."

"Okay, well, if she does, make sure you find me. Otherwise I'm just gonna plan to steer clear. She's kinda scary."

I nod. Don't I know it.

It's just shy of seven o'clock when I arrive at the clinic. I'm the only one here, which means I'll have plenty of quiet time to get caught up on paperwork. I make myself a strong cup of coffee, then head back to my office.

Because we've yet to transfer over to a digital filing system (something Helen, our newly hired office manager, will be administering), we're still inputting handwritten patient notes into our online system. It's time consuming but isn't particularly challenging. Or it usually isn't. Today it's proving to be as easy as nailing Jell-O to a tree.

Despite my best efforts, all I can think about is J.T. and what could be causing him so much distress. When we went to bed, I was convinced his mood had nothing to do with me, and as I looked at him this morning, I was still sure of the same thing. But there were plenty of times last night—in those lonely hours when sleep eluded me and speculation stole my train of thought—that I wasn't so sure. Did he run into his ex? Did she realize what a crazy fool she was and now she wants to get back together with him? Or is something physically wrong with him? His mom has dementia. Is it hereditary? Is it possible that he went to the doctor and got some bad news about his health—*oh god*. What if he's got cancer? Or a brain tumor? Or maybe his ex has a brain tumor, and now he's feeling conflicted. Is he going to leave me to take care of her while she's dying—

Ugh!

Frustrated, I slap shut the patient folder in front of me and sink back into my chair. I hate that I'm acting like one of those insecure women in a Hallmark movie. Why can't I just accept that he's working through something, and if I needed to know what it was, he would tell me—

I hear the clinic's front door open, followed by the familiar sound of ice sloshing against plastic. That's Daisy with her daily iced caramel macchiato. An unsettling thought suddenly springs to mind. I hate the idea of involving her in my love life, but it's becoming pretty obvious I need another opinion on this situation, or I'll never be able to get any work done.

"Good morning, Daisy."

"Oh, hey, Mac." Her eyes narrow as she starts to peel off her jacket. "What are you doing here? You're supposed to be at the free clinic."

The free clinic . . .

My eyes snap wide.

Daisy called me shortly after I left work yesterday, asking if I could cover for Renee Bradford, the on-site doc of the free clinic where we volunteer. Apparently she had a family emergency and had to head out of town. Since I have only three patients on my docket, and both Tracy and Andy have scheduled deliveries at the hospital, I agreed to help. However, Daisy's call came in while I was trying on nighties, so I wasn't as focused on work-related issues as I probably should have been.

"You forgot, didn't you?"

I nod sheepishly, and she rolls her eyes.

"I'm sorry," I say. "Were you able to reschedule my patients to next week?"

"All but that icky friend of yours," she says, referring to Caroline, while she hangs her jacket on the back of her chair. "She said she *had* to see you today, so she'll just drive over to the free clinic so you can see her there."

The free clinic is a solid twenty-minute drive from here—and not in the friendliest of neighborhoods. If it were any other patient, I'd be concerned that something was wrong. But knowing Caroline, she probably just wants the scoop on my love life.

"You should probably get going if you want to get there when it opens."

"Right," I say. But I don't make a move to leave.

"Did you need something else?"

"Yeah, actually, I do."

It doesn't take long to recap the events of the night, and by the time I'm done, Daisy offers me exactly what I was hoping for: a very confident diagnosis.

"He's just self-protecting because he's scared of getting hurt again."

"Really? You don't think he's dying of cancer or something?"

She shakes her head. "You guys are moving pretty fast—not that that's a bad thing—but it probably caught him by surprise." I nod. I sort of feel that way myself sometimes. "My guess is that he's starting to feel really comfortable with this happy little world you've created, but with that happiness comes the fear of having it all taken away from him again. His ex did a serious number on him. There are bound to be some residual bruises he's got to learn to work through." She pauses to take a pull from her green straw. "But that doesn't mean he's not totally invested in you," she quickly adds, and places a reassuring hand on my forearm. "He's not intentionally pulling away from you. His subconscious is just demanding he take a little breather so he has time to assimilate and stabilize his feelings. It's actually a very healthy response. It shows that he's mature and taking this relationship seriously. He's not the type to just hop into bed with someone and not worry about the aftermath. He cares about how this is affecting both of you."

"That's so true," I say over a relieved breath. "He's not the kind of guy to do something without thought. He's very mindful of his actions. That's one of his most attractive qualities."

"You just need to give him a little extra room to work through all of his feelings, but it will be okay. He'll come back around once he's feeling more secure."

Daisy's astute observations instantly calm my worries. Of course he's feeling a little insecure—after what he's been through, that makes perfect sense!

I give her a grateful hug, then return to my office to gather my things—and find my faith in our relationship further renewed when I read the text J.T. just sent:

I'm sorry I didn't get to see you before you left.

And even more sorry for last night. I've got a lot going on in my head right now—I will fill you in soon.

I miss you.

My poor guy. He's clearly going through something difficult, and yet he's still thinking of my feelings . . .

I miss you too. And it's okay. We're good. Really, really good. <3

Despite my exhaustion, I still navigate my busy day at the free clinic with a spring in my step. J.T. and I *are* good, and the fact that he's willing to share his troubles with me only solidifies that point and his commitment to our relationship.

I head into my two o'clock appointment and find a smiling Caroline waiting on the exam table.

"What's up, hooker?"

"Hi, Caroline. How are you?"

We exchange a quick hug, and then I drop down onto the stool beside her.

"I'd be better if we weren't in the fucking ghetto." She scowls as she takes in the less-than-impressive surroundings. "Are you working off community service hours or something?"

"No," I say, silently praying her baby is born wearing earplugs. "I'm just covering for the usual doctor who had a family emergency. This is where I volunteer every other week."

"Well, they need to add your name to the sign then. I drove around the block like five times thinking I was at the wrong place. You know there's a nasty homeless dude talking to his feet out in the parking lot, right?"

I sigh. "Yes. That's Tom. He's got some issues, but he's harmless. So, how's everything?" I ask, making my way over to the sink to wash my hands. "Are you feeling good?"

"Yeah, I guess. I'm tired as fuck, and I can't stop farting, but otherwise I'm fine. How about you? Tell me all about this new cock who's rockin' your block . . ."

I cringe, not only at her choice of words but at the callousness of her delivery. J.T. is *so* much more than a body part.

"He's great," I say while pumping soap onto my hands. "He's sweet and funny and thoughtful and just . . ." I sigh contentedly as images of my handsome guy dance through my head. "He's everything I ever wanted—"

A soft knock on the door cuts off my sentimental train of thought.

One of the nurses must need something—

"Oh fuck," Caroline blurts out. "I totally forgot. The baby daddy is coming today."

"What?" I quickly glance over my shoulder. "He's here? That's him knocking?"

She nods over a budding smile. "That's why I had to keep the appointment today—'cause he said he'd come."

"Really?"

"Yeah. He said he wants to be involved."

I exhale a monumental sigh of relief. I've always thought that Caroline would be a good mom, but going it alone is never easy—even for the most resilient women.

"Oh my god, that's fantastic, Caroline."

"I know, right? I was going to tell you when I got here, but I totally forgot. I swear I can't remember shit these days." She shakes her head absently. "Fucking pregnancy brain . . ."

"So, are you guys back together then?"

"Not officially, but I'm sure it's just a matter of time. It's okay that he came, right?"

"Yes, of course," I say, turning back to the sink, smiling. "Tell him to come in."

"Come on in, babe," she calls out, just as I reach for a paper towel—

"Sorry I'm late."

The familiar sound of his voice in this very unfamiliar setting steals my breath and sends a chill up my spine. I quickly turn toward the door and gasp as I take in the person standing in front of me. It's J.T.

My J.T.

His brown eyes snap open, impossibly wide, and his jaw drops in shock—the same shock that's cementing me where I stand.

Unable to move.

Unable to breathe.

J.T. is the baby daddy . . .

Chapter 13

I grip the edge of the countertop, my body suddenly swaying like a sapling in the wind.

No.

No, no, no . . . this isn't happening.

J.T. can't be the baby daddy.

Caroline said she was in a relationship with him—that he got spooked when he found out she was pregnant.

But J.T. hasn't been in a relationship since his ex—

"Mac—" he starts to say in a soft voice at the same time Caroline crows over him.

"See, I told you my baby came from good stock. We're gonna have some damn pretty Christmas cards, aren't we?"

Christmas cards?

NO!

He's supposed to be on my Christmas card, not yours!

Oblivious to my distress, Caroline bursts out laughing while I grapple to grip the counter even tighter, my breath growing shallower by the second.

This can't be happening.

J.T. is my guy.

HE'S MY JAKE RYAN!

All the delicious memories of our time together start spiraling through my mind like photographs in a cyclone—late-night chats, walks with Rerun, movies by the fire—but they feel far away from me now—distant, like I'm not sure if they're even mine.

"Well, I guess I'll have to do intros, since neither of you seems capable," Caroline goes on, then turns to J.T. and says, "Babe, this is Dr. Huntress, but you can call her Mac." Her use of the word *babe* prompts a wave of nausea to swirl through my gut. "We went to high school together like a hundred years ago. I used to copy her homework, and now she's delivering our baby. How crazy is that?"

J.T.'s chin trembles as a mountain-size knot slides down the length of his throat.

"Hello . . . Mac."

The waver in his voice makes my stomach turn again.

I'm going to be sick.

I'm going to throw up all over him.

Or die.

Shit.

I'm going to die right here—

"And this is Jake," she says to me. "But everybody calls him J.T."

The familiarity with which she speaks of him forces a disturbing image of the two of them *TOGETHER* to come to mind. Bile races up my throat, and I quickly cover my mouth with my hand.

"Oh my god, girl, are you okay?" Caroline questions.

Tears flood my eyes, and I start to shake my head.

"Mac . . ." J.T. reaches for my arm, but I bat his hand away before he can make contact.

Wincing against the nervous twinge in his voice, I swallow the acrid, sour burn and grunt out, "I'm sorry. I—I have to go. Reschedule for next week at my clinic."

I push past J.T. and run out the door and down the hall.

"Mac!" I hear him call after me, but I don't stop.

I can't stop.

Blinking against the tears, I burst into the doctors' lounge and pull my bag from the locker against the wall. My hands are trembling as I grab my car keys and head for the exit.

"I'm sorry. I have to go," I cry out to April, the front-desk attendant. "I've met with all my scheduled patients. Everyone else can see Jane!"

I hate to saddle the on-site nurse practitioner with all the remaining patients, but there's no way I can stay here. I can't properly tend to patients while horrific images of my boyfriend and my free-loving high school classmate are bouncing around in my head.

How could he be with her?

With HER?

And now she's having his baby.

My god, she's having his baby!

They're going to be tied together for life.

Forever!

How long was he with her?

Was he lying to me about his ex?

Was he ever even married?

Has he been playing me this whole time . . .

The same panicked cycle of thoughts ricochets around in my brain the entire drive home—and only intensifies when I storm into the kitchen and see his opened box of cereal still sitting on the counter.

"Son of a bitch! How many times have I told you to close the box or they'll go stale!" I grab the box and chuck it against the wall, sending a spray of colorful pebbles raining across the room. Rerun barks, but rather than vacuum up the fallen goodies like he normally would, he wisely retreats to the safety of his pillow.

I stomp around the house, screaming, "Close the damn box!" over and over again, while a cocktail of emotions threatens to boil out of me:

anger, disappointment, confusion, embarrassment, shock, disgust . . . each one as suffocating as the next.

How could he do this?

All this time I've been stressing about my own stupid lie that doesn't even involve him, and he does this—

He does this!

A fucking baby—

"*Mac . . .*"

The sound of his voice from behind instantly silences my rant, though it does nothing to dilute my mood. Teeth clenched, I whip my head over my shoulder to face him. I'm not at all surprised that he followed me home, considering how many times he called my cell on the drive, but seeing him here, in the space *we've* been sharing, makes me sick.

His brows furrow above red, bloodshot eyes. "I'm so sorry. I had no idea you were her doctor—"

"Is that really the kind of guy you are?"

"Wh-what?"

"She's six months pregnant, *babe*. Where the hell have you been for the last six months?"

He starts to shake his head. "No, it's not like that. I didn't—"

"How long were you with her?" I go on, refusing to let him interrupt me. "You said you were alone since your ex. But she's six months pregnant, *babe!*"

"Mac, I didn't know—"

"Yeah, I heard you!" I lurch toward him, prompting him to reel back in shock. "You didn't know I was her doctor! But it's a good thing I was, right? Otherwise I never would have known you're going to be a fucking father!"

Overwhelmed by the unfamiliar rage in my voice, I stomp away from him and into the living room, a trail of Fruity Pebbles dust lying in my wake.

"Mac, please just let me explain—"

"*Explain what?* That you were lying to me the whole time we were together? What happened to how much you *hate* being lied to?"

"No, Mac. *Dammit*, it wasn't like that. Remember I told you about that nigh—"

"*Shit!*"

Tears may blur my vision, but I'm still able to make out the car that's just pulling up in front of the house on the opposite side of the driveway from J.T.'s truck. "You have to leave!"

"What? No. I need to explain—"

"My mom is here," I growl as I face him again. "My mom and my sister and her bridesmaids are here. I'm not doing this right now—not with them here."

"But I need to explain—"

"Just go! *Please.* I can't do this right now."

He sighs through a pained expression. "I don't want to leave you like this—"

"You don't have a choice," I snap back while swiping at a hot tear that's sliding down my cheek. My mom's head would literally explode if I introduced her to J.T. right now.

Hey, Mom, sorry to break the news, but Michael, the wealthy superdoctor, doesn't actually exist—but this guy does—and he's great! So great that he's about to have a baby with Caroline Fuller. You remember her, right? My friend from high school who you called a loose trollop with a trucker's mouth? Yeah, they're going to have a baby together. Isn't that fantastic! Can I get you a glass of champagne to celebrate?

"I need you to leave right now."

Rerun barks as if reiterating my demand.

J.T.'s shoulders sag. "Promise you'll call me as soon as they're gone. We have to talk about this."

"Yes. Fine."

He raises his hand like he's going to try to touch my face, but I'm shaking my head in refusal before he can even make the movement. "Not right now. Just . . . you need to leave."

He drops his hand—and his head. "Okay. I'll wait for you to call me."

Rerun follows him out the back door, while I stand at the living room window, willing myself not to burst into all-out hysterics.

How did this happen . . . everything was so perfect . . .

J.T. makes his way down the driveway with Rerun hot on his heels just as Mom, Hope, and the girls climb out of the car.

My shuddery breath catches.

Please don't talk to them. Don't say anything to them . . .

As if aware of my thoughts, he casts a sad glance back toward the house, then simply acknowledges my visitors with a quick nod before he climbs into the truck and drives away.

I exhale hard. Thank god.

I quickly run to the bathroom to splash some cool water on my face.

"Mac Daddy, where are you?"

I swallow through the thickness in my throat and call back to Hope, "I'm here. Just a sec!"

The sound of chirping women fills my house as I blot my face dry and head toward the kitchen.

"Mackenzie Rose, what in heaven's name is going on here? Were you robbed or something?"

Mom's scowled greeting as she observes Rerun tending to the mess on the floor only solidifies my rationale for sending J.T. away. A complicated love affair is a lot messier than spilled cereal.

"Nothing, Mom. Just a little accident. And it's nice to see you too."

"Oh, stop it," she grouses. "You know I'm happy to see you. I just assumed you'd have your house tidy, knowing we were coming."

From over her shoulder Hope mouths the words *she's insane* while making the *crazy* twirling motion with her fingers.

"And who on earth was that man storming down your driveway?" the crazy old woman continues. "He looked positively distraught."

"Yeah, who was that?" Harper, the single of the two bridesmaids, asks, her green eyes wide and hopeful. "He's really cute."

"That wasn't Michael, was it?" Hope asks.

"Of course that wasn't Michael," Mom snips. "Neurologists don't wear jeans and drive beat-up pickup trucks."

"So, who was he?" Hope persists.

Two hours ago, the answer to that question would have been obvious, but now I'm not so sure who he is . . .

I sigh and say, "That's J.T. He's just the handyman."

◆　◆　◆

He's just the handyman.

The words haunted me all night—and still as I roll out of bed, alone, this morning. Of course J.T. isn't *just* the handyman, but he's also not *just* my J.T. anymore either. Whether he's a liar or not has yet to be determined, but he is most definitely the father of Caroline's baby, and that fact still makes my stomach sour just as badly as it did yesterday. For so many reasons . . .

I lumber down the stairs in search of coffee but instead find Hope and her bridesmaids camped out in the living room watching TV. They're giggling like schoolgirls, so it's hard to hear what's got their attention, but just as my foot hits the hardwood floor in the foyer, I hear Hope and one of her bridesmaids reciting the lines of the movie, and it becomes painfully clear what they're watching.

I swallow a pained sigh.

"Oh, Mackie-pants, look!" Hope calls out from the couch. "It's *Sixteen Candles*! We were just flipping channels and it was on—right at the beginning! Harper's never seen it. Can you believe it?" I glance over Hope's shoulder to where Harper is nestled up in the corner of the couch under a blanket. Despite the bride's enthusiasm, she looks unimpressed. "How many times do you think we watched this that summer with Amanda?"

I force a smile and say, "Too many."

Head down, I make my way into the kitchen and pour myself a cup of coffee. Hope appears just a moment later, looking worried.

"Is everything okay with you? You've seemed a little off since we got here."

I take a sip of my coffee as I consider how best to answer. While I'd welcome an outside opinion on my troubling situation, I'm not sure that Hope's the right person to give it. Even though she entrusted me with the biggest secret imaginable, I'm not entirely sure I can trust her to keep *my* secret from Mom. Not because she's a tattletale, but because Mom is officially running off the rails. She's wound up tighter than a kindergartner's shoelace, barking out orders and criticisms like they're the oxygen she needs to breathe—she's earned her *wedding Nazi* moniker a thousand times over, and unfortunately her hostility is starting to wear on Hope. She confided in me last night that her blood pressure has been steadily climbing, and while it's not at concerning levels yet, given her condition, we don't want to do anything to aggravate it . . . which is exactly why I can't answer her honestly.

"I'm just tired. How about you?" I glance at her still-undetectable belly. "Are you two feeling okay?"

"Yep, we're good." She grabs a powdered doughnut from the box on the counter and takes a hearty bite. "I'm super excited to finally meet Michael. He's still coming to dinner tonight, right?"

Shit!

I sputter over the coffee in my mouth.

I never came up with an excuse for Michael's absence, because I'd been planning on bringing J.T. to dinner with us instead. I quickly scour my brain for something viable while Hope takes another bite, her blue gaze fixed expectantly on me.

"Um, actually, no. He . . . had a family emergency and had to head out of town."

She gasps. "What happened?"

What happened?

Good question . . .

"His . . . uncle had a stroke."

"Oh no. Is he going to be okay?"

I conjure up my best worried face. "They're not sure yet. They're running a bunch of tests."

"Oh my god, Mac. That's so sad." She lays a consoling hand on my arm. "No wonder you don't seem like yourself. You must be so worried."

Despite the guilt swelling in my throat, I nod.

"Well, Mom will be disappointed not to see him," she goes on, breaking off another piece of doughnut and tossing it into her mouth. "But she'll get it. She knows how important it is to be supportive of your family."

She no sooner finishes the thought than Mom yells out from the top of the stairs, "Hope Anne, you better not be eating any of your sister's junk food! You're not built like her—you have curves and they *will* expand! That wedding dress barely fits as it is! Nobody wants to watch a bride waddle down the aisle!"

Hope levels me with an annoyed look before she screams, *"I'm eating carrots,"* sending plumes of powdered sugar spraying from her mouth. "I swear to god, Mac, that woman"—she motions toward the ceiling with what's left of her doughnut—"is in for a *very* rude awakening when she finds out the truth."

I nod. Yes she is. Though *your* rude awakening isn't the only one I'm worried about . . .

As expected, Mom wasn't particularly understanding when I told her about Michael's family emergency on our way to the bridal shop. Thankfully, though, Candace, the owner of the shop, was foolish enough to have *carnation*-pink dresses waiting for us rather than the requested *flamingo*-pink dresses, so all Mom's hostility was quickly rerouted her way. Sorry, Candace; your ignorance is my savior!

Because Hope had already narrowed her selection down to just four dresses, it didn't take long to decide that the floor-length, sleeveless chiffon with a V-neck, ruched bodice was the best choice. Besides being Hope's favorite, the wedding Nazi astutely determined that the style adequately covered Harper's "chunky rump," Meghan's "floppy tummy pooch," and my "flat chest that you got from your father's side." Had I the presence of mind, I would have reminded her that my dad's mother actually had a solid set of D cups (they weren't noticeable because they drooped to her ankles and she refused to wear a bra), but I was too busy thinking about J.T. and his future child to do so.

Though Caroline insists on being surprised, I already know the sex of the baby; it's a boy. And just because J.T. said he was never planning on going the *Dad* route, I can't help but think he'll enjoy having a son. In all the babies I've delivered, I've yet to meet a father who was disappointed when a little boy arrived—even the ones who claimed they wanted a girl. I can't imagine J.T. will be any different.

Sighing, I lean my head against the passenger window. I wonder what he'll look like. Will he have J.T.'s strong jawline and those kind, almond-shaped eyes, or will he favor Caroline with her upturned nose and that wild, almost-savage look that always seems to be lingering behind her gaze? My heart twists as I think back on what she said when I asked her if they were back together: *Not officially, but I'm sure it's just a matter of time . . .* They're going to be a little family. The three of them—

"Mackenzie." From the driver's seat, Mom swats my arm, demanding my attention.

"What?"

"Did you call the restaurant and remind them that we're only *five* for dinner?"

I sigh. She overenunciates the head count like it hurts her tongue. "Yes. I told them we're only *five* for dinner—"

"Because a last-minute change like that can throw off their seating strategy for the entire evening."

"Seating strategy?" Hope questions from the back seat.

I glance back at her and roll my eyes.

"That's ridiculous, Mom," she goes on, smirking at my response. "A little change to *our* reservation isn't going to affect anybody else's."

"Well, you don't know that." She fires her a stern look through the rearview. "We have no idea what kind of impact a last-minute change will have on their planning."

"Our reservation isn't for three hours, Mom. That's not last minute."

The stink eye quickly reroutes to me.

"When it comes to reservations at a place like the Grove, three hours *is* last minute."

"Fine," I grumble, exhausted by her constant pecking. I can see why Hope's blood pressure is climbing. The wicked witch is off her freaking rocker. "It's last minute, and we're going to ruin the entire seating strategy for everyone. The restaurant will go under because of all the business they're going to lose, and it's all our fault."

"Was Michael's uncle taking proper care of himself?" she goes on, ignoring my sarcasm. "Did he follow a healthy diet and have an exercise routine?"

"I don't know—"

"Because you have to take responsibility for your own health. Nobody's going to do it for you. How old a man is he?"

"I don't know. Old."

"How old?"

"*I don't know.*" I cast her a tired look. "Probably about your age."

The dig is intentional and provides me just a taste of the levity I so desperately need. Hope and her bridesmaids giggle from the back seat, while Mom snuffs in disapproval.

"Laugh while you can, ladies. Before long, your breasts will be sitting on your lap, and growing old won't seem so funny. Of course, that doesn't apply to you, dear," she adds, reciprocating my insult over a pointed look right at my chest. "When you're old, you'll finally be able to appreciate taking after your father's side of the family."

I shake my head and sigh. Given her behavior, I already do.

We're about a mile from my house when my phone chimes, indicating I have a new text message. My breath shallows as I pull it from my bag.

Please don't be a message from J.T.

I can't handle hearing from him right now . . .

It's from Caroline.

Shit.

I'm not sure I can handle hearing from her right now either.

The *intimate* visual of the two of them that's been haunting me since yesterday's visit returns to my thoughts, prompting me to cringe as I reluctantly tap the screen and open the text:

EMERGENCY!

The disgusting thought instantly disappears.

Are you okay? Baby okay?

I need to see you.

Are you okay? What's wrong??

I HAVE TO SEE YOU!

Her unwillingness to answer my questions is not only frustrating but concerning. Quite often when someone is experiencing something traumatic, they're incapable of responding to direct questions; they're too focused on removing themselves from the situation to think clearly. If something has happened to her or the baby, that could be why she's responding the way she is . . .

Go to the nearest hospital immediately!

No. I have to see YOU!

Which hospital are you closest to? I will meet you there.

The little dancing bubbles appear on the screen, indicating a response is coming, but after a moment, they disappear . . . without a message.

Caroline, where are you? Do I need to call for an ambulance?

My fingers grip the phone tight as I stare expectantly at the screen. Still no response.
Dammit.
Something's very wrong.
I'm just about to press the "Contacts" button to dial her number when the thinking bubbles reappear and her response finally pops up.

Russet Ridge Urgent Care. I'm almost there.

Russet Ridge. That's just a few miles from here.

Okay. I'll meet you there soon.
I'll call ahead and let them know you're coming.

"Sorry, guys, but it looks like we're going to have to change the reservation to four. One of my patients is having an emergency."

"What?" Mom shrieks.

At the same time Hope says, "Oh no. What's wrong?"

"I'm not sure," I go on while googling the phone number for Russet Ridge. "But I need to leave as soon as we get home."

"Well, this is just perfect," Mom grumbles. "They'll probably put my picture on the wall like a mug shot and never allow me to make another reservation."

I shake my head in frustration. Trust me, old woman, if any of us is going to earn a mug shot today, it'll be me . . . for killing you!

◆　◆　◆

My tires squeal as I tear into the urgent care parking lot. Caroline told me she lives near *my* clinic—in Metro Chicago, so she must have been out here in Naperville shopping or visiting a friend or—*oh god*. My heart suddenly sinks to the floorboards. She was probably with J.T. *Shit.* That means he might be here too. *Double shit.*

Dread weighs down my steps as I climb out of the Jeep and hustle toward the building. *I'm a professional. I can put personal feelings aside and do my job. I can do my job—*

Caroline suddenly steps out from behind some shrubs that line the front walkway.

I come to a screeching halt.

"Hey, Mac."

"Hi." I quickly size her up while I catch my breath. She doesn't appear to be in any pain or discomfort. "Are you okay? What's going on? I got here as fast as I could."

"Uh . . ." She smiles sheepishly. "Nothing's actually wrong."

"What do you mean? Your text said there was an emergency."

"Yeah. Sorry about that."

My shoulders sag, and my bag slides down my arm and into the bend of my elbow. "So, you're okay?"

She nods.

"And the baby's okay?"

"Yup." She pats her stomach. "Kicking the balls out of me like always."

I shift my stance to one side. "So you're both fine?"

"Uh-huh."

"Then why did you tell me you had an emergency? I dropped every-thing I was doing and came racing over here. I canceled my family plans to meet you." Truth be told, I was grateful for the disruption, but fab-ricating an emergency to your doctor is *never* okay. "I've been worried sick that something happened to you or the baby . . ."

Her smile slopes down into a frown. "I'm sorry, but I *had* to talk to you, and I figured that was the best way to get your attention."

I blink hard. *Get my attention . . .*

"You don't *ever* send your doctor a fake *emergency* message," I snap. "That's not something you joke around about."

"I'm not joking. I *had* to talk to you *in person.*"

"What could you possibly have to say to me *in person* that warrants a fake emergency?"

The moment the question crosses my lips, I already know the answer. And she knows I do. She folds her arms over her big belly and levels me with a knowing glance.

Oh god.

No.

No way.

I'm not doing this here. Not right now.

I quickly turn and head back toward the parking lot.

"Mac, wait! We have to talk about this."

I wave my hand dismissively. "Nope. I'm not doing this right now—"

"Yes, you are!"

"No, I'm not!"

"Mac—" I hear her footsteps quicken behind me, so I pick up my pace. The doctor is now running *away* from her patient.

Physician of the freaking year, that's me!

"Mac, you don't know what's really going on!"

"Oh yes I do!" I call back through my clenched jaw. "J.T.'s your ex. He bailed when he found out you were pregnant, and now he wants to be back in the picture so you can be a happy little family. I get it just fine!"

"He's not my ex!" she cries out, right as I step off the curb and into the parking lot. "He was just a one-night stand!"

A one-night stand.

The words sucker punch me straight in the gut.

I stop dead in my tracks.

The one-night stand.

Holy shit.

I'd completely forgotten about it.

He was mortified by the experience, but I thought it was funny—at least, his reaction to it was—

My stomach suddenly wrenches as conflicting emotions start to burble up inside me: this is good news; he didn't lie about being in a relationship, but . . . *oh god.*

His one-night stand was *Caroline!*

"He said he told you about it."

I drop my head and nod. Yes, he did tell me about it.

"It was one stupid night," she goes on, her words winded from her efforts to catch me. "I went to a bar with some girls after work, and one of them knew one of his friends, and we all just started hanging out. He was celebrating . . . something, I don't know, and we all got pretty shit-faced, and somehow we ended up at my place—"

I raise my hand again, this time a silent request for her to please stop explaining. Thankfully, she listens and instead says, "He didn't even know about the baby until two days ago."

What little anger I'm still harboring for him instantly disappears beneath her unexpected confession. I turn over my shoulder, jaw hanging in disbelief.

"He didn't?"

She shakes her head. "I called him the day before the appointment. We hadn't seen or spoken to each other since that *one* night."

"Oh my god." I drag a shaky hand through my hair as a sea of regret swells hard and heavy in my chest. That's why he was acting so different—so distant—the other night. He'd just found out he was going to be a father . . . and the baby's mother was someone he didn't even know.

"I had no idea you two were together," she goes on. "I never would have let him come to the appointment if I had. But once he found out about the baby, he said he wanted to be involved however he could. He says he wants to do the right thing by me . . ."

I nod absently. Of course he wants to do the right thing, because J.T.'s a good guy . . . No, J.T.'s a *great* guy, and I wouldn't even let him explain what was going on.

I swallow hard. "Did he ask you to come and talk to me?"

She snorts. "Ohmygod, no. He'd kill me if he knew I was here. He specifically told me *not* to talk to you. He said that you were going to talk to him when you were ready, and he was going to respect that and wait for you and that I needed to stay out of it."

"So why are you telling me then?"

"Chicks before dicks, baby. There was no way I was going to let you suffer, thinking that your guy was some kind of asshole who just runs around knocking people up. As soon as he told me you wanted your space, I knew I had to track you down. I stopped by your house first—"

"You went to my house?" The terror in my voice has nothing to do with the fact that she somehow managed to find out where I live—which

is beyond concerning and will need to be addressed at some point—but that she went to *my* house, where *my* mom is! She could have blown up my entire world in a matter of seconds.

"Yeah, but you weren't there," she continues, oblivious to my state of mind. "So that's when I decided to call you. You're not pissed, are you?"

I shake my head, more relieved than she could ever imagine. "No. I'm not pissed. I'm glad you told me. I'm just . . ." I sigh, overwhelmed by the sheer magnitude of information that's come to light in the last few minutes. "It's just a lot to take in."

"I know, and I'm really sorry. I'd never hurt you on purpose."

"I know."

"He's a good guy, Mac. And he's crazy about you."

I drop my head and smile. I know that too.

"*And* I'm pretty sure he's going to be a kick-ass dad."

I glance down at her stomach, and even though I'm not completely *okay* with all this yet, I can still answer her with a sincere, "I think so too," because I *do* think J.T. will be a kick-ass dad . . . because J.T.'s amazing. This baby will be lucky to have him. A thought suddenly comes to mind. "Can I ask you something?"

She nods.

"It's kind of personal, so if you feel at all uncomfortable, you don't have to answer."

"Oh my god, girl." She rolls her eyes. "You've been further up into my cooter than half the guys I've had sex with—and that includes *your* boyfriend." She snorts, unconcerned that it's *way* too soon for jokes like that. "There's nothing too *personal* between us. What do you want to know?"

"Why did you tell me that you were in a relationship with the baby's dad? Why didn't you just tell me the truth?"

Her smile quickly fades, and her gaze drifts down to the ground.

Uh-oh.

Too personal.

"It's okay." I reach for her arm. "You don't have to answer."

"No, it's cool." She slowly raises her head. "I was embarrassed. Nobody wants to advertise that they got pregnant from a one-nighter, you know? I guess . . . I don't know." She shakes her head while fighting a laugh I'm not sure she's feeling. "I guess it seemed like making up a relationship that ended badly was easier than admitting the truth. Does that even make sense?"

The irony in her reasoning isn't lost on me. I nod. "More than you know . . ."

Chapter 14

Sunday, 2:28 p.m.
Eleven days until the stupid wedding
Two minutes until J.T. is scheduled to arrive

I'm ready to talk. Come by at 2:30 tomorrow.

I'll be there.

On the surface, the message I sent him last night appears simple, as does his response, but the truth is it's layered with more depth than any cell phone screen has ever displayed.

To me, those two little sentences represent my sincere regret for reacting the way I did (my lack of trust in his feelings causing me the most anguish), my willingness to accept this new situation (no matter how foulmouthed and challenging it may be), and *most importantly* my heartfelt desire to be a part of his life. Because what's become clear to me over the last forty-eight hours is that—baby or not—my world works better when J.T. is in it.

I smack the phone down on the counter and start pacing the kitchen. This has become my routine since the Nazi and the rest of the wedding party left an hour ago: stare at the phone, get excited, then get nervous, then get excited again, then pace the room to keep my sanity.

Rerun's so familiar with the cycle he doesn't even lift his head anymore, though his furry eyebrows still scrunch up like caterpillars every time I take another lap.

"What if he doesn't feel the same way about me?" I ask him, again, as I circle the island. "What if over the weekend he realized that having a baby—*and* a Caroline—in his life was going to be too much for him? What if he thinks he won't have time for me? It's possible, you know." I level him with a serious look. Still nothing more than the waggling eyebrows. "Relationships take a lot of time *and* a lot of work. It's not just eating takeout and having great sex. It's about actually *doing* life together. Even the hard stuff. Like emergency trips to the vet and crazy parents and . . . babies . . ." I rake my fingers through my hair. "I want to do all that stuff with him, bud. I really, *really* do. But what if he doesn't want to do it with me—"

Woof!

Rerun cuts off my neurotic rant with a thunderous bark and, as quickly as his old joints allow, hoists himself to his feet. He makes his way over to the back door and presses his snout up against the jamb, his entire body wiggling in anticipation.

My heart starts to hammer against my ribs. "I know, bud. I'm ready to see him too."

Rerun barks again—three *woofs* in quick succession, and then through the kitchen window I see J.T. arrive at the side gate. He unlatches the lock with familiarity and starts to make his way across the backyard but slows when he sees me watching him. Our gazes lock, and my breath catches. *I've missed you so much.*

He offers a tentative wave that makes my heart twist with deeper regret for how we ended up here. Nothing between the two of us should ever be tentative . . . I hold my position at the island and nod him inside with a nervous smile.

It's no surprise that Rerun lumbers right into him. J.T. gives him a generous pat and says, "Hey, buddy . . . ," but keeps his eyes trained on me.

"Hi," I say.

"Hi."

"How are you?"

"I've been better. How about you?"

"Same."

He nods slowly, his attention shifting away from me.

I clear my throat of the emotions starting to swell there and say, "Do . . . you want some coffee?"

"Sure. Yeah."

Looking painfully uncomfortable, he shuts the door and makes his way into the house, Rerun waggling happily at his side.

I fill up two mugs—creamer in mine, nothing in his—and return to the island, where he's now standing. Logistically speaking, it's a déjà vu of the first time we shared coffee in this kitchen, but the circumstances that led us to this moment couldn't be more different.

"This is good," he offers after taking a drink.

His gaze is steadily shifting between me and the mug.

"My mom brought it."

"How'd the visit go?"

"Okay."

I take a drink. My gaze is as unpredictable as his.

"Did you get the dresses squared away?"

"Yep. They're appropriately ugly."

The corner of his mouth twitches. *God, I love that mouth.*

"So, she went with the pink?"

"Flamingo pink," I clarify. "Do not be confused."

He offers the faintest grin. "Flamingo pink. Noted."

I raise the mug to my lips and take another drink.

I hate this small talk.

J.T. and I don't do small talk . . .

Silence fills the room.

I take another drink.

He takes another drink.

"So . . . the weather guy said it might rain later this week—"

"I can't do this anymore." I cut him off, incapable of one more second of this awkwardness.

"*What?* No." He slams his mug down, sending coffee sloshing over the edge. "Mac, please—"

"No, not that—not *us*. I mean I can't take any more of this stupid small talk when all I want to do is tell you how sorry I am for the way I acted on Friday. I should have let you explain everything, but I was just *so* shocked I couldn't think straight—"

"No, you don't have anything to be sorry for." He quickly rounds the island and grabs my hands. They feel warmer and stronger than the last time we touched. "It's my fault—"

"No, it's not. You didn't even know about the baby until the night before the appointment. You were still trying to process everything . . ."

Lines of confusion splinter across his forehead.

"I talked to Caroline. Or . . . she talked to me."

"Oh god." Looking a bit sick, he scrubs a heavy palm across his chin. "I asked her not to talk to you. I told her that I wanted to be the one to tell you what happened. I didn't want you to have to hear it from her."

"I know. And I am grateful you wanted to be the one to tell me, but she was just looking out for me. She wasn't trying to make you look bad or beat you to the punch or anything. She just wanted me to know the truth, because she knows how important you are to me. She didn't want me thinking I was falling in love with an asshole."

My confession surprises me almost as much as it does him.

I let out a little gasp as his eyes grow impossibly wide.

"You . . . you're . . . *what?*"

I never would have imagined I'd be professing my love in the middle of a conversation that was birthed from my boyfriend's baby-producing one-night stand, but here we are. It's happening *right* now, in my kitchen, with an old dog as our audience.

John Hughes couldn't have scripted it better himself.

I shrug over a sheepish grin and say, "I am. I'm falling in love with you."

"I . . . uh . . ."

Oh crap.

I knew it . . . It's too much for him!

I drop my head. "You don't have to say anything—"

"I'm falling in love with you too."

My breath shallows beneath a sudden flutter of hopefulness. "You are?"

He steals my hands back and drops his head so our eyes meet. "Yes. *God, yes.* Since the day I saw you screaming for the Cubs, which is why I didn't know how to tell you about the baby. When she called me that afternoon, it was like she ripped the rug out from under me. I was completely blindsided. All I could think about was you and how this was going to affect what we have. Because this thing we're doing"—he tightens his grip on me—"this is the best thing that's ever happened to me. *You're* the best thing that's ever happened to me. And I don't want to lose you."

My heart twists at the familiarity of his words, nearly identical to the thoughts that have prevented me from telling him the truth about Michael. A truth I'll tell him once things settle down a bit—we've both suffered way too much emotional drama for one weekend. Right now, I just want to enjoy this moment together . . . "You're not going to lose me." I press our mingled hands against my chest and squeeze them tight, a reassurance that I'm speaking the truth. "I'm not going anywhere."

"But . . . this baby. It's going to change everything. This isn't what you signed on for. I'd understand if you wanted out—"

"I don't want out. I want you. And if this baby is a part of you, then I want the baby too."

His dark brows cinch in concern. "You say that now, but what if you feel different in ten, or twenty, years? I don't want you resenting me for changing the course of our lives."

Ten or twenty years . . . I love that he's talking about our future.

"I won't resent you. I could never resent you."

He starts to smile, but before he fully commits, his attention averts away from me and to our mingling of hands. He stares at them for a long, concerning beat before he swallows so hard I can hear it. In a near whisper he says, "And you don't think less of me for getting myself into this situation?"

The vulnerability in his question forces my throat to swell with a thick, painful ache that brings tears to my eyes. *Oh, you sweet man . . . Old wounds run too deep . . .* I untangle my fingers from his, press my palms against his cheeks, and gently raise his head so he's looking at me. The slight quiver of his chin reaffirms the answer I'm about to give him.

"The only way I could think less of you is if you *weren't* stepping up and doing the right thing, but you are. Because you're a good, integrous man. It's one of the qualities that made me fall in love with you."

He pinches his eyes shut tight, as if savoring my words, before he leans forward so our foreheads are pressed together. His breath blankets my face in long, warm spurts—like he's been holding it for days—before he finally whispers, "Thank you," and then kisses me.

The kiss is soft and tender and, just like the text I sent, declares his truest feelings for me. Feelings that leave me confidently saying, "You're going to be a great dad."

From beneath my lips he lets out a weak laugh. He pulls away from me, shaking his head. "I have no clue how to be a father."

"Yes you do. From what you've told me about your own, you've got a pretty great example to work from."

"Yeah, I guess. But the circumstances were *so* different. How is this even going to work? Do I only see the baby on weekends and holidays?"

"I don't know. That's something you and Caroline will have to work out."

"Caroline." He sighs. "How am I going to deal with *her* for the rest of my life?"

I grin. "She's a lot."

"*So* much. I can't believe I—ugh." He buries his face in his hands. "I was so drunk."

Despite the seriousness of the topic, I can't help but laugh. My ego needed that stroke.

"I know." I nuzzle his arm with my knuckle. "If it makes you feel any better, I *do* think she's going to be a good mom. Deep down there's actually a pretty decent person under all that . . . filth." He glances up at me, and I shrug. *Way deep down* . . . "But I think it will be better for everyone if I'm no longer her doctor; I've decided to transition her over to Andy."

"Good idea." Just like with Claire, busy schedules haven't allowed for J.T. to meet my partners, either, but he's heard enough about them to know they're all good, trustworthy people. Andy will take good care of Caroline *and* his baby. "You know I never would have come to the appointment if I had known—I mean, I had no idea *you* were her doctor. I feel awful about that."

"I know you do, and I appreciate that, but there's nothing you can do to change how it all went down, so you just have to let it go, okay? Try to chalk it up to a painfully awkward story we'll tell at dinner parties someday."

"Or weddings . . ."

I blow out an appalled snort. "Uh, no. Our goal is to make it through the wedding without *any* mention of babies."

"Your mom still hasn't figured it out?"

"Nope. And I'm definitely not going to be the one to tell her."

"You really think she'd be that upset? I thought grandbabies were always good news."

J.T.'s never formally met my mom to appreciate just how naive his question is. I level him with a steely look. "Yes. She's going to be *that* upset. She lives and dies by outward appearances. Throwing an out-of-wedlock baby into the mix is going to shatter the picture-perfect image she presents to the rest of the world."

"So, *our* situation will probably send her over the deep end, huh?"

"Oh yeah."

"I'm really sorry we weren't able to do the whole dinner thing last night," he says, remorse once again stealing his expression. "I hate the idea of showing up at a family wedding and never having met any of them. I mean, other than the little hello as I was leaving the other day, but they didn't even know who I was. Do you think maybe we should drive up and see them this weekend, just so everybody's familiar come wedding day?"

I've given this a tremendous amount of consideration over the last forty-eight hours, and while the big reveal definitely makes me nervous, I think I've come up with a pretty sound plan to survive it: I'm going to spring J.T. on Mom during the rehearsal. That way there will be lots of witnesses to help temper her reaction. Because if there's one thing my Martina experience back in high school taught me, it's that my mom doesn't like to lose her cool in front of an audience.

"You're sweet to think of that," I say, "but there's already too much going on. You can just meet them at the wedding. It'll be fine."

Chapter 15

Twenty-six hours until the wedding

I run my fingers down the lapel of the charcoal suit coat and grin. As it hangs here now, on the back of the laundry room door, I can appreciate what a handsome suit it is. But come tomorrow, when *his* frame is filling out every tailored inch of it, it's going to be a truly spectacular sight—not that his current ensemble is anything to sniff at.

I glance down the hall and into the kitchen, where he's standing at the counter waiting for the coffee to brew, wearing nothing but his navy cotton pajama pants. My grin widens. Yeah, those look pretty spectacular too . . . He must sense my gawking, because he suddenly turns and looks at me.

"Can I help you?"

His tone is as playful as the smirk on his face and immediately sends my thoughts racing to the bedroom—and the things we *could* be doing to each other up there. Unfortunately, though, I'm on a tight, Nazi-scripted schedule that won't allow for any deviation, no matter how sexy he might be.

"Just admiring the view," I say back to him. He gives his butt a little waggle that makes me burst out laughing. *Good Lord, you are cute* . . . I zip the suit up in the garment bag along with my very pink dress, then head into the living room and add it to the pile of other luggage sitting by the door.

"Is it time?" Coffee in hand, J.T. walks out of the kitchen, a sad look on his face.

I nod.

He hands me the mug and sighs. "I should have asked if he could reschedule."

"No, you shouldn't have. You don't want him to think you're not interested. You absolutely need to be there."

Earlier this week, a former client of J.T.'s from Rockford—the guy who worked for the big developer—reached out to him and asked if he would be interested in working with them on a renovation project (converting an old library into urban lofts) in the city. Of course he was thrilled at the offer. It's exactly the kind of thing he was hoping to get into, but the powers that be are only in town to discuss the details this evening, which means that J.T. won't be able to make the three-hour trek to Grand Rapids with me for the rehearsal and accompanying dinner, as we'd originally planned—at best he'll get there around eleven o'clock tonight, which is when I plan to tell him about Michael. Considering everything we've been through, I can't imagine it will upset him but figure a good night's sleep—and some great hotel sex!—will help cushion any blows he might experience.

The turn of events has J.T. feeling guilty, but I think it actually works in our favor. Unlike my original plan, which had only family and the wedding party in attendance, ripping off the J.T. Band-Aid at the wedding—in front of Mom's gallery of hoity friends—has to yield us the best possible results. The bigger the audience, the better!

Although explaining Michael's absence *before* the wedding may still prove to be a bit of a challenge . . .

"I just feel like me not showing up until the actual wedding is going to wind your mom up even more. I don't want her annoyed with me before I even meet her."

"It'll be fine," I assure him. "She'll be three drinks in by the time she slides on her wrist corsage. Nothing in the world will be bothering her. Now, would you be a gentleman and kindly help me with my bags?"

We load up my Jeep and say our goodbyes through the driver's window.

"I'll see you tonight. I'll be the one in the slinky black nightie," I mutter between our succession of kisses. He groans happily against my lips. "And I'll see *you* on Sunday." With a little assistance from J.T., Rerun stands up on his hind legs and leans his big panting mug into the window. I give him a hearty scratch and a kiss on the head.

"Drive safe," J.T. says.

"I will."

"I love you."

He's said those words to me at least a thousand times over the last week and a half, and they still make my insides flutter with excitement.

"I love you too."

I slide the gearshift into reverse and slowly back down the driveway, my heart swelling at the pair of them watching me. My guy and my dog. Samantha Baker, eat your heart out.

◆ ◆ ◆

The lobby of the Pebble Creek Lodge is every bit the craftsman-style masterpiece the website boasts it is: gleaming hardwood floors, dark-leather furniture, exposed beams showcasing the meticulous framework of the enormous building. There's even a monstrous stone fireplace situated against the far wall (logs currently crackling despite the sixty-eight-degree afternoon outside) with a collection of rocking chairs lined up in front of it. It's the kind of place where Lady Mary would kick off her riding boots after a grueling day hunting pheasants and scowling—definitely *not* the kind of place a crazed mother of the bride will lose her cool when she learns her eldest daughter has been lying to her about the man in her life.

I check in at the front desk, adding J.T.'s name to my account so he can pick up a key when he arrives later tonight, then head to my room to freshen up before the rehearsal. After a quick shower, I touch up what little makeup I wear, then slide into the celery-colored jersey wrap dress I bought last summer for Daisy's graduation party. Mom will undoubtedly say it's too simple for the occasion, but I think it's perfect, a sort of understated elegance. And Claire told me it made my green eyes *pop*, so I'm considering it a good choice.

According to the Nazi's detailed itinerary, tonight's rehearsal (and tomorrow's ceremony) will take place in the chapel located in the northern wing of the building. Following the little signs posted throughout the property, I navigate my way down countless hallways and corridors before finally arriving in front of two enormous wooden doors, each with a small cross emblazoned across its center.

I pull hard on the thick, burnished handle and step inside. Wow. Much like the lobby, its vaulted ceiling and walls are outlined by thick oak beams the same honey color as the rows of pews, but it's the floor-to-ceiling wall of glass—just behind the pulpit and framed by a rise of natural stones—that's the most striking feature. It faces a wooded area so dense with varying shades of foliage you'd think we were tucked away in an English forest rather than in a man-made building on the outskirts of Grand Rapids, Michigan. I've been wondering why Hope elected to have a late-morning service rather than an evening one, but now I know . . . with the morning sun peeking through those trees, they're in for some breathtaking wedding photos.

"Macaroni!"

From the front of the sanctuary, where the bridal party, my parents and extended family, Reverend Howell, and all of Whitman's guests are gathered, Hope cries out my least favorite nickname, prompting all heads to turn in my direction.

Thank you, Hope . . .

I offer a timid wave, while Hope hurries up the aisle to greet me. Amazingly, her baby bump is still undetectable—and strategically hidden under her floor-length, peasant-style dress—but as she leans into me for a hug, I can *feel* my future niece or nephew inside her.

"Thank god you're here," she whimpers into the crook of my neck. "I'm losing my freaking mind."

Aware of our audience, I keep my expression pleasant as I quietly respond. "What's going on? Are you okay? Is the baby okay?"

She sniffles. "Yes. I'm fine—we're both fine. It's not me. It's *her*."

Of course I want to know what's causing my sister so much distress—though I don't need to ask who the *her* is who's causing it—but first I need to be sure that she's physically okay.

"What was your blood pressure the last time you checked it?"

Her body shudders against mine as she searches for a calm breath—and the answer. "Um . . . one twenty-five over eighty."

"And when did you take it?"

"Last night."

"Okay. That's good." I stroke her back with a reassuring hand. While it is higher than when we last spoke two days ago, it's still within normal range. Though the continued increase is a bit concerning . . . "So, what's she doing that's got you so upset?"

"She's a freaking lunatic," she growls in a restrained whisper, her breath fiery against my skin. "She's got split personalities or something. She's all bossy and bitchy to me and Dad and even the poor wedding planner, but the second anyone else comes around, she clams up and turns into this like . . . bobbleheaded Stepford wife. She's all polite and sweet and—*ugh!* Her smile is so scary! It looks like someone painted it on her face. I swear to god, Mac, it's like a real-life Jekyll and Hyde."

Despite my sister's obvious anguish, I consider this incredibly encouraging news. Just as I'd hoped, Mom is too concerned with putting on a good show to express her true feelings. So long as she's introduced to J.T. in front of people, we should be good to go . . . "Just try and ignore it as best you can," I advise in my most calming big-sister voice. "Twenty-four hours from now this will all be over, and you'll be a happily married lady getting ready to have a family with that sweet guy up there. It'll all be worth it. But for now, you need to get yourself together, because the crazy woman is headed right for us."

Looking every bit Laura Bush in her navy St. John suit, Mom makes her way up the aisle, while Hope composes herself, subtly dabbing her eyes as she pulls away from me.

"Hello, Mackenzie." Mom sizes me up from tip to toe as she extends her arms to hug me. She feels more rigid than usual, like an ironing board without the cushiony cover.

"Hi, Mom. You look very nice."

"Well, thank you, dear."

And you look very nice too . . .

"What happened? Why are you late?"

"I'm . . . not." Confused, I glance down at my watch. It's not even five o'clock yet.

"Oh, for heaven's sake, didn't you check your email?"

"No. I was driving."

"Well, Tammy sent out an updated itinerary over two hours ago." She sounds exhausted by my very rational explanation. "The rehearsal was pushed up to four forty-five. We've all been standing here waiting for you."

I glance over her shoulder at the two dozen or so people either standing near the raised stage area or sitting in one of the pews. Contrary to her perturbed state, no one else seems the least bit put out to have been waiting for me for a whopping eleven minutes.

"Now we're going to have to rush through it," she goes on. "We absolutely *have* to be out of the chapel by five fifteen, and you still have to meet everyone. Come on . . ."

With a disgusted wave, she orders us to follow her back down the aisle.

"I'm sorry," I mutter to Hope. "I had no idea you changed the time."

"It was *her*," she grouses through gritted teeth. "She demanded the floors be cleaned before the ceremony because she found a dirty spot back behind the pulpit."

"Behind the pulpit?"

"Yes. And the hotel stupidly said they would do it, but it takes like seven hours, and then they have to allow enough time for it to dry. They have to start by five thirty or it won't be ready in time."

I roll my eyes. Hope was right. She *is* insane . . .

On the advice of Tammy, the wedding planner, Hope has kept the rehearsal itself as simple as possible, limiting the guest list to only the wedding party and immediate family, with the exception of Carol and Steve, our favorite aunt and uncle, and their son, David, and his partner, Phillip.

The four of them wave to me from their seats in the fifth row, while Phillip, sitting on the aisle, adds to the greeting by whispering, "Somebody call the fire department, this girl's smokin'," as I pass by.

I cast an appreciative glance over my shoulder. Coming from Phillip, the J.Crew-worthy dresser, that means a lot.

We catch up to Mom where she's now standing with an older couple I've never seen before.

"Jim, Cathy, this is my oldest daughter, Mackenzie." Mom's voice is dripping with unfamiliar sentiment as she turns to me, now wearing that scary, plastered-on smile Hope warned me about. She ushers me closer with a nudge to my lower back. "Darling, these are Whitman's parents. Jim and Cathy Gentry."

Darling? Oh, please . . .

"It's nice to meet you both." I shake hands with Cathy first, then her husband. Like their son, each has a kind, warm smile and one of those firm handshakes that suggests their small fortune (raising prize cattle) was earned through hard work and jaw-strapping grit. "Good midwestern stock," Grandpa Harold would call them. The kind of people you can always count on, even though they're Buckeyes fans.

"So, this is the famous doctor, huh?" Mr. Gentry's smile widens. "We've heard a lot about you, young lady."

"Only good things, I hope."

"Oh, stop that." Mom gives my arm a playful swat while forcing out a sound that's probably meant to be taken as a laugh but instead comes across more like a goose being slaughtered.

"What kind of doctor?" Mrs. Gentry inquires.

"I'm an obstetrician."

"Oh . . ." She clutches her chest. "I just love newborns. They're so fresh and new and smell so good."

I smile, grateful that Hope's baby will have at least one normal grandmother.

"That must be so rewarding," she goes on. "Have you been doing it long?"

"Just over ten years now."

"Oh, that's just wonderful. You must be so proud." She glances at Mom, who's obnoxiously quick to reply, "Well, of course we are. She's done very well for herself, haven't you, dear?"

I nod. Yep, I sure have. Glad you noticed . . .

"I'm sorry to interrupt, but we should really get started with the rehearsal, since we're pressed for time." The suggestion comes from an intense-looking woman with a clipboard in her hands. This must be Tammy, the abused wedding coordinator. "Assuming everyone has arrived, that is . . ."

"Yes, everyone's here," Hope says.

"No," Mom interjects. "We're still waiting on Michael."

Michael?

Shit.

My eyes snap wide.

"But Michael's not *in* the wedding," Hope counters.

"Yes, I'm aware of that, dear," Mom answers, her tone still remarkably friendly despite the correction. "But he's Mackenzie's special guest. It would be impolite to start without him."

She glances back toward the doors to see if my imaginary boyfriend sneaked in when we weren't looking.

"Where is he, darling?" She turns back to me, smile fading.

Despite my confidence in the audience theory, my heart starts to beat faster. I glance around the sanctuary, taking in all the new and familiar faces.

Please, don't let me down . . .

"He's actually not going to be able to come tonight—"

"He's not coming?"

I shake my head, nerves braced in anticipation of Dr. Jekyll appearing and rearing her ugly head. I wish I could tell her right now—extinguish the *Michael* myth and get it over with—but I need an informed J.T. and a roomful of impressionable wedding goers present for it to work.

"He was called away on a work matter, but he assured me he'll be here first thing tomorrow. He's really looking forward to meeting all of you."

She stays stone-still for a long, pulse-pounding beat before her gaze softens, and that phony smile once again settles on her face. She looks directly at Mrs. Gentry and says, "Her boyfriend is a neurologist, so you can imagine how busy he is . . ."

"Oh, I'm sure," Mrs. Gentry says over an approving nod.

My stomach turns. Great, now the poor Gentrys are in on the lie too . . .

"So, we're good to start then?" Tammy asks eagerly.

"It seems we are," Mom says. "Go ahead and stand by your sister, dear."

She motions toward the stage area, where the rest of the bridal party is starting to assemble, while I exhale a shaky sigh of relief.

That definitely could have gone better, but at least my theory holds: as long as there's an audience, we'll be good to go . . .

◆ ◆ ◆

Even though Mom knew my date wouldn't be attending the rehearsal dinner, she still instructed the waitstaff to leave the empty chair at the table beside me—a silent, subtle reminder that she is not happy with me. Her antics aren't really bothering me, though. Besides the fact that she's stationed at a table on the other side of the room, throwing back vodka tonics and cackling like a bludgeoned goose, I'm having a surprisingly fun time at the geriatric table, where I'm babysitting Aunt Ginn while Whitman's elderly family members keep me thoroughly entertained.

Along with his grandmother Eva—who's nowhere near her deathbed despite that being the excuse for the speedy nuptials—are Pete and Ida, his great-uncle and -aunt; second cousin Barb, also born during the FDR administration; and Barb's boyfriend, Dang, the sixty-four-years-young Chinese man she met online. Barb and Dang are just back from a three-week trip to Europe and, from the stories they're telling, had a surprisingly wild time. (Apparently, the Sex Machines Museum in Prague is the best in the world . . .)

"What'd you say it was called?" Grandma Eva asks over a hearty laugh.

"A voyeuristic chamber pot," Barb cackles back.

"Yes. Chamber pot," Dang adds.

Dang's English isn't very good and is mostly limited to repeating exactly what Barb has already said, though he does it so enthusiastically—lots of nodding and smiling—that it's more funny than annoying.

"It had a mirror on one of those swivel things"—Barb makes a back-and-forth motion with her hand—"so they could give the voyeur a few different shots."

"Good Lord, that's disgusting!" Great-Aunt Ida bursts out laughing.

From behind the rim of his whiskey glass, Uncle Pete adds, "I suppose it's all about getting the right angle."

"Oh, stop it!" Ida swats her husband in the arm, and he starts to chuckle.

"The wildest was the hand-operated vibrator," Barb goes on, shaking her head like she can't believe what she's saying, which makes good sense, because I can't believe what I'm hearing. "It looked like a first-century telescope. It was made of metal and wood and had gears and levers on it. Was about this big"—she extends her age-spotted hands in front of her, at least fifteen inches apart—"and had this great big handle that you had to crank—"

"Yes. Crank," Dang offers while demonstrating a cranking motion with his hands.

I sputter on the wine in my mouth.

"You had to crank it yourself?" Grandma Eva asks.

"I don't think there was any rule on *who* had to do the cranking," Barb answers.

"Yes. Crank," Dang says again.

Uncle Pete snorts.

"What's the Chinaman talking about?" Aunt Ginn barks out from beside me. Along with having loose lips, she's now practically deaf, a horrible combination that will undoubtedly give J.T. a run for his money when he's babysitting her during the ceremony tomorrow.

"Vibrators," Barb calls out to her from across the table.

"Vibrators?" Aunt Ginn looks more confused than she usually does. "What the hell is that? Did Ellen give those away on her Christmas show?"

"Lord no!" Ida crows.

"That's an episode I would've watched," Pete chides.

"This is a riot," Grandma Eva mutters, then takes another sip of wine.

I hang my head. She's right. This is a riot of sorts. It's like Blanche and Sophia crashed the set of *Sex and the City* and the director just kept on filming.

"It's a gadget people use during sex," Barb clarifies for Aunt Ginn.

"Yes. For the sex."

And there's Dang again.

Barb continues, "They're long and make buzzing sounds . . ."

"What the devil are you talking about?" Ginn levels Barb with a frustrated look. "The only long, buzzing thing I know about are wasps, and nobody wants one of them near their cooter."

I snort.

"No, they're not insects." Barb waves off Ginn's comment. "I said they were sex toys. We saw them at a museum when we were on vacation in Prague."

"And they just had them sitting out there on display, huh?" Pete asks.

"Well, they sure as hell weren't demonstrating them," Barb answers, prompting everyone but Ginn to roar with laughter, including me.

Cooters and vibrators may not be discussion points for most dinner conversations, but they're certainly keeping me entertained—

"I need to see you in the foyer immediately."

Mom is suddenly leaning in over my shoulder, her flammable breath tickling my ear.

"What? Why?" I turn to look at her. "Is Hope okay?"

"Of course. Why wouldn't she be?" I follow her annoyed gaze to the head table, where Hope is looking like the belle of the ball, laughing joyously beside her friends.

I shake my head. "No reason."

"I need to talk to you about your speech."

"My speech?" I turn back to her. "What about my speech?"

"Who's gonna preach?" Aunt Ginn, world's worst eavesdropper, suddenly barks out, prompting everyone at our table to turn in our direction. "Nobody said there was gonna be a sermon. I came for the booze—not a sermon."

"Oh, for god's sake," Mom mumbles before she quickly adopts her scary smile and, in a loud and restrained voice, says, "No, Ginn. Her speech. I need to talk to Mackenzie about the maid of honor speech she's going to deliver."

"Oh no, are you uncomfortable speaking in public, dear?" a concerned Barb asks me.

"What—no." I shake my head, still startled by the sudden swing in conversation.

"I just need to make sure it sounds okay," Mom cuts in. "The last time she spoke in public, she actually referenced a Dr. Seuss book. Can you believe that?" She pats my shoulder in that condescending way of hers. "A children's book, for goodness' sake. It was ridiculous."

I sneer up at her, a twenty-year-old grievance stirring in my gut. My high school valedictorian speech was *not* the last time I spoke publicly, you twat, and using *Oh, the Places You'll Go* as an analogy for what the future held for us was not ridiculous; it was insightful!

"The last thing I'd want is for her to embarrass herself in front of all these people," Mom goes on. "I'll have her back to you in a minute. Come along, dear."

Despite the overwhelming urge to flip her the bird, I lay my napkin on the table and follow her out into the foyer.

"Mom, I know how to deliver a speech."

She makes a snorting sound that echoes through the empty corridor. "I beg to differ. Now, hurry up and tell me what you plan to say. They're about to clear the dinner plates."

I sigh. I haven't really planned anything. When Hope asked if I would say a few words before the dessert course, I figured I'd just say something about the occasion, how great it is that we can all join together to celebrate these two wonderful people and—

"Hey, there's my beautiful girl."

My breath hitches on a terrified gasp at the sound of J.T.'s voice from behind me.

What the—NO!

What is he doing here?

He wasn't supposed to be here until late tonight . . . Mom's brow cocks, her narrowed gaze instantly settling in just over my shoulder.

FUCK.

He can't be here now. Not now!

I haven't told him yet.

He doesn't know about Michael.

And there's no audience.

I DON'T HAVE AN AUDIENCE!

"Mac?"

Heart hammering against my sternum, I slowly turn to face him. My throat instantly swells at the sight, so handsome in his steely-gray button-down shirt and charcoal pants.

He offers a hesitant smile and starts toward me, his eyes momentarily darting away from me over my shoulder toward Mom.

Shit.

Shit. Shit. Shit.

"I was able to get away early and wanted to surprise you."

I swallow hard, feeling like I might throw up. "Well . . . you . . . sure did."

"You look beautiful." He cups my elbow with his hand and gives me a polite kiss on the cheek. Against my ear he whispers, "Is this your mom?"

I nod, my voice too tangled up in fear to respond.

"Mrs. Huntress," J.T. says, releasing me and heading straight toward the devil herself, his hand stretched out in greeting. "It's so nice to finally meet you. I'm—"

"Oh, I know who you are," Mom coos, an unsettling glimmer in her eye. "You're the one and only Dr. Michael."

Michael.

Michael.

Michael.

The name reverberates like gunfire inside my head, prompting my breath to catch in a painful-sounding whimper.

J.T. casts me a quizzical look but then turns back to Mom. "Michael? Um . . . no, I'm—"

"Oh, good god! You're the handyman." Mom recoils as recognition finally sets in.

Shit.

"Uh, yes." His hand drops back to his side. "Well, technically I'm a contractor, but I am the one who did the work on Mac's house. I think you saw me there a couple weeks ago—"

"Where is Michael?" Mom aims her attention to me, her scary smile suddenly, terrifyingly, nonexistent.

SHIT!

"Who's Michael?" J.T. questions.

"Her boyfriend," Mom answers before I can even formulate a response. "The neurologist she's been dating."

"What?" J.T. turns to me. "Mac, what's she talking about? Who the hell is Michael?"

I shake my head, terrified by his reaction, and furious with myself for not telling him before—

Dammit, I should have told him before!

"No—nobody. He's nobody. We broke up—I mean—"

"You broke up?" Mom snarls, too disgusted to let me air my entire confession that Michael is no more real than the bogeyman. "You

209

broke up with the neurologist for him? You told me he was *just* the handyman."

"*Just* the handyman?" The look of betrayal on J.T.'s face is heartbreaking—and mine to own. I quickly reach for his hands.

"You're not *just* the handyman. I never said that—not the way she's implying—"

"Mackenzie Rose, what on earth is going on here? Where is Michael?"

"There is no Michael!" I scream at her. "I made him up."

"What?"

She reels back like she just got a whiff of something rotten.

"I made him up, Mom! Michael doesn't exist—he never has!"

"*You made him up?* Why would you do that?"

"Because a handyman wasn't good enough." J.T. slowly untangles his hands from mine and starts to back away from me. "You had to make up a guy that was good enough for you and your family because *I* wasn't . . ."

My heart twists as memories of our talks about his ex's horrific betrayal start to cyclone through my mind.

"No. God, no! That's not it at all! That has nothing to do with any of this."

I reach out for him again, desperate to explain that I was lying long before I met him—that it doesn't have to do with him at all—but this time he raises his hands, prohibiting the movement.

"God, I'm such an idiot . . . ," he mumbles. "I . . . I did it again—I can't go through this again."

My stomach sinks with regret as he takes off down the hall, head hanging low beneath the weight of the world's greatest misunderstanding.

"*Wait!*" I call after him. "Please let me explain! I was going to tell you! I swear, I was—just let me explain!"

"You need to explain to me first."

Just like when I was a kid acting up at church, Mom pinches my arm, demanding my attention. "Why did you lie to me?"

"Because it's a hell of a lot easier than telling you the truth!" I snarl, while wriggling out of her grip.

"Lying to me is easy for you?"

"Yes! The truth only earns me criticisms, so I lie to you—I've been doing it my whole damn life!"

"Criticisms? What on earth are you talking about? I don't criticize you—"

"Ohmygod!" My jaw drops so hard I'm surprised it doesn't dislocate. "All you ever do is criticize me! My house is too messy, my dog is too old, my food is too fattening, my boobs are too small—"

She shakes her head in that dismissive way of hers, prompting my blood to pump even harder than it already is.

"You have spent your life picking apart everything I do. Nothing is ever good enough for you—"

"That's not true—"

"Yes it is! Especially my love life! You're constantly harassing me about whether or not I'm dating anyone—"

"All mothers do that—"

"Not the way you do! You berate me about it: *Why aren't you dating anyone? Are you putting out those tennis player vibes again? You don't want to die alone, do you?*" The tone I'm using to mimic her sounds more like Fran Drescher than my mom, but it's still making the point. "And god forbid I actually *have* a boyfriend, 'cause that's when the *real* judgment starts. *Where did he go to school? What do his parents do? Does he own or rent—*"

"I do *not* do that."

"*Yes* you do! You just did it with him." I cast a heartsick glance down the hallway that J.T. just vacated. "I'm in love with him, Mom. He's the guy I've been waiting for—"

"The *handyman?*"

"Yes! The fucking handyman!" I throw my hands up in the air. "And the fact that you keep calling him that is the very reason I made up Michael the Neurologist in the first place—before I even met J.T.—because it was easier to create the *perfect* guy you couldn't find anything to complain about than to tell you the truth. That's why I lie to you—that's why everybody lies to you—because the consequences that come from being honest are too impossible and humiliating to live with! It's the only way we can survive!"

"*We?* No, no, no. This is all about *you*, Mackenzie. *You're* the one who insists on butting heads with me and making things difficult. You've always been this way, ever since you were little. You've always twisted everything I've said so I'm the bad guy—"

"No, Mom! It's not just me—"

"Well, I don't have these kinds of issues with your father, and certainly not with your sister. Hope and I have always gotten along without any of this kind of drama. She would never lie to me the way you did. It would never even cross her mind—"

"She's pregnant." The very instant the forbidden words cross my lips, a wall of regret slams into me, and I gasp.

"Wh-what? What did you say?"

"Nothing. I—I didn't say anything—"

"Yes you did." She takes a step closer to me. "You said that Hope is—"

"Hope is what?"

I whip my head to the right and see Hope standing just outside the ballroom doors. Her cherubic cheeks are still aglow with the happy energy of the room she just exited, but the confusion in her eyes suggests she's not feeling quite as smiley on the inside.

"*Hope is what?*" she asks again, shifting her gaze between Mom and me.

I swallow against the sickening feeling now rising in my chest, silently willing Mom to keep her damn mouth shut.

Please have the good sense to stay quiet.

Please don't say anything—

"Are you pregnant?"

I wince.

Hope's face falls as pale as her pretty dress.

"You told her?"

"I—I'm sorry. I didn't mean to—"

"How could you do that? You promised you wouldn't say anything—"

The betrayal in her voice, reminiscent of J.T.'s, makes my stomach start to turn.

"So, it's true? You're pregnant?"

Eyes now glistening with tears, Hope turns to Mom but doesn't answer her question. She doesn't need to. The devastation on her face says it all.

"I can't believe this. You intentionally kept this from me. Both of you." Her fiery gaze darts back and forth between us. "My own flesh and blood lying to me about the most important events in their lives. You two are just . . . unbelievable!"

With a huff, she stalks back toward the ballroom, while Hope snarls, "It's not all about you, Mom!" after her, then turns to me and growls, "I hope you're happy. You just ruined what was supposed to be the best day of my life!"

"Hope—"

"Don't, Mac!" She levels me with a fiery gaze of her own. "Don't even try to make this right. I told you something in confidence and you just shit all over me—my freaking maid of honor just destroyed my entire wedding. Thanks a lot!"

She stomps down the hallway, leaving me completely alone . . . and completely guilty of doing exactly what she said. I did just ruin her entire wedding, along with the best thing that's ever happened to me . . .

Chapter 16

10:15 p.m.
Three hours since the blowout with Mom and Hope
Twelve hours and forty-five minutes until the fucking wedding

Knock. Knock. Knock.

Eyes raw and itchy from crying, I rap on the door of the honeymoon suite, praying Hope will talk to me. I didn't chase after her when she stormed away from me earlier—like me she needs lots of space when she's angry—so instead I've been searching the hotel grounds for J.T., because he won't answer his phone when I call or text.

I started with our room, confirming with the front desk that he'd actually retrieved his key when he arrived—he had—but when I got upstairs, the only evidence he'd been there was the damp bath towel hanging on the back of the bathroom door. Otherwise, there was no indication he'd even set foot in the room.

Our room . . . *Dammit, what have I done?*

I wandered the hotel grounds, scouring the pool area, restaurant, and both bars, and I inquired with any hotel staff I encountered, but no one had seen him. And when I finally took a trip around the parking lot and didn't see his truck anywhere, the heartbreaking reality of what I'd done finally settled in: J.T. was gone, and it was all my fault.

I collapsed onto a cement median and cried a sea of regretful tears before the crisp night air got the better of me, and I finally came inside to see if I could make some inroads with Hope, assuming she hasn't fled the scene to get away from me too—

The door opens.

It's Whitman.

He steps out into the hallway, leaving the door cracked behind him. His usual boy-next-door smile is nowhere to be found. "She doesn't want to see you, Mac."

"I know, and I totally get it. I just want to talk to her for a minute to try and explain . . ."

"No."

"I know she's mad, and she has every right to be. I totally messed up—"

"Yeah you did!" Hope yells from deep inside the room.

"Hope! Honey, please just talk to me—" I make a move for the door, but Whitman stops me with a raise of his hand and a firm shake of the head.

"No!" she screams out. "Go away!"

"Hope—"

"It's not a good idea," he cuts me off.

"But I need to talk to her—"

"No, Mac. She's really upset, and with her blood pressure the way it is, I don't think we should do anything to aggravate it."

My heart twists at the worry in his voice.

He's right.

She doesn't need any unnecessary stress, no matter how badly I need resolution.

"Have you taken it lately?"

"Not since last night—"

"You need to take it now."

"Okay."

"Like, *right* now. As soon as I leave, I want you to go in there and take it, and then text me the results."

"Okay," he says again. "I will. I promise."

Given the situation, his reassurance is more kindness than I deserve. "Thanks."

He offers a weak smile. "You're welcome."

I start to walk away but turn back and say, "I am really sorry about what happened . . ."

"I know," he says. "And deep down she is too. She just needs some time."

Back in my empty room, I peel off my dress and climb into the shower. The hot water provides little soul comfort, but it does ease some of the tension from my shoulders and neck. With a Benadryl and a bottle from the minibar, I might get some sleep tonight.

The only thing I brought to sleep in was a naughty little black number with minimal fabric, so I pull on the Michigan T-shirt I drove up in and wrap the hotel robe around me instead. I'm just climbing under the covers when there's a knock on the door.

J.T.!

I hop out of bed and race to answer it.

Oh.

"Hi, Dad."

"Hey, Goose. How you doing?"

I drop my attention to the floor and shake my head. "Not good."

"Do you want to talk about it?"

Just like when I was a kid, the tenderness in his deep voice makes me feel safe somehow, like I can share my feelings without any judgment. I step back, inviting him in. He squeezes my arm as he passes, then makes his way to the guest chair near the sliding patio door while I climb back under the covers. I pull my knees to my chest and hug the blankets.

We sit quietly for a few moments before he finally says, "So, it sounds like things got pretty heated with your mom and your sister . . ."

"Yeah."

"You okay?"

My chin starts to quiver, and I shake my head. "I screwed up, Daddy. I ruined everything . . ."

My throat swells with a deep, painful ache that makes it impossible to talk. I drop my head against my knees and start to cry.

"No, no, sweet girl." The mattress sags beneath my feet as he moves over to the bed. He rubs my blanketed calf. "You didn't ruin anything. You just had a fight. That's all it was."

"No, it wasn't just a fight," I protest over a sniffle. "I betrayed her confidence. She's never going to forgive me."

"Well, I know it feels like that right now, but I think we both know that's not true. Look at me. I've ruined plenty of things for your sister over the years, and she's always forgiven me. Remember her sixth birthday, when I brought home the Bugs Bunny cake instead of the one with the Cherry Blossom Girl on it . . ."

"Strawberry Shortcake," I correct over a sputtery laugh.

"Right, right, Strawberry Shortcake." He chuckles. "She vowed never to talk to me after that, remember?" I nod. I do remember. I'd just passed my driver's test and was feeling incredibly grown up. I couldn't imagine how anyone could be so immature that they'd ruin their whole birthday party over a stupid cake. "Or prom. Boy, that was a doozy." He sighs. "I had the audacity to ask her date for his home phone number. You'd have thought I asked for a stool sample by the way she reacted . . ."

Again, I nod. Not because I witnessed the event—I was neck-deep in medical school by then—but because I distinctly remember hearing about it a few days later from Mom, though looking back, it's hard to remember if she was on Dad's side or Hope's . . .

"For a kindergarten teacher, your sister lives a fairly dramatic life," he goes on. "She always has, and she's really good at drawing people into her mood, too, but don't be fooled. This is just a little blip on the screen of your relationship. Everything's going to be just fine, and the wedding is going to go off without a hitch."

While I appreciate his optimism, bad birthday cakes and prom-date embarrassments do *not* carry the same weight as outing an unplanned pregnancy.

"I don't think it's that easy this time, Dad."

"Why? Because her exciting news didn't come out exactly the way she planned?"

Clearly Mom filled him in on the details.

I nod.

"Well, it seems to me that *your* exciting news took a hit in the process too."

My exciting news? Swiping back the moisture from my eyes and nose, I slowly raise my head. "What do you mean?"

He grins. "Something about a handyman . . ."

My cheeks warm at the mere mention, but with the flush comes the reminder of what I've lost. I drop my head again. "I ruined everything with him too."

"How do you figure?"

"I lied to him. Well, not really to *him*, but I lied to Mom, which resulted in hurting him." Images of his pained expression the last time I saw him suddenly flash through my mind. I clench my teeth, disgusted with myself. "I never meant to hurt him," I go on, zeroing my attention in on the downy comforter I'm strangling in my lap. "I was just trying to get Mom off my back, so I made up a story and—*dammit!*" I push the blanket off with a frustrated sigh and raise my head to look at him again. "Why does she have to be so critical of everything I do? Why can't she just accept people and situations the way they are instead of shitting all over them? Why does she have to be such a bitch?" *Bitch.*

The word grates against my tongue like sandpaper. I sigh. "I'm sorry. I didn't mean to say that—"

"It's okay, Goose. Sometimes you just have to get it out. And you're right. Your mom can be . . . challenging at times for you and your sister. Over the years, I've learned that's just her way of coping with her insecurities."

I snort. "Insecurities? She's the bossiest, most self-confident woman I've ever met."

He chuckles under his breath. "Well, sure, that's the face she puts on for the outside world, but underneath it all your mom is probably the most insecure person *I've* ever met. She feels like she pales in comparison to just about everyone, especially you."

"*Me?*"

He smiles at my disbelief. "You know that Mom and I got married very young, right?" I nod. Dad was a junior in college, Mom a wide-eyed freshman. They met at a social the second day of school and have been together ever since. It's a true old-fashioned love story. "And you know that your mom planned to be a nurse but never completed her education—"

"Because she got pregnant with me," I say, well aware of the story.

"Actually, no. You were just a well-timed excuse. The truth is she failed out of the program before the end of sophomore year. The university asked her to leave."

"Really?" Mom has always claimed that, like so many other women in her generation, she only went to college to earn her MRS degree. The thought of her flunking out never even crossed my mind . . .

"Really. She was understandably upset, but more than that she was embarrassed."

"Why? I mean, I'm sure it was disappointing, but not everyone's cut out for college—especially the nursing program; it's really challenging."

"Because your mother's a driven person," he explains. "And she comes from a line of other driven people who have been very successful in their careers." I think back on my mom's family. Along with Grandpa Harold, my medical mentor, Uncle Steve is a patent attorney, and before she passed Aunt Diane ran national fundraising campaigns for various cancer research organizations. Grandma Pearl, her mom, never worked outside the home, but she did graduate from college with an English degree. Though I've never been fortunate enough to see them, I'm told she penned out a few novels in her day . . . "I think that's why she's always worked so hard to create a picture-perfect home life," he goes on. "If she couldn't be recognized as a successful nurse, then at least she could be recognized as a successful homemaker."

I admit that this information gives me a surprising amount of insight into what makes my mother's crazy clock tick, but I fail to see how it relates to me. Dad must recognize the confusion on my face, because he continues with his explanation before I even have to ask him to.

"Sweetie, you are a smart, beautiful, talented woman who excels at everything you've ever put your mind to. You were valedictorian of your high school class, graduated college with honors, have a thriving medical practice, purchased a home on your own . . ."

As always, his recognition of my accomplishments makes me feel good, but *he's* not the one I have a problem with.

"Too bad Mom doesn't feel the same."

"Oh, but she does," he says. "You've seen the way she talks about you to other people. She's immensely proud of you—"

"Not when it comes to my love life. Apparently that's more important to her than any of my other accomplishments."

He inhales a deep breath and, on the exhale, says, "Actually, I think your love life is the thing she's most proud of . . . or envious of."

I level him with a tired look.

"I'm serious," he says over a firm nod. "Even though I know your mother loves me and is happy with the life we've made together, I don't doubt that if given the opportunity, she would go back and do things a little differently."

"No she wouldn't." I quickly toss the covers off me and reach for his hand. "She's crazy about you. She wouldn't do it differently—"

"No, no, no." He squeezes my leg. "That's not what I meant. I have no doubt she'd still have chosen me—the fates would have seen to that—but I think she might have enjoyed the opportunity to take her time finding me. She was just a kid, still living at home, when we got married. She went straight from her father's house into mine. She never had an opportunity to live on her own and discover who she was, let alone figure out what she wanted in a partner."

"Is that a nice way of telling me it's *good* to be an old spinster?"

He laughs. "No, honey. I'm telling you that there's something to be said for taking your time and finding the right one."

My heart twists at the tenderness of his words. "Yeah, well, a lot of good it did me. I finally found the *right one*, and he won't even talk to me, no thanks to Mom."

"She feels worse about that than you know," he says, and by the sincerity in his tone, I almost believe him. "And I have a feeling your guy is going to come around."

"I appreciate the optimism, Dad, but you don't know him. You don't know what he's been through—and why what happened was as hurtful to him as it was."

He leans in a bit closer, locking eyes with me. "You're right. I don't know him, but I know *you*. And any man you deem worthy of being the right one will be smart enough to know a good thing when he's got it. Trust me, honey, your guy will turn up. And in the meantime, you need to get some sleep. According to the schedule you've got to be downstairs for hair and makeup in about"—he glances at the clock on the nightstand—"eight hours."

I sigh. "I know."

He gives my leg another pat, then pushes himself off the bed.

"You gonna be okay here?"

"Yeah."

"All right, then. Good night, my little Goose."

He steps forward and plants a kiss on the top of my head, just like he did when he tucked me in when I was little.

"I know it's hard," he adds as he's heading for the door, "but try and cut your mom some slack, okay? This wedding has been pretty stressful for her, and now that we've got a baby in the mix, it . . . well"—he throws his hands up and laughs—"this weekend has definitely taken an unexpected turn."

"I'll try," I concede. "And congratulations, *Grandpa.*"

He grins. "It suits me, don't you think?"

"Definitely."

He gives me a parting wink and then disappears out the door, while I settle back under the covers, desperately trying to buy into the things he just assured me of. If Mom is as insecure as he claims, then I suppose I can see how she might tear me down to make herself feel better—like a bully on the playground. And if *I'm* the catch Dad thinks I am, then maybe there is hope that J.T. feels the same and will give me a second chance.

Please, god, give me a second chance . . .

Chapter 17

10:48 a.m.
Twelve minutes until the damn wedding . . . but who's counting?

Oh, happy day.

Hope, the other attendants, and I have been holed up in a small anteroom just outside the chapel for the last three hours, getting our hair and makeup done. While the bride has managed to engage in silly, nervous banter with the other girls, she's yet to speak to me. This isn't entirely surprising, but it is disappointing—and also a bit concerning, as I'd really like to examine her.

According to the text Whitman sent last night, Hope's blood pressure climbed up to 132/87. While it's still a way from dangerous, it makes me uneasy. I never want to see a patient's BP on the rise, especially when we're still four weeks out from the due date. I instructed him to keep her in bed, with her feet propped up and a bottle of water pressed to her lips. The doctor in me desperately wants to slap a cuff on her arm right now, but the remorseful big sister is holding back for fear of making a scene in front of the other bridesmaids. Based on the amount of champagne they're offering her—which she refuses on the grounds of keeping a clear head—they're still not aware of her condition . . . and I'm not about to out her again.

And despite my countless texts and voice messages, J.T. won't talk to me either. I could easily burst into a fit of regretful tears right now, but Hope's delicate state has me swallowing my own heartache and instead focusing on getting her through this day without any additional drama.

Just let us survive this freaking day . . .

"Ugh. You've got something weird going on back here. Sit down. I need to fix it." Looking annoyed, Jasmine, the hairdresser, drags me back to the salon chair on the other side of the room. She fusses with something at the back of my head, then douses me with another layer of Aqua Net. "There we go." She steps back to evaluate her work. "Now you're good. Remind me of your count . . ."

"Thirty-seven."

"Now it's thirty-eight."

"Thirty-eight. Got it."

Jasmine insisted we all know the exact number of bobby pins used to secure our twists and curls so we could be sure to remove every single one before we climb into bed at the end of the day. I'd grumble at having to fish out thirty-eight if I hadn't heard that Hope's count was seventy-four. Along with Mom's enviable curves, she also inherited the thick-hair genes.

I take in my reflection as I rise out of the chair: The pink dress fits well but does little for my figure—not that there's much figure to work with—and though I feel like a sheet of drywall that's been spackled and primed, the makeup artist did manage to cover up the dark bags I came in with, so I consider that a win. I'm not so sure about the halo of pale-pink flowers pinned to my head, but they could withstand a category 5 at this point, so I'm stuck with them whether I like them or not. All in all, I'd say I'm a perfectly respectable-looking attendant, as are the other girls (who are currently sucking back mimosas while they update their posts with prewedding pictures), while Hope, on the other hand, is a true vision in her ivory gown. She mentioned to me a few days ago—when she was still talking to me—that she had to ask the seamstress to let it out some in the midsection, but you wouldn't know it by looking at her. She's every bit the voluptuous Botticelli beauty she's always been, and that baby secretly growing inside her provides an angelic glow no makeup artist could ever reproduce.

Tammy, the wedding planner, suddenly charges into the room, clipboard in hand, and cries out, "Who's ready to get married?"

"I am!" Hope crows, sounding like the epitome of an excited bride.

"Damn straight you are," Meghan chirps back, her glass raised in a salute.

"Well, I should think so. You're absolutely stunning," Tammy says, air-kissing Hope's cheeks. "All of you are. And all the boys are looking pretty sharp, too, although we did have one little hiccup with Charlie's ascot . . ."

Charlie is Whitman's cousin / best man, who will be escorting me up the aisle at the conclusion of the ceremony. He's sweet—and cute as a bug with schoolboy dimples—but sadly is *exactly* my height. That wasn't an issue last night when I was wearing flats, but now that I'm in three-inch heels, I'm starting to think maybe it could be.

"What happened to Charlie's ascot?" Mom suddenly appears in the doorway.

It's the first time we've seen her today . . . the first time *I've* seen her since my little chat with Dad. I had hoped she would look different to me somehow, more like the vulnerable person Dad said she was, but as I see her now—the epitome of self-confidence in her silver, tea-length dress and coiffed hair—I can't help but think he's mistaken. There's no way that a lifetime of insecurity is hidden beneath all that chiffon and lace.

"Oh, there was just a little tear in the fabric," Tammy says easily while she kneels to fiddle with the buttons on Hope's bustle. "I just had to put in a few quick stitches, but it's looking good now. Can you believe how gorgeous all of these women are?" she asks, wisely changing the subject. "Just look at them. And your baby girl . . . she's stunning, isn't she?"

"Yeah she is!" Harper cries out, and Meghan adds, "The most beautiful bride ever!"

Hope beams at the attention from her giggly friends, while that ridiculous smile slowly returns to Mom's face, though this time it's accompanied by a strange twitch of her lower lip.

Without even looking at me, Mom says, "Yes, you're all gorgeous. Especially you, sweetheart." She looks directly at Hope, smile spreading, lip twitch deepening. "You *are* stunning. You're going to take Whitman's breath away."

Hope adopts a disturbed smile of her own and says, "Aww, thanks, Mom. You look beautiful too."

My stomach wrenches.

Apparently she also inherited the bullshit gene . . .

"All right. I think you're about as perfect as any bride can be," Tammy says to Hope. "Let me just get a quick peek at the rest of you." From where she stands in the center of the room, she takes a visual inventory of me, Meghan, and Harper. She nods with approval, then says, "All righty, all that's left to do is walk down the aisle."

She motions for Mom, me, and the other bridesmaids to follow her out into the hallway, where we'll assemble with the rest of the family and bridal party, just as we rehearsed yesterday, but before we're able to, Mom says, "I just need a quick minute with my daughters, if that's okay . . ."

Tammy glances down at her watch but astutely doesn't say anything about the time. "Yes, of course."

Mom ushers Hope and me to the corner of the room by our elbows, like children caught swiping candy from the jar. In a clipped voice she says, "Clearly this weekend has taken an unexpected turn"—her gaze darts to Hope's belly—"but today is not the time or place to discuss it." The twitch deepens. "There are two hundred and eighteen people in that chapel, and we're not about to make a spectacle of ourselves." Now the right side of her mouth is joining in. *Twitch. Twitch. Twitch.* Like little jackhammers are tucked up under her lips. "We've worked too hard to put this wedding together to let it fall apart now. Everyone just put on your best smile"—*twitch, twitch, twitch*—"and get through this day looking like the capable and lovely Huntress women we are, understood?"

It's the worst pep talk in history, but it still motivates Hope to say, "Absolutely."

Mom turns to me, her lips now in full seizure mode.

I cringe, half expecting her head to start spinning. "Okay."

"Good. Then let's have a wedding." With a satisfied nod, she turns to leave but casts a quick glance over her shoulder and says, "You both *do* look beautiful," before she stalks out of the room.

"What the hell was that lip twitch?"

"I don't know . . ." Hope mutters absently, clearly unaware that she's actually talking to me.

I take advantage of her befuddled state and, with a gentle touch to her arm, say, "Are you feeling okay?"

"What?"

"Are you feeling okay? I saw that your blood pressure was climbing again—"

"*Ugh, stop.*" She yanks her arm away from me. "You don't get to ask me how I am."

"Hope, please. I'm worried about you—"

"*No.* You made it perfectly clear last night that you don't care about me—" She winces.

"*What?* What's wrong? What hurts?"

"*Nothing.*" She pinches her eyes tight and inhales a deep breath through gritted teeth. "I'm fine. It's just a little gas."

"Hope—"

"I'm fine."

"Sweetie, please just let me check you out real quick—"

"*I said I'm fine,*" she growls. "Just do like Mom said and walk down the damn aisle already."

Despite the worry now rattling my veins, I comply with a reluctant nod, because agitating her any more won't help the situation. I head out into the hallway, where the rest of the bridal party is assembled. Tammy was right. The boys do look nice in their tailed suits and ascots. My throat starts to swell again. *J. T. looked so good in his suit . . .*

"Hey, Goose." Dad comes in from my side and gives me a hug. "How are you feeling today?"

"Don't ask."

"Well, you look beautiful."

"Thanks. You're not too bad yourself." I tap the rose pinned to his lapel.

"How's the bride holding up?"

"She says she's fine, but I have other thoughts."

"The baby?"

I nod. "I'm worried about her blood pressure, but she won't let me check her out."

"Okay, it's go time, people!" Tammy suddenly calls.

"I'll talk to her," Dad assures me while giving my arm a gentle squeeze. "Maybe she just needs a few minutes of quiet."

"Yeah, maybe," I say, even though my gut is screaming otherwise.

"Mac, I need you up here, please," Tammy orders.

"Better get going, Goose. And don't worry about your fella. I'm sure he'll turn up. I've got a good feeling."

I sigh. I wish I did . . . Tammy hands out the bouquets—fresh-cut pastel roses tied together with silken, ivory-colored ribbons—and we take our positions, me at the front of the pack, alone, with Meghan and Harper linking arms with their respective groomsmen behind me.

"Here we go . . . ," Harper chirps.

"Dun, dun, duunnnn," Brandon, her groomsman, singsongs from beside her.

"Remember, chin and eyes forward," Tammy instructs me while fussing with my hair one last time. "And smile. A big beautiful smile like your mom's."

I roll my eyes. Sure thing, Tammy.

She opens one of the big wooden doors that leads into the chapel. Today the pew ends are adorned with romantic sprigs of ivy and rosebuds and filled with happy, well-dressed guests. As expected, it's a lovely event. The stringed quartet segues from the unfamiliar piece they've been playing to the recognizable Pachelbel's Canon, prompting all heads to turn toward us.

"And now you're walking . . . ," Tammy instructs from behind the door.

I swallow back my nerves, force out a smile, and begin my solo march down the aisle. My cheeks flush hot as all the attention in the room settles on me. I do my best to ignore their wide eyes and whispered greetings and instead keep my attention fixed up front—on Whitman, Charlie, and Reverend Howell—but Dad's hopeful words, *Don't worry about your fella. I'm sure he'll turn up*, start gnawing on my brain, and I find myself wondering if maybe he's right. As subtly as possible, I survey the bride's side, hoping to see my fella blended into the crowd . . . I don't. The only person who catches my attention is my cousin David. He's on the exterior aisle about halfway down, scowling at me. My eyes narrow in confusion until I see that Aunt Ginn is sitting beside him.

Shit.

He was not supposed to be the one babysitting . . .

I offer him my most apologetic look, then recommit my attention back to the pulpit. Despite my mood, a genuine smile tickles my lips as I see Whitman fidgeting with schoolboy excitement. My heart softens with gratitude—and a bit of disappointment. Hope found herself a good one.

So did I . . .

"You look great," Whitman mutters as I take my position on the step.

"And really tall," Charlie adds.

Reverend Howell chuckles under his breath.

Stifling a giggle of my own, I turn my attention back toward the doors but stop short when I see that, from her front-row seat, Mom is staring at me rather than the rest of the processional. She blots her eyes with a tissue and offers me a smile that looks even stranger than usual thanks to the still-present lip twitch—an involuntary movement, I've determined, that comes from trying to restrain her anger. Clearly, she's just realized how much taller I am than Charlie and how unbalanced we're going to look when we're walking up the aisle.

I blow out an exhausted breath and watch as Harper and Brandon, then Meghan and Chad, make their ways down the aisle; their smiles are wide, their strides confident, just as Tammy instructed. Whitman offers each of the girls the same kind greeting he did me as they take their positions on my right.

"How's she doing?" I whisper to Harper, who's standing nearest me.

"*So* great."

I smile. Even though she's oblivious to the real meaning behind my question, I take her enthusiasm as a good sign. Hope is doing great. Everything's going to be fine . . .

"You ready for this, man?" Charlie mutters to Whitman.

"Oh yeah," he whispers back to him. "More than ready."

The musicians slowly transition into the traditional wedding march, prompting Meghan to squeal and say, "Here we go . . ."

"Enjoy your last breaths of freedom," Charlie teases.

My heart starts thundering with the same palpable anticipation that's humming through the room as the doors swing open and Dad and Hope appear in front of us.

"My god . . . ," Whitman mutters as he takes in his bride for the first time.

My heart swells at the reverence in his voice.

Yeah, she got a good one . . .

Dad is all prideful grins and stifled tears as they take their first step down the aisle. I glance at Mom and see that she's already reaching for another tissue. I can't see her mouth to confirm, but I can't imagine her lip is twitching anymore. What could she possibly find wrong with this perfect image?

Hope's smile, already as radiant as the sun after a summer storm, seems to grow bigger and brighter as they pass the first row of pews, then the second—

"Aaaaaaagh!" She lets out an agonized wail and falls to her knees.

My breath catches.

I know that sound too well . . .

A collective gasp explodes through the chapel as Dad kneels next to her, saying, "Sweetie, what's wrong? What's wrong?"

"The baby . . . ," Whitman mutters.

"Baby?" Mrs. Gentry gasps, then turns to her husband, who looks as stupefied as she does.

Whitman and I exchange a quick glance and then leap off the stage and race up the aisle, while Mom scrambles out of her seat, tearing away the floral adornments hanging across her pew, crying, "Mackenzie, help her! *Please, god,* help her, and the baby!" from behind us.

The word *baby* spreads through the chapel like wildfire, inciting the guests to gather on the interior aisles for a better look at what's going on. Ignoring their curiosity, I drop down onto the floor next to Hope. "Sweetie, what's going on? What are you feeling?"

"Aaaagh! It hurts—"

"I know it does—"

"It hurts so bad, Mac." She pounds the floor with her fist. "And I'm wet—" She winces beneath the tears streaming down her cheeks. "I'm wet! Everything's wet. My water broke!"

Contrary to her assessment, being wet doesn't necessarily mean her water broke—it's possible she just lost control of her bladder. And the pain could very well be Braxton-Hicks and not active labor. That's what I'm hoping for, anyway.

"What's wrong?" Whitman pleads.

"I don't know yet . . ."

Because she's on all fours, I reach under her and gather up the dress so I can get a look at the floor below. *Dammit.* The puddle has a familiar pinkish hue to it.

I sit back on my haunches and quickly formulate my plan.

"Hope, I need to examine you to see if you're dilated, okay?"

Teeth clenched in pain, she's only able to nod her response.

"Dad, you and Mr. Gentry need to clear everybody out of the back rows; push them up to the front."

I'm not at all comfortable moving her at this point, so the least we can do is offer her a little privacy. These are *not* the kind of wedding photos you want showing up on your Facebook feed.

"Right," Dad says.

"Let's go, people. Move to the front!" Mr. Gentry steps right into action.

"What can I do?" Mom cries helplessly.

Truth be told, I'm the only one who can actually *do* anything right now, but the anguish on her face suggests she needs a purpose, or she's going to lose her mind.

"You're going to sit behind her so she doesn't have to prop herself up."

Without concern for her $1,000 dress, Mom heeds my instruction and drops to the floor. We slowly transition Hope from her knees to her butt, then carefully get her cradled in Mom's lap while Dad, Mr.

Gentry, and now the other groomsmen corral all the guests to the front of the sanctuary.

I hike my own dress up above my knees so I can move without impediment, then crawl around Hope so I'm kneeling at her feet. Using her dress as a modesty curtain, I spread her legs apart and, mentally removing myself from our personal ties, pull down her wet undies—*oh shit*. That's a head.

"Tammy!" I call out, aware that she's been watching nervously from the back corner of the chapel.

"Yeah?"

"I need you to call 9-1-1 and tell them to send an ambulance here right now—"

"Oh god!" Hope cries out. "What's wrong?"

"—and then I need you to bring me some hand sanitizer and some clean towels," I go on with my instruction.

"Okay," Tammy says, then takes off toward the door with her phone already up to her ear.

"Whitman, get over here, and hold her hand!" I order while putting my hands in place to help guide the baby out.

Without hesitation, Whitman sprints over and drops to the floor beside Hope's shoulder. "It's okay, babe. I'm here," he says, voice trembling with fear. "It's going to be okay."

"Mac, what's wrong?" Hope wails out again.

"Nothing's wrong," I reassure both of them in my calmest voice. "Your baby has just decided to come a little early—"

Whitman gasps.

"No!" Hope cries. "It's too early! I'm only thirty-six weeks! That's too early!"

"Oh my god." Mom starts to whimper. "That's too early—"

"Mom . . ." I level her with a steely look that shuts her up, as intended. "Everything's going to be fine. I've delivered plenty of babies at thirty-six weeks."

"But it's too early!" Hope continues. "We have to stop her from coming!"

Now Mom gasps. "It's a girl?"

"A girl?" Mrs. Gentry echoes Mom's excitement.

"Hope, listen to me." The authority in my voice instantly silences both of them. In fact, the whole chapel goes quiet. The only sound I can hear is my own heartbeat. "Your baby is coming *now*. I'm going to ask you to start pushing in just a second—"

"*What? No!*" She slams her fists down onto the floor and struggles to push herself into a more upright position. "I can't have my baby here—not in front of everyone!"

"Oh dear," Mom whimpers.

"I knew this was going to be a good wedding!" someone who sounds a *lot* like Aunt Ginn yells out from one of the pews.

"There's nowhere for them to go, Hope," I continue, ignoring the outburst. "There's only one way into this room, and it's behind me. Do you want two hundred people walking past you right now?"

Her entire face pinches together in agony, and she shakes her still-veiled head. "No . . ."

"Okay, then we're going to have the baby right here. And it's going to be just fine."

"Are you sure?" she sputters.

"Yes, I'm sure."

"Your sister knows what she's doing," Mom adds while stroking her forehead. "She'll take care of you."

Surprised by her vote of confidence, I glance her way and see that her lip is now practically twitching off her face—

"Here you go . . ." An out-of-breath Tammy suddenly runs up with the towels and sanitizer. "The paramedics should be here any minute."

"Good. Thanks." I squirt a heavy dose of sanitizer onto my hands and, while scrubbing them, instruct Tammy to get down on the floor beside me. "You're going to hand me towels as I need them, okay?"

She nods quickly. "And once the baby's out, I'm going to pass her off to you."

"Okay. Got it."

"*Aaaagh!*" Hope screams again, louder this time, as another contraction hits.

"You're doing great, sweetie. So great . . . ," Whitman wisely encourages.

I glance down and see that the baby's head is already crowning.

Holy crap, this girl's coming fast.

"Hope, I need you to give me a big push, okay?" I look up over her dress and see her nod at my instruction, but the nervous tears tumbling down her flushed cheeks suggest she's not really hearing me. "Hope, *now.*"

She bears down. "*Aaagh!*"

The baby's head slides out a smidge farther.

"Good, Hope. Good," I tell her.

"You're doing great, babe," Whitman adds, though his fingers are looking a little purple beneath Hope's grasp.

"Do it again," I order. "As hard as you can."

She inhales a deep, shuddery breath.

"*Aaaaaaaaaagh!*"

"Yes, that's good." I wipe the area with a towel, then pass it off to Tammy, who hands me a fresh one. "You're doing great. Give me another really big one."

She whimpers, then bears down. "*Aaaaaaaaaagh!*"

The baby's entire head appears.

I wipe it clean again, allowing for a better grip as I cradle her little head in my right hand.

"Good girl, Hope! Just give me one more big push—"

"It hurrrrrrrts! It hurts so bad!"

"I know it does, but you're almost done, sweetie. I just need one more really big push to get her out—"

235

"You can do it, honey," Mom assures her over an encouraging nod.

"Keep pushing, Hope!" Whitman's dad calls out excitedly.

"Come on, Hopey!" my dad cries out.

"Just like taking a dump!" Aunt Ginn adds.

"Oh good god," Mom mumbles.

"Ow . . ." Whitman lets out a little whimper of his own as Hope engages in the notorious final-push hand strangle.

"AAAAAAAAAAAAAAAAAA—"

The baby's right shoulder starts to emerge.

"That's it, Hope," I say. "Keep pushing—"

"AAAAAAAAAAAAAA—"

And the whole shoulder's out.

"Get the towel ready," I tell Tammy.

"AAAAAAAAAAAAAAAAAAAAAAAAAAAAAAAAAAGH!"

And the other shoulder.

"Okay, Hope, no more pushing. She's here. Your girl is here . . ."

Chapter 18

I gently pull the baby out the rest of the way, while Hope collapses in a breathless heap against Mom's lap. As expected, she's little—five pounds at best—and her wrinkly skin is the color of an overripe raspberry, but that will change once we get her breathing.

I quickly transfer her slick body into Tammy's waiting arms and start wiping inside her mouth and over her nose to expectorate the mucus. I've never done this without a suctioning bulb before, but it does the trick, because she lets out a hearty wail that prompts the entire chapel to break into a round of yelps and applause.

"Oh my god," Hope cries over a winded breath. "That's our baby . . ."

"You did it, sweetie," Whitman chokes out.

With Tammy's help, we wipe the baby off a bit, then carefully raise her up for the new parents to have a look.

Hope's face explodes beneath the world's biggest smile, though the slight bobble of her head suggests that, along with her happiness, she's also feeling dizzy. Her blood pressure must be through the roof.

"My god, would you look at her," Mom says. Not only is her lip still twitching, but now her chin is quivering, too . . . because she's crying. The twitch was in an effort *not* to cry. "She's perfect. She's absolutely perfect. Dan!" she calls out to my dad. "Did you see? We have a grand-daughter! I'm a grandma!"

"I see her!" he calls back, his voice thick with emotion.

"She's just beautiful!" Whitman's mom gapes from a distance.

The chapel doors suddenly swing open behind me, and two paramedics come storming in with a gurney and loads of medical equipment; a handful of security and hotel staff are hot on their heels.

"We've got a preterm delivery at thirty-six weeks," I inform them while quickly backing out of the way so they can take over. "Baby's heart rate appears a bit accelerated, but otherwise breathing normally. Mom has possible postpartum preeclampsia."

"What?" Hope calls out. "What's wrong?"

"Nothing's wrong," I assure her. "I just want them to be aware of your blood pressure before they transport you."

One of the paramedics drops down to check on the baby, while the other grabs the blood pressure cuff from the bag and heads toward Hope.

"You're a doc?" the medic tending to Hope asks me.

I nod.

"She's an obstetrician," Mom says proudly.

"She's also my big sister," Hope adds, sounding a bit disoriented. "And the maid of honor . . ."

"Well, you're lucky she was here," he says. "She saved the day, from what I can see."

She locks her wobbly gaze onto me and says, "Yeah. She did. She's the best."

I smile. I guess she's not mad at me anymore . . .

"All right, Mom's pressure is high but stable," the medic reports.

"Yeah, baby looks good too," the other medic says. "Do you want to take care of the cord, Doc?"

"Sure."

I take the clamp and scissors from his hand, then set off tying the umbilical cord.

"Do you want to do the honors?"

Looking a bit shell-shocked, Whitman nods, then scoots down beside me.

"Right here . . ." I point to the appropriate spot, and with a nervous hand, he takes the scissors and makes the cut.

"Way to go, Whit!" the best man, Charlie, cries out, and the entire chapel erupts in another round of applause.

"I can't believe this is happening," Whitman says over a befuddled laugh. "One minute she's walking down the aisle, and the next I'm a dad . . ." He blinks hard, like the reality of the moment is starting to settle in. "I'm a dad," he says again.

"Yeah, you are."

"And she's . . ." He shifts his attention down to his little girl. "She's so beautiful. And . . . small . . ." His voice trails off, lost amid the raucous chatter of the excited crowd and whatever thoughts are running through his mind.

Recognizing the fear on his face, I reach for his hand. "It's going to be okay."

He blinks hard. "Is it? I mean . . . can I even do this?"

His question is nearly identical to the one J.T. asked me, prompting the immediate response I give back to him.

"Yes, you can. And you're going to be great at it."

"You think so?"

My chest swells at the vulnerability in his eyes, so much like what I saw in J.T.'s . . . "Yeah," I say. "Trust me, I know a good dad when I see one."

Seventy-four minutes later . . .

Not only did she carry her baby to thirty-six weeks without anyone realizing she was pregnant, but Hope also had the world's shortest labor and the fastest hypertension rebound (she returned to a comfy 118/77 on the ambulance ride over), and now she's propped up in the hospital bed looking as fresh and vibrant as a Summer's Eve commercial while she and her bridesmaids swoon over beautiful baby Ella. I could easily strangle her on behalf of every other woman on the planet if I didn't love her so much.

"Motherhood suits her, doesn't it?" Dad joins me in the doorway, where I've been watching Hope and her guests. After a thorough examination, the doctors determined that the baby was healthy enough to be seen by visitors, so long as they were in good health and promised not to handle her. Everyone agreed to the terms except for Mom. Up until about ten minutes ago, she was racking up more baby-holding time than Hope and Whitman combined.

"Yeah, she's a natural."

"Your mom wants to talk to you for a minute."

"About what?"

He shrugs.

"Do I have to?" I offer up a weary look that makes him smile. Other than her surprising compliments during the actual delivery, Mom and I haven't had a whole lot of interaction since the baby arrived, which has been sort of nice. Turns out cooing over grandbabies is more enjoyable than berating your children.

"It will be fine," he says. "I promise."

With a sigh, I head out the door and find her standing at the end of the hallway, in front of the window that overlooks the parking lot.

"Hey, Mom."

"Oh, hi, honey. Come here for a minute, would you?"

She walks over to the little love seat against the wall and picks up Hope's veil. While the rest of us are still wearing our wedding attire, Hope was fortunate enough to shed all hers as soon as we got here.

"I need you to run this down to my car."

"Okay. I'll do it when I head back to the hotel in a while—"

"No. It needs to be right now."

"Why?"

"Because I don't want it to get wrinkled."

"But it's just lying here. It's not getting wrinkled—"

"For goodness' sake, Mackenzie"—she cuts me off with a pointed look—"please just take it down to my car."

I sigh. "Fine. I need your keys."

"Oh, right. Just a second."

Looking surprised by my request, she hustles back to Hope's room and returns a moment later with her valet key in hand.

"Here you go."

She presses it into my open palm, but rather than releasing it, she collapses her hand around mine and squeezes tight, just like she did when I was little and she was helping me cross the street.

Confused by the show of affection, I lift my head and find her eyes glinting with emotion—and her bottom lip pulsing just like it was back at the chapel.

She's trying not to cry . . .

"What you did today was very impressive," she says, locking eyes with me. "The way you took charge of the situation . . . you were so calm and collected. You knew exactly what to do—"

"That's my job," I cut in, voice wavering.

She smiles. "Yes, I know it is. And you do it very well. I don't tell you that enough, but you do." She squeezes my hand tighter. "You do everything very well, Mackenzie. You always have. It's quite enviable."

My throat grows thick beneath her unfamiliar sentiments.

"I wouldn't change anything about my life," she goes on, "but if I had to do it all over again, I'd probably like to be a little more like you."

It's not exactly an apology, but it's still about the nicest thing she could possibly say to me. I swallow against the ache building in my chest and say, "Thanks, Mom. That means a lot."

She locks her gaze onto mine and smiles—a *genuine*, loving smile that's about a thousand times more meaningful than the one a padded bra earned me. It's a smile that leads me to believe things might be a little different between us moving forward. I hope so, anyway . . .

"Now then." She gives her head a righting shake, getting back to business. "Be sure to lay this out nice and flat on the back seat so it doesn't wrinkle. She's going to need this in a few months when we have another ceremony."

I nod while giving my head a subtly amused shake.

I guess short-lived praise is better than no praise at all.

Under her watchful eye, I drape the veil over my left arm and make my way to the elevator at the end of the hall. I'm just stepping into the car when she calls out, "Good luck!"

Good luck?

I cast a confused glance over my shoulder just in time to see her give me a big Fonzie-style thumbs-up before the steel doors slide shut and I start my descent down to the lobby.

"Good luck?" I mutter. What the hell is she talking about? I just delivered a baby in front of two hundred people, and she's wishing me luck to open a car door?

Becoming a grandma is definitely having an effect on her . . . My flamingo-pink, placenta-splattered dress and cemented-on crown of flowers earn me plenty of attention as I walk through the busy lobby and out the front doors. The warm spring sun shines bright overhead, prompting me to visor my eyes with my hand so I can see where I'm going. I don't remember exactly where Dad parked the car—we were all moving at a panicked pace when we got here—but I do remember that the parking lot was over an embankment just on the other side of the driveway in front of me, where an ambulance is currently parked and unloading a patient.

Allowing them all the room they need before I try to pass, I back up toward the building and start fiddling with Hope's veil. Compared to her dress, it's very simple with its two tiers of delicately embroidered flowers, but there's something about the glimmering sheen of the sheer fabric that makes it look almost magical, like something you'd see in a fairy tale—or at the end of a really good movie . . . My heart sinks as I think back on the last six weeks: the frustration with my friends, the horrible dates, the Jake Ryan epiphany . . . I thought that at thirty-nine I was *finally* getting a grip on my love life, but I'm no better off than I was when I was fifteen: head over heels for a guy who's too good to be true . . . a guy who doesn't want me because I was a fool.

The ambulance suddenly roars to life, and a heart-wrenchingly familiar song emits from its speakers. That same dreamy song that plays during the closing scene of *Sixteen Candles*.

A tortured wail stirs through my gut.

Of all the songs in the world, it has to be *that* one?

"Oh my god, I love this song," the female paramedic chirps to her partner as she climbs into the passenger side of the rig.

I shake my head, agonized and heartsick.

Me too, girl . . . me too.

She slams the door shut and the rig takes off, but the song still plays as clear as a bell through my head. I pinch my eyes shut, pained by images of that perfect moment—when the car pulls away from the church and Jake is standing there waiting for Samantha . . . Tears start to well in my eyes. I had him. I had *my* Jake, and now he's gone . . . Heart heavy with regret, I raise my head and—

Ohmygod.

It's him. It's my Jake—*my* J.T.

His old pickup is parked on the opposite side of the driveway, and he's leaning up against it, staring at me.

My heart hammers hard as our eyes lock for a tenuous beat before he raises his hand up into a timid little wave.

A hopeful whimper escapes me, and I raise my hand and wave back at him.

Good Lord, that old truck is so much sexier than a red Porsche . . .
Stomach fluttering, I step off the curb and hurry toward him; he does

the same, and we meet at the cement median in the middle of the driveway.

We stare at each other with schoolyard awkwardness for what feels like an eternity before we both say, "Hi," at the same time.

He grins. "Hi."

"Hi."

"How did you know I was here?"

"I followed you from the wedding."

"You were there?"

He nods.

"I didn't see you."

"I was hiding out on the groom's side."

"Oh. So . . . you saw?"

He nods again. "You were amazing."

My cheeks flush beneath his compliment, and I drop my head. "I didn't think you were ever going to talk to me again."

"Neither did I," he confesses. "But thankfully somebody talked some sense into me."

I raise my head. "Who?"

"Third floor." He nods toward the hospital.

I turn and look up to find my mother staring down on us from the same window I found her in front of just a few minutes ago. My heart softens as her *good luck* offering finally makes sense. She gives me another thumbs-up and then disappears out of sight.

Sneaky old bird, she doesn't care about the dumb veil . . . I turn back to him. "What'd she say? When did you talk? H-how did she even get ahold of you?"

He grins at my barrage of questions. "She called me this morning— like an hour before the wedding—apparently got my cell number from the front desk. I gave it to them when I checked in yesterday."

I blink hard. Hotels don't usually give out personal information. That means there's probably a front-desk clerk balled up crying in the fetal position right now . . . "And what'd she say?"

"First, she apologized, and then she just talked about how wonderful you are and how I'd be an idiot to let you go."

"*My* mom said that? Are you sure you weren't being crank called?"

He chuckles. "Yeah, I'm sure. She was great, Mac. She reminded me that we all have things in our past we might not want the people we love to know about, but that if we don't share with them, they'll never get to know who we really are, and the relationship will suffer because of it."

My heart warms at the thought of her saying those words, and not just because they speak to my relationship with him, but also to my relationship with her . . .

"We both did stupid things before we met that came out at really inopportune moments," he goes on, "but it's all out there now—all of the embarrassing ugliness is out there, and we can move on and start building a life together. And that's what I want, more than anything, Mac." He reaches for my hand. "I want to build a life with you. I want to take your old dog to the park, and pay the bills, and get groceries, and raise another woman's child with you—"

I burst out laughing, my heart overflowing with love for everything he's professing. "I want those things too," I say, sniffling back my tears. "I do. I want to do all those things with you too."

He cradles my face with his hand and leans forward to kiss me. It's a loving and tender and deliciously familiar sensation that somehow erases all the upset and replaces it with reassurance that what he's saying is true: J.T. and I are going to build a life together: a beautiful life filled with ordinary things and other women's children. The kind of life I've been dreaming of. The kind of life they make movies about . . .

Three months later . . .

"Uh, Mac. I need you down here . . ."

The confusion in Andy's tone matches the expression on his face. Given the circumstances, both are a little concerning. I leave my post at Caroline's left side and hustle down to the end of the bed, where he and Nurse Becky are tending to the screaming newborn.

"What's wrong?" Caroline growls, her demonic active-labor voice still in full effect. "Let me see him! I want to see my baby!"

"Is something wrong?" J.T. asks from Caroline's right side, eyes wide with concern.

"Not exactly," Andy mumbles under his breath.

Offering me a befuddled shrug, he quickly steps out of the way, allowing me a good look at the—

"Ohmygod." I blink hard.

"Right?" Nurse Becky mutters from behind me.

"What?" Caroline screams. "What's wrong?"

"Are, um—is there—uhhh . . ."

I'm too shocked to formulate an entire thought. By all accounts I'm looking at a healthy, beautiful baby boy. It's just . . . well . . .

"Any chance you have African American heritage?" Andy asks hopefully.

"What?" Caroline snaps.

"Or maybe there's a history of hyperpigmentation in your family?" he continues. "Where the skin might take on a slightly darker color than the parents'?"

"What? *No!* What the fuck are you talking about?" She grabs the bed rail and starts hoisting herself up to see the baby, while Andy turns his attention to J.T. and asks him the same questions.

J.T. shakes his head. "Not that I know of."

Okay.

Andy and I exchange a knowing glance just as Caroline's gaze makes its way to the end of the bed and she gets a good look at her son for the first time.

She gasps. "Holy fuck. He's black."

I nod. Yes, he is. He most certainly is.

"*What?*" J.T. steps in for a look.

"Is there any possibility you were with a black man around the same time you were with J.T.?" Andy asks her.

"No."

"You're sure?"

She shakes her head and starts to say no again, but before the word actually crosses her lips, she pauses, and her sweaty brow starts to wrinkle in consideration. "Oh . . . wait . . ." An icky, wry grin starts to tug on her lips. "Reggie. Holy shit, I forgot about him." She licks her lips, clearly lost in thought. "Damn, he was a tasty morsel. . ."

"Oh my god." I glance up at J.T. just in time to see the color drain from his face, along with all the excitement that's been building inside him for the last four months. It wasn't an immediate process, but he's grown to love the idea of becoming a dad. He casts me a tortured look, then storms out of the room.

"Ah shit," Caroline mutters. "Now he's pissed."

"You think?" Nurse Becky mutters.

"It's okay," I assure her. "He'll be fine. Just enjoy your baby."

I give my hands a quick scrub, then take off to find him. After a few minutes of searching, I track him down on the other side of the building, standing in front of the nursery's window, looking at all the babies.

I sidle up behind him, wrapping my arms around his waist and resting my chin on his shoulder.

"You okay?"

He sighs while absently dragging his thumb over my engagement band. He does that a lot. "Not really."

"You're disappointed . . ."

He nods.

"The idea of being a dad sort of settled in on you, didn't it?"

"Yeah."

"I think I know something that might cheer you up . . ."

I didn't plan on telling him this way, but all things considered, I think it's the perfect time.

I ease my grip on him and slowly reposition myself so that I'm now standing with my back to him. I wrap his arms around my waist and press his palms flat against my stomach, holding them in place with my hands. With my gaze fixed on the beautiful little bundles squirming in the bassinets in front of us, I say, "In about seven months, you'll be looking at our little one through this window . . ."

He stays completely silent—and completely unmoving—for a long beat, before he finally says, "Are you serious?"

I raise my attention higher so I can see his expression in the window's reflection when I answer his question. "Yes. We're going to have a baby."

A prideful grin starts to spread across his face, and as if John Hughes scripted it himself, his top teeth settle in on that plump lower lip of his. My insides flutter with delight as he gently grazes his fingers across my belly.

"Oh yeah. That *definitely* cheers me up."

ACKNOWLEDGMENTS

Endless gratitude to:

My husband, Terry, who will always wait for the movie version but still listens to my scenes (even the kissy ones) without complaint.

My kiddos: Grace, who reminds me that pursuing a passion—no matter how exhausting—is always worth the effort, and Becca, who silently assures me that even the slowest-blooming rose smells just as sweet.

My sisters and parents for always believing in my talents, no matter how many times I painted the angel.

Anita Howard, faithful bestie and incomparable critique partner, for joining me on the ledge so I don't have to jump alone.

Amy Moore-Benson, the dream agent I don't deserve, whose wisdom and encouragement make me a better, more confident writer.

My exceptional editorial team, Maria Gomez and Selina McLemore, for making me laugh in the midst of the chaos and providing brilliant insights that turned this story into a masterpiece.

Angela Cook and Mary Frame, who keep my stories—and love scenes—moving at the right speed.

The Heathers (Hernandez and King) for braving the early-draft waters.

The Goat Posse for boundless love, support, and tin can humor.

Rebekah Crane, Tonya Kuper, Kerri Maniscalco, and Amy Rolland for perfectly timed text messages that always lift my mood.

My fourth-floor hens—past and present—for keeping my snark on point and the spotted dick in supply.

The *real* Mac Huntress for lending me his exquisite name.

The incomparable John Hughes for providing a lifetime of entertainment and an education on storytelling no classroom could offer.

And most importantly to my Heavenly Father, who sees me for the unruly, ragged mess I am—and loves me anyway.

ABOUT THE AUTHOR

Photo © 2013 Stacy Bostrom

Bethany Crandell, author of the young adult novel *Summer on the Short Bus*, lives in San Diego with her husband, teenage daughters, and two destructive puppies. *The Jake Ryan Complex* is her first adult novel, though it still carries the heart and humor of teenage exuberance. For more information, visit Bethany online at www.bethanycrandell.com and www.facebook.com/AuthorBethanyCrandell, and @bethanycrandell on Twitter.